"I'm having our baby, Dominic… In about five months."

Dom saw the rise of color in Zanna's face and heard the pitch in her voice. When he moved his lips, nothing emerged, as if he were in the depths of Casco Bay, struggling to surface.

"It's okay," she said. "I'm not expecting a lot from you, but it would be nice if our child had a father to connect with. That's all I'm asking."

"Zanna…" His voice broke, and he inhaled, calming himself. "I…uh…"

She held up a palm. "Don't say anything. We'll talk later." Then she spun around and ran back along the grassy ridge, sliding down the sandy bank of dune to the beach below.

"Zanna! Wait!" He watched her land, almost losing her balance and continuing down the road to town. Never looking back.

A cloud passed across the sun, darkening the waters of the bay and chilling the air. Dom wiped a hand across his face, waking himself up to what had just happened. He had a sickening feeling he hadn't measured up…

Dear Reader,

The Officer's Dilemma is the third and final book in a short series of Harlequin Heartwarming romances set in the fictional small town of Lighthouse Cove, Maine. It, and the first two novels—*His Saving Grace* and *The Christmas Promise*—center on an impulsive teenage prank that ended in tragedy. Although all three books refer to some of the consequences of that sad time for the Winters family in the Cove, their main focus is on redemption and forgiveness—for the characters who played a role, directly or otherwise, and for the Winters family itself.

Families, with their complex and often contradictory dynamics, have been a never-ending source of interest for me as a writer of Heartwarming romances. The emotional ups and downs of families, the eccentricities, flaws and endearing traits of parents, children and siblings provide stories of people striving to overcome adversity, to reconcile with past mistakes or lapses in judgment. Yet in the end, our fictional families surmount these challenges with the right amount of forgiveness and love.

For Suzanna (Zanna) Winters, the heroine of *The Officer's Dilemma*, forgiveness, acceptance and trust in love are the end goals of a difficult, painful journey. One that was only possible with the love of a good man.

To families!

All the best,

Janice Carter

HEARTWARMING

The Officer's Dilemma

———

Janice Carter

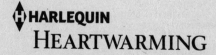

HARLEQUIN®
HEARTWARMING™

Recycling programs
for this product may
not exist in your area.

ISBN-13: 978-1-335-58481-6

The Officer's Dilemma

Harlequin Enterprises ULC
22 Adelaide St. West, 41st Floor
Toronto, Ontario M5H 4E3, Canada
www.Harlequin.com

Printed in U.S.A.

Janice Carter has been writing Harlequin romances for a long time, through raising a family, teaching and on into retirement. This is her sixteenth romance and she has plans for many more—along with plenty of personal family time, too.

Books by Janice Carter

Harlequin Heartwarming

For Love of a Dog
Her Kind of Hero
His Saving Grace
The Christmas Promise

Visit the Author Profile page
at Harlequin.com for more titles.

With love to my husband, Peter, who has been with me all the way.

Acknowledgments

A big thank-you to author Dawn Stewardson for reading, brainstorming and moral support.

A special thank-you to Petty Officer Second Class Reid McDougall for inside tips about the Navy, creative ideas and general enthusiasm for plotting!

PROLOGUE

"ZANNA!" A WOMAN called out.

Dominic Kennedy jerked his attention away from the two former classmates he'd been chatting with to the door of The Daily Catch. Snowflakes and a gust of winter blew into the small bistro as the woman entering stamped her boots on the doormat. Laughing, she shook off her woolen hat, showering those nearby in wet snow. Dom was oblivious to the roar of joking protest from the people she sprayed. Every nerve in his body was on full alert as he watched the tall redhead. *Suzanna Winters*. Or Zanna, as she'd told him almost eighteen years ago when he last saw her, weeping at her younger brother's grave.

She unbuttoned her parka, draping it over a hook already heaving with coats, and hugged the woman who'd greeted her. Her face was flushed—not simply from the cold, Dom was thinking, but maybe from the attention.

The Zanna Winters he remembered would have dodged the stares by slinking inside—if she'd have come to the party at all. But this woman was light-years away from that nineteen-year-old. Her once flame-colored hair had mellowed to a burnished mahogany and the low-necked sweater over slim black jeans accented curves the lanky teen he'd had a crush on back then definitely never had.

"That Zanna," commented the woman at Dom's elbow. "Always making an entrance. And just before midnight on New Year's Eve!"

Dom stiffened as the graveside memory of a tear-streaked face and choked question—*does the pain ever go away?*—flashed in his mind. Ignoring the couple beside him, he tracked Zanna's slow movement around the knots of people on her way to the bar. The bartender leaned across the counter to hug her, sparking a twinge of envy in Dom. He was vaguely aware of the woman at his side asking him a question but mumbled "Excuse me," and headed toward the bar.

By the time he reached her side, Zanna was perched on a stool, holding a glass of white wine and chatting animatedly to the bartender. Dom couldn't recall the guy's name, so he caught his attention by raising an index finger as he interrupted, "Another IPA?"

Zanna turned her head as the bartender said, "Coming up." She studied Dom for a second or two before asking, "Have we met? You look familiar."

"Dominic Kennedy. Dom."

Realization crept across her face and she nodded. "Brandon's funeral. You came over to give me a hug after everyone else had left."

Setting a glass of ale in front of Dom, the bartender interrupted, saying, "Glad you could come tonight, Zan, and thanks again for helping out after the storm. All of us volunteers appreciated having a warm place to work, with electricity."

Zanna shrugged. "I was relieved the old generator kicked into action, Ted. And lots of people helped out those couple of days."

Ted Nakamura—a friend of Zanna's cousin, Ben. Dom remembered him now and was about to introduce himself when someone else came up to the bar, getting Nakamura's attention. An awkward lull settled, so Dom picked up the ale and took a sip, aware of Zanna's gaze. He didn't want to talk about her brother's funeral at a party, so he said, "I heard the town was shut down for a few days before Christmas."

"I assume you weren't here then?"

"No. Unfortunately I missed Christmas itself because my ship was caught on the fringes of the same storm. Just got here a couple of days ago. I'm here for two weeks then off to the Mediterranean."

"Your ship? Navy? Coast guard?" She peered over the rim of her wineglass, sipping, but keeping her eyes on his.

"Navy."

"Hmm. No uniform tonight?"

He caught the twinkle in her eye. "Here?" He gestured to the crowd behind them.

She grinned and Dom's heart gave a small flip-flop. He was about to move closer to mute the background noise when someone shouted, "Five minutes, folks! Get ready for the countdown."

"Oh gawd," Zanna muttered.

"Not a New Year's Eve countdown fan?"

"Not even a New Year's Eve party fan. I only came because Ted there—" she nodded toward the other end of the bar where Ted was uncorking a champagne bottle "—insisted.

Told me I needed to take a break from being my usual workaholic self and have some fun. Though this definitely isn't my idea of fun."

"Mine neither."

"Oh? Then why are *you* here, Mr. Kennedy?" One eyebrow arched in a tease.

"My mother made me come."

Her laugh rolled down the bar.

"Four minutes!" cried someone else.

"Shall we go?" Dom impulsively asked.

"Go?"

"Outside. Cool night air and—"

"Escape all that hugging and kissing at the stroke of midnight," she finished with a grimace and plunked her half-empty wineglass down. "Yes!"

Dom grinned and began to work his way through the room, aware that Zanna was following him and that some people were asking her where she was going. He didn't stop until he reached the jumble of coats at the door and by the time she reached his side he was zipping up his down ski jacket.

Zanna plucked her coat from the hook. "One of the benefits of coming late to a party. Your coat's always on top of the pile." Then, slipping into it, she breathlessly exclaimed, "Let's go!"

Dom pushed open the door as a shout of "Ten!" sounded from the crowd milling in the center of the bistro. The quiet, cold night rushed at him as he closed the door behind them. Turning to Zanna, he asked, "Where to?"

"The water," she said, pointing to the harbor fencing opposite the bistro. She strode across the snow-covered boardwalk, and leaning her elbows on the flat top of the railing, gazed out into the dark. For a moment Dom felt she'd drifted away. To the past?

"I can't remember the last time I looked out on this view in winter," he said, looking in the same direction. "Maybe when I was a teen."

"I'm guessing you haven't been home much since college days and the navy."

He sensed her watching him. "Hardly at all. Holidays mainly."

"Miss it?"

"Not really, to be honest." He looked at her and smiled. "I've been lucky to realize my youthful dreams of travel and adventure. Except for my mother and an uncle, the navy is my only family. How about you?" When she didn't reply, he added, "Was running the family hotel your dream?" He regretted the question when he saw her hesitation. "I mean, I heard you've been back in the Cove for two or three years. Was that part of your long-term plan?"

She turned her attention back to the water. "No, but then life always throws curveballs, doesn't it?"

So, she didn't want to talk about it. Dom mentally kicked himself for letting the conversation flow into serious territory, away from the light tone at the bar. Recovering that earlier mood suddenly seemed beyond his ability.

Finally, she said, "By the way, I want to thank you."

"For?"

"All those years ago, at Bran's funeral. You were the only one who got what I was going through. Everyone clustered around my parents and forgot about me. At least, that's how it felt." She raised her head, meeting his eyes. "You helped me…when you told me the pain would get better." Her eyes were glistening, and not from the cold air.

"And did it?"

"Eventually. Like you said at the time, a little bit every day."

Dom wanted to pull her into his arms, the way he'd held onto her as a sobbing teenager. But the woman next to him wasn't that girl. She'd had a life apart from his—back then and certainly now. Maybe if they hadn't both gone their separate ways to college... Dom switched back to the present. There was nothing to be gained by such futile thinking.

Zanna turned her head to the hotel, lit up like some fairy-tale castle, on the hill overlooking the harbor. "I should get back," she said, her voice soft and almost regretful.

At least that was how Dom wanted to interpret it. He didn't feel ready for the night to end, not yet and not like this. "Coffee? A nightcap?" The hope in his question lingered between them.

"My assistant is waiting to go home. I promised I'd be back shortly after midnight."

Dom kept the disappointment out of his voice. "Okay, I'll walk with you."

"It's right there!" She gestured to the hotel on the street above the harbor boardwalk.

"Still..."

She shrugged and led the way up the stairs

leading to the main road. Except for the jingling strings of Christmas lights and decorations bobbing in the gentle breeze off the water, the night was quiet.

When they reached the front door of the hotel, Dom was overwhelmed by a feeling of uncertainty he hadn't had since he'd been an insecure teenager. But something in Zanna's face when she started to bid him goodnight spurred him to say, "So what you said before, about escaping all the hugging and kissing? Think you can tolerate a goodnight hug?"

She laughed aloud and Dom knew he didn't want to let this magical woman go, not yet. He gently wrapped his arms around her in a long embrace and closed his eyes, letting his mind drift back to that day years ago and the girl he'd yearned for throughout high school. He wished the night could last forever.

CHAPTER ONE

THE BRIDE WAS LOVELY; the groom, handsome.

Zanna Winters shifted on the metal folding chair. Draped in white linen, the seats were pretty but uncomfortable, though she knew her fidgeting had more to do with the wedding, despite its perfection.

Her cousin Grace was radiant next to her adoring groom, Drew Spencer. A late afternoon outdoor wedding suited the couple. Baskets of potted plants along with porcelain jugs of spring flowers were scattered throughout the garden. It was too early for Aunt Evelyn's roses, but Grace had wanted May rather than June. The wedding reflected both Aunt Evelyn's and Grace's style—low-key but classy. Zanna bet the pair's witnesses, Ella Jacobs and Grace's brother, Ben, would be joining the bridal queue soon themselves, as they'd recently announced their engagement.

Zanna was happy for all of them. The event

could be in a wedding planner's brochure, an item Zanna knew she'd personally never want or need again. After officially ending her brief marriage to a serial womanizer almost a year ago, Zanna had decided she was relationship shy. That was the crux of her impatience to have this ceremony over with. She just wanted to grab a canapé or two and flee as quickly as etiquette permitted.

But that wasn't going to happen. Family members had duties and obligations. They weren't allowed such escapes. Zanna's assigned task was to ensure that some of the older guests were comfortably seated in the gazebo while champagne and appetizers were served after the ceremony. Other guests would mingle in or around the large tent-like structure, but Aunt Ev was convinced that everyone over sixty needed a chair. Surveying the heads in front of her, Zanna figured her job would be easy. There was her mother, Jane, sitting next to Henry Jenkins, a long-time family friend; Drew's parents and an uncle; a couple of people from the Historical Society; and a former business associate of Uncle Charles. Of course, there might be a few gray-haired guests behind her, but not many. Zanna guessed the total attendance was no more than fifty people.

Grace had insisted on a small wedding with no dinner, no speeches except for a toast and no wedding cake. *Well, good for her, though the absence of a cake is disappointing.* The sound of applause roused Zanna as she realized her cousin was now legally wed. The beaming bride and groom faced the guests and, hand in hand, floated down the grassy aisle. Their joy was almost hard to take.

Zanna's Las Vegas elopement hadn't been joyful, though she'd thought she was happy at the time. But thinking you're in love isn't the same as *being* in love, and how often in her life had thinking been confused for being? Too many instances to count. She suddenly thought of the last time she'd felt the magical buzz of a connection with a man. The bright day was instantly eclipsed by the memory of warm eyes and a hug on New Year's Eve. *Don't go there today, Zanna. Be kind to yourself.* Still, the mellow tone of Dominic Kennedy's voice and his comforting arms lingered all these months later.

But that was a memory she'd rather not entertain today. The guests followed the couple across the lawn to the gazebo where tables and chairs had been set up. Zanna started toward her mother and Henry, who were sitting at the front. Aunt Evelyn had already slipped away to the kitchen and Zanna noticed that Uncle Charles was being taken care of by his son, Ben, who was leading him to the gazebo. No sign of Ben's fiancée. Zanna figured Ella's assignment was to be at Grace's side, ready to help with anything Grace needed. Taking a deep breath and vowing not to allow herself even a drop of self-pity on her cousin's wedding day, Zanna reached her mother and Henry.

"Wasn't it lovely, dear?" Jane dabbed a tissue at her eyes.

"Yes, it was. Now let's head over to those chairs Aunt Evelyn's reserved for you in the gazebo."

Henry frowned. "No need for special treatment, Suzanna. We're not infirm!" His indignation belied the cane leaning against his chair that, given the uneven ground of the lawns around the Winterses' family home, was the reason for Zanna's assistance.

"It's my pleasure to walk you over to seats

that everyone else here would give an arm and a leg for."

Henry sighed. "Righto. Lead the way then." He held onto Zanna while he grabbed his cane and stood up. His hip replacement months ago had been a success, but now the other hip was giving him grief. Aunt Evelyn's fear of either Henry or Zanna's mother, who had low blood pressure, stumbling was reasonable, yet Zanna knew aging was something neither of them willingly accepted, unlike Uncle Charles, whose health had deteriorated since his heart surgery last year. He'd finally surrendered to the demands of his family and had retired, handing over the family company to Ben. Zanna knew that must have been quite a struggle for her uncle, whose unyielding tenacity was a family legend.

Henry slipped his free arm through the loop of Zanna's elbow while her mother did the same on Zanna's other side, murmuring, "Grace looks beautiful, doesn't she? I'm so happy for her. And so do you, darling. Green was always your color and—" Jane studied her with a slight frown "—you almost seem to be glowing yourself."

Zanna knew her face was red—not because

of the compliment, but the fact that her mother was uncannily close to the mark. "Grace does look lovely," she replied, thankful when her mother let the subject drop. Once Henry and Jane were seated, she added, "I'll make sure the champagne gets to you."

"Dear, we'll be fine. The catering staff are making the rounds. Go and enjoy yourself."

Right. Not much chance of that, Mom. "Can't just yet. I've got to check on other people—who aren't infirm either," Zanna added, winking at Henry. She worked her way around the clusters of chatting guests to guide Drew Spencer's parents and uncle to the gazebo. They didn't really need her help with chairs either, but Zanna had known better than to argue with Aunt Evelyn about it. When the Spencers were seated next to Henry and Jane, the tinkling of a silver bell signaled the start of Ben's toast to the happy couple.

Later, when her mother mentioned how sweet Ben's toast had been, Zanna could barely recall more than a few words. He'd prefaced it with a remark about Drew's arrival in the Cove last summer to undertake a lighthouse survey, and Zanna's thoughts had instantly swept to the subsequent fundraising for the Cove's lighthouse restoration and her brother's memorial. The pain from Brandon's drowning nearly eighteen years ago had subsided into a muted sadness. She knew her mother felt the same, though they seldom spoke about the tragedy. The lighthouse restoration was almost complete and plans for some kind of ceremony were underway. Zanna was on the committee of three organizing the project, along with Henry and Grace.

The vibration of her cell phone in her dress's jacket pocket interrupted her thoughts. She ducked out of the way of two women bearing trays to answer.

"Suzanna Winters?"

"Speaking."

"This is Alex Corelli at Gateway Living. We were speaking last week?"

"Oh, yes. Hello, Alex."

"We'd like to set up a meeting with you."

Zanna hesitated. This was the call she'd been waiting for, yet now she felt herself wavering. Did she really want to go through with it? She cleared her throat. "Umm, sure. That would be fine. When were you thinking?"

"Well, there are a few hoops to jump through

before we have a serious conversation—a building inspection for a start and then a more intensive tour of the locale to see how it would work with our Gateway Living concept."

Zanna closed her eyes, relief oozing out of her. Okay, so only an information meeting. She had to keep that in mind. "Fine."

"Perfect. We'll organize something and get back to you about the meeting date etcetera. Probably next week sometime. Does that work for you?"

"Perfect. I…uh… I'm looking forward to it." Zanna tucked the phone back into her pocket. Perhaps this was the perfect time to slip away. If someone said anything about her leaving, there was always the excuse of the hotel. She'd left her very capable assistant, Rohan, in charge, but there were two check-ins later today. *Only* two for the Mother's Day weekend and the hotel was currently at just twenty percent capacity. Memorial Day was coming up at the end of the month and she was hoping to book at least fifty percent capacity for that holiday. She hadn't yet reached desperation level, but that could change if summer bookings failed to materialize.

A potential rescue had arrived a week ago,

when Alex Corelli had phoned to say that Gateway Living, a company that built and managed exclusive retirement homes for seniors, was interested in having a discussion about her hotel. If Gateway Living ended up making her a reasonable offer, she should probably jump at it.

For the past year the idea of selling the hotel had drifted in and out of her increasingly exhausted mind, but she was worried how the family, especially Uncle Charles, would react. The Lighthouse Hotel had been a town landmark for more than a century, its construction begun in the early 1900s by the family patriarch, Hiram Winters.

What worried her more was her mother's possible reaction if Zanna were to leave the Cove. She suspected Jane was lonely in Bangor, where she'd been living since divorcing Zanna's father when Zanna was in college. Her recent hints that she was considering a move back now that Zanna had settled there could lead to hurt feelings and disappointment. There'd been enough of those emotions between them over the years.

Zanna surveyed the crowd of wedding guests enjoying themselves. For a few seconds she felt completely out of sync with the scene, watching through the eyes of an outsider. It was a peculiar sensation she'd begun experiencing as a preteen and even more after her mother had told her she'd been adopted. The stunning revelation came on the eve of Zanna's departure for college. Not a good start for the exciting adventure Zanna had been anticipating.

A waiter paused in front of her with a tray of champagne and Zanna instinctively reached for a glass before she remembered. No more alcohol for her, for at least the next five months. Instead, she snatched another canapé and scanned the grounds, noting that everyone had someone to talk to. Of course, nothing was stopping her from joining any of the conversations, but frankly, she didn't feel like being social. Rohan was probably ready for a break, and she had to make sure the rooms were ready for the new check-ins. Although the reception was due to continue for at least another hour, Zanna was keen to leave. She was exhausted, a common state these past few months. Taking a deep breath to gird herself for the obligatory goodbyes, she headed across the lawn to the gazebo.

On the way, she met Ben, who looked a

bit frazzled with his loosened tie and flushed face. "You're not leaving, Zanna?"

"Work commitments, Ben. By the way, I liked your toast." It was a white lie because she hadn't actually been listening, but he was a good speaker and adored his sister, so Zanna figured the speech had been loving.

"Thanks, Zan. Well, if I can't persuade you to linger a bit longer, come to an after-party that I've organized at The Lobster Claw. About nine. I've asked some people who weren't part of the inner circle invited to the wedding. Grace and Drew won't be there though, because they want to get an early start on their road trip."

"Road trip?"

"The honeymoon."

"Oh. Where are they going? Grace has been keeping it a secret."

Ben laughed. "Because she was getting tired of the eye-rolling."

"Huh?"

"Drew has planned a grand tour of lighthouses along the coast of Maine and up into Massachusetts."

Zanna couldn't contain a big grin. "Seriously?"

"See? That's why she decided to keep mum about it." He shook his head. "The guy's a complete nerd about lighthouses."

"Well, he *is* the coast guard officer in charge of their maintenance for the whole state."

"Yeah, and although the trip doesn't sound romantic—"

"I'm sure he'll have no trouble at all making it a romantic getaway."

"I hope so, for Grace's sake. Anyway, think about coming tonight, Zanna. I'm sure you could use some time off from the hotel. It'll be fun."

Recalling the last party she'd attended in the Cove, the one on New Year's Eve, she tried not to grimace. "Thanks, Ben. I'll see."

An hour later she'd traded her uncomfortably tight silk sheath and matching jacket for the tailored navy trousers and cream blouse she usually wore on duty at the hotel. Zipping up the trousers, she reminded herself to order a few more pairs in larger sizes.

Rohan had departed shortly after her return, heading back to Portland. He'd recently expressed an interest in taking tourism and hotel management college courses similar to ones that Zanna had taken. Although that charmed her, she knew replacing him would be difficult. Not many ambitious young people wanted to work in the Cove these days. She was getting by with two room attendants and Rohan on the front desk.

Zanna checked the computer a second time, scrolling through the room allocations. The four-story hotel had a total of eight rooms on each floor, a dated ballroom/dining room currently being used for storage and a single elevator. When she and Mark, her ex, had moved in almost three years ago they'd undertaken some basic renovations—new doors on the rooms to accommodate the card key system, safes in the closets and upgrades to the bathrooms. Another innovation had been the PIN code lock on the front door, to be used by guests after midnight. She had her ex to thank for the idea, his most important contribution to the hotel as far as Zanna was concerned. They'd also purchased new linens and beds for some of the rooms but then funds had dried up, along with their enthusiasm. Not to mention their marriage.

It was almost five and Zanna figured the wedding reception must be wrapping up. Her mother had wanted to stay longer and would get a ride back to the hotel later. It was an opportunity for Jane to have a visit with the family, as well as old friends like Henry, before heading back home in the morning. Despite Zanna's efforts to persuade her mother to stay a few extra days, she'd insisted she had social obligations. Zanna had stifled a scoff at that. Book club and golf were hardly priorities, though she grudgingly admitted her mother had a better social life than she had.

Her last big social event had been the party at New Year's and Zanna had gone only at the urging of a friend. The town's pre-Christmas ice storm had caused turmoil. She'd offered the hotel as a depot for emergency supplies and helped some seniors in town get settled back into their homes. It had been exhausting, and a party was exactly what she'd needed, although she wouldn't have gone if Ted Nakamura hadn't pressed her. The old maxim "If only I knew then what I know now" rose up.

A sudden rush of loneliness hit, yet another reminder that her divorce had set her on a totally different, and probably solitary, course for the future. *Be honest with yourself, Suzanna Winters.* Loneliness might have been one factor in deciding to go to that party, even in flirting with the attractive naval officer, the adult version of the teenager who had comforted her at Brandon's funeral. But it was the instant attraction that caused her to flee the party early with him. Zanna sighed, lowering her forehead onto her cupped hands. *Where are you now, Dominic Kennedy?*

DOMINIC KENNEDY STOOD on the threshold of the back room in The Lobster Claw. He couldn't remember the last time he'd been in the pub. Maybe once or twice over the past few years when he'd been home on leave. He had no idea this part of the pub, meant for private parties, even existed. The room was dark, but he could make out the shapes of people bobbing on the makeshift dance floor to the loud pulse of music or mingling in small groups, shouting to make themselves heard. A revolving disco ball strobed the room in neon streaks. Dom wondered if it was the same disco ball that had revolved above the Lighthouse Hotel ballroom at senior prom eighteen years ago. How many disco balls could there be in the Cove anyway?

After watching the crowd for another minute, he began wishing he hadn't taken Ben Winters up on the invite to come to his sister's after-party. When he'd bumped into Ben this morning, he'd barely recognized him—hardly surprising when they hadn't seen each other since Brandon Winters's funeral all those years ago. A lifetime, Dom thought. He, Ben and the rest of their senior year cohort were packing up and heading for various colleges when Brandon drowned that Labor Day weekend. The tragedy had rocked the entire town and Dom still had conflicting emotions about all of it.

But when Ben had greeted him so warmly, he'd felt a surge of friendship, though to be honest, he and Winters had been basketball teammates rather than actual buddies. They'd been in the same high school class but had moved in different social circles.

Ben had said, "Come to the party. See some of the old gang, at least the ones who ended up back here." The remark took Dom back to their senior year when almost everyone had vowed never to return to the Cove because they'd been hungry for adventures beyond the small Maine town. He'd heard Ben had only returned to the Cove a little more than a year ago, to take over his family business.

Dom found himself accepting, mostly because he'd always liked Ben and the invitation had been so enthusiastically genuine.

But now that he was here, well... He usually avoided parties like this. The last exception he'd made for his personal rule had been months ago, when he'd been home for the Christmas holidays. And he was still wrestling with his conscience after that New Year's Eve party. So why was he standing here like a gawky teenager, all nerves and no confidence?

C'mon, Kennedy. Be honest. You came because you thought there was a good chance of meeting another Winters. The woman in practically every one of your thoughts since New Year's Eve. Suzanna. Being part of the Winters family, she could be here. But maybe he should leave now before it was too late. He was about to go when a voice stopped him.

"Hey, you made it!" Ben was holding a half-empty glass of beer. "I've just ordered some snacks and there's a bar set up inside." He grasped Dom's forearm and led him into the room. As they wound their way through the knots of people, Dom strained to identify any of the partygoers as Zanna. When they reached the small bar in a back corner, Ben asked, "What'll it be? I've got a tab running so be my guest. But the bartender isn't doing cocktails, right, Gary?"

"Nope. Beer and wine only tonight."

Gary looked vaguely familiar. "Uh, make it a small beer."

"Sure." As he pulled on the keg spigot, Gary said, "You're from the Cove, aren't you?"

"Yeah."

"Portland High?"

"Yep."

"Gary Kowalski. I think you might've been in my brother's year. Glen Kowalski?"

"Oh, right. What's Glen up to these days?"

"Married with two kids. Works for this guy here." He jerked his head toward Ben, who was now talking to a woman farther along the bar.

"Very nice. Give him my congratulations."

"Sure." He handed Dom the glass of beer. "Have you moved back to town then?"

"Oh, no. Just home on leave."

"On leave? Are you in the military?"

"Navy." Dom sipped some beer and glanced

around. He noticed that Ben was mingling, playing host.

"Very cool. How long you here for?" Gary asked.

"A couple of weeks."

"Well, that gives you time to reconnect with people. I work here at the Claw, so pop by sometime."

"Sure."

Gary turned aside to take a drink order from someone else. Dom moved to the end of the bar and surveyed the room. Still no sign of Zanna. Maybe he'd finish his beer and then go. He turned his back to the room and swallowed another mouthful. *Heck. Why wait till I'm finished? Now's as good a time as any to escape.* Plunking the glass down he swung round and bumped into someone setting an empty glass next to his.

"Sorry," he said. The rest of whatever he might have said lodged in his throat while the steady bass reverberating in the room dimmed at his own heartbeat. She was every bit as beautiful as he remembered, even in the semi-dark with the disco ball's light flickering across her face. A face that paled as she recognized him.

"What are *you* doing here?" She raised her voice above the music.

"Looking for you, Zanna," he quipped, keeping his tone light.

Her frown tightened. "I meant, you're supposed to be overseas."

"I came back." She leaned toward him, pressing a finger against one ear. Muffling the background noise, he guessed. "Want a drink?"

She shook her head. "I was just leaving."

"Same here. I'll walk you out." Dom took her by the elbow to steer her into the crowd. He felt her slight jerk at his touch but, undeterred, reached for her hand as they moved through the crowd. As they emerged into the quieter, main area of the Claw, she pulled her hand from his clasp. Dom continued on ahead and when they were finally out on the sidewalk, the cool night air brought him to his senses.

She stood in front of him, the streetlight's amber glow highlighting her deep auburn hair and the pale freckles strewn across the bridge of her nose. Her dark jeans topped by a loose turquoise shirt hinted at curves that Dom didn't remember from New Year's Eve.

He swallowed hard. "I'll walk you back to your place," he finally managed to say.

"It's okay. I'll be fine." Then she asked, "How long will you be in town?"

"A couple of weeks. And I *will* walk you back." He started heading toward Main Street and the hotel. When she caught up to him, he asked, "Or would you like to go for a coffee somewhere instead?"

"You've got to be kidding. This is the Cove, remember? Everything but pubs and a few restaurants are closed for the night."

Right. That was the reason for their escape to her hotel that night—someplace warm and cozy to continue their animated conversation from the party they'd fled. "Yeah," he mumbled, unsure what else to say. When the hotel loomed ahead, he suggested, "Maybe a coffee tomorrow morning, then?" He watched the shifting expressions on her lovely face. She felt as unsure as he did.

"If I can get away. I'm a bit shorthanded at the hotel right now but…okay… I guess if you're going to be in town for a bit, we should set some ground rules."

Well, that's a giveaway about where we stand, he thought. "Sure. Guess we'd better."

She looked away then, avoiding his eyes. "Text me in the morning. Use the hotel number. I'll be working the desk first thing."

As she resumed walking, Dom called out, "Zanna? I'm glad we met tonight. I…um… I was hoping we would."

She turned to look at him, nodded and continued on. Dom waited until she pushed open the hotel front door and went inside before releasing his pent-up breath in a long, tortured sigh. The first hurdle of returning to the Cove had been accomplished. If only he felt relief, instead of this anxious uncertainty about Zanna Winters.

CHAPTER TWO

"EVELYN WAS DISAPPOINTED you left the wedding reception early yesterday," Zanna's mother said after the server took their brunch order.

"Rohan needed a break."

"How much longer can you manage with just the two of you on the front desk? That's not a good situation."

"Tell me about it," Zanna mumbled.

"Pardon?" Jane leaned forward from the other side of the table.

"I can't afford to hire more staff until I know for sure how this season is going to shape up."

"Is business that bad?"

"It will be if more bookings don't appear. But don't worry about it," she hastened to add at her mother's frown. "I have some ideas."

The frown deepened. "You're not considering selling it, are you? Charles would be—"

"Upset. I know, Mom. But he doesn't own this…this white elephant. I do."

"It's been in the family for more than a hundred years. It's a Winters legacy."

"Maybe it's time the Winterses got over themselves."

"What do you mean by that?"

Zanna shrugged. "The whole pillar of the community and founding father image is old. No one thinks like that anymore." Now Jane was shaking her head. Zanna wished she hadn't let herself get drawn into this conversation, which she figured would lead nowhere and only dampen their Mother's Day brunch.

"But it's history."

"Precisely my point, Mom. *History*."

Their eyes locked until Jane lowered hers and stirred some sugar into her mug of coffee. When she looked up again, she softened her tone. "Darling, don't do anything rash. If you need help, I have more than enough money. You don't have to wait for your inheritance from me."

Zanna teared up—something she was prone to do recently—but was saved from response by the arrival of their food. She glanced around the busy room while the server placed their plates before them. Mabel's Diner had chosen not to take reservations for Mother's Day brunch.

The food was a welcome distraction from an emotional talk about money, and Zanna quickly tucked into her waffles. She didn't glance up until her mother commented, "I can't remember the last time I saw you eat with such relish. And waffles of all things, with bacon!"

"I'm starving," Zanna managed to say around a mouthful of waffle. "And I said no to the whipped cream so…"

"It's an observation, dear, not a judgment."

"How're the eggs Benedict?" Zanna asked, changing the focus.

"Delicious, though I'd have preferred smoked salmon to ham. I can't believe they've already run out of the salmon and it's only eleven."

Zanna looked over her mother's shoulder to the door, noticing the lineup was now extending outside. "We came at a good time. I guess they're working fast in the kitchen to accommodate as many as possible."

"They should have taken reservations. I don't understand the reasoning."

"Sam Hargrave, the owner here, told me they get a lot of late cancellations and even no-shows. He can't afford the potential loss of revenue from unused food and the wages he has to pay."

"Still…" Jane shook her head as she cut another piece of brioche and egg.

"I've changed the cancellation policy on bookings for the same reason, Mom. Maybe Frank Morgan was able to absorb the no-shows when he managed the hotel, but I can't afford them."

"Aren't deposits a matter of course for bookings?"

"I haven't cancelled the deposits, but often refunds were issued up to forty-eight hours before the reservation. I increased the cutoff to seventy-two hours."

"I wonder how Frank's enjoying retirement. Do you ever hear from him?" Her mother suddenly asked.

Zanna was grateful for this topic shift to the hotel's former manager who'd run the hotel after her father's death fifteen years ago. "I think Henry Jenkins might occasionally be in contact with him, but I bet he's playing lots of golf in Florida and not missing the Maine cold at all."

Frank Morgan had not only rescued the

hotel from bankruptcy, but his management until three years ago had allowed Zanna to continue her life of adventure far from Lighthouse Cove. She'd considered hiring another manager after Frank left, but decided to return to Lighthouse Cove with her then husband, naively thinking the move could save their failing marriage.

Jane smiled. "He deserves an enjoyable and long retirement."

"He does. By the way, I heard Grace and Drew are honeymooning on a lighthouse road trip," Zanna said, steering the talk away from the past.

"Isn't that sweet!"

"I guess, but not very romantic."

"Why isn't it?"

"Well, it's his work, right? I mean, doesn't he get enough of lighthouses?"

"But he knows so much about them, and I suppose he wanted to show them to Grace, so she could see what he loves about his job."

"Surely Grace has had enough of lighthouses," Zanna muttered and immediately regretted the gibe as her mother flushed. They'd both successfully been skirting the topic that they always avoided on Mother's Day—the fact that one of Jane's children, Brandon, was no longer there to celebrate with them.

Their server returned with a coffeepot in hand, a timely interruption. "A refill, ladies?"

"No, thanks," Zanna put in before her mother could say yes. She glanced back at the line of people waiting to get in, thinking it would be rude to linger. And then she spotted someone in line. *Dominic Kennedy.* Bumping into him at the after-party last night had been a shock and she hadn't been very welcoming. Not that basic etiquette was at issue here, she told herself. Although he was the father of the child she was expecting, his sudden return to the Cove had complicated her plans, including the special one meant for this morning. She'd intended to use the brunch to say *Happy Mother's Day, Mom, and by the way, you're going to be a grandmother!*

Now, rather than emailing Dominic to relay the news, she'd have to tell him in person. Which worried her. How would he react? Would his response reveal something about the man—the father of her child—that she wouldn't want to know?

Zanna asked for the bill as the server was about to walk away.

"Are you in a rush, dear?"

"Umm, no, no, Mom. It's just that they're so busy today I figured it'd be best to ask for it as soon as possible. But don't hurry, please. Take your time!"

"I'm getting mixed messages from that, Zanna. Anyway, I should be on my way back to Bangor, but let's get together soon. Perhaps I could help you go over your finances. I used to help your father with them years ago, when we were still…"

Zanna could fill in the rest. *Still together as a family…still whole.* "Mom, this is your day. The perfect end to Grace's wedding weekend. I love you and will always be so very grateful that you're my mother."

Jane pulled a tissue out of her suit jacket and blew her nose. "I was lucky to have two wonderful children."

"Brandon and I were the lucky ones." She was about to search for her own tissue when the server came with the bill. Just in time. Zanna had always hated public displays of emotion. "Do you want to linger a bit?" she asked as her payment was taken away.

"No, quite all right, dear. I couldn't eat another bite anyway."

There was a piece of brioche with part of an egg remaining on Jane's plate and for a mad second, Zanna was tempted to steal it with her fork.

"Would you…?" Jane asked, obviously noting her expression.

"Oh, no, Mom! I'm stuffed." She glanced down at her own empty plate, smeared with syrup, and remembered she needed to order another size up in her work dress trousers. She checked the front of the diner again and sighed. There was no chance of evading Dominic, who was chatting to the slight, gray-haired woman standing next to him. His mother, she guessed.

Jane got up to leave and Zanna followed. As she drew closer to Dominic, she pretended to search through her purse, hoping to pass the line without his noticing her. *No such luck*.

"Hello, Zanna." His tone and the light glint in his dark blue-gray eyes told her he'd detected her ruse and found it amusing.

"Oh, hi, Dominic."

He glanced at Jane. "I guess you and your mother had the foresight to get here early." The woman at his side cleared her throat and he said, "Oh, sorry…this is my mother, Marie. Uh, Mom, this is Zanna Winters. She's—"

"The owner of the Lighthouse Hotel. Nice to meet you, Zanna. You were very generous with your help after the ice storm last Christmas. I was one of the volunteers working out of the hotel that day."

"It was wonderful how so many people came out. Very nice to meet you, too, Mrs. Kennedy." Zanna smiled and was about to move on when she felt her mother elbow her. "And this is my mother, Jane Winters."

The mothers smiled and exchanged greetings while Zanna avoided eye contact with Dominic. The diner hostess called the people ahead to a table and Zanna quickly said, "We should get going. Happy Mother's Day, Mrs. Kennedy," and turned to leave.

Dominic stopped her, his hand on her forearm. "Were we getting together later today or…?"

Aware of the interest from the other two women, Zanna pretended she'd forgotten their parting words last night. "Oh! Right. I'm busy today but maybe call tomorrow morning? About nine?"

"I will." He held onto her arm a second longer, as if emphasizing his determination.

Zanna nodded to Mrs. Kennedy again and followed her mother around the rest of the line out onto the sidewalk, where Jane stopped. "Dominic Kennedy. His name is familiar, Zanna, but I don't recognize him. Refresh my memory."

"Dominic was in Scouts. Maybe that's where you heard of him? I'll walk you to your car, Mom," Zanna said, impatiently tugging at her mother's jacket sleeve.

Jane stood still, thinking. "That's right! He was the older teen who took Brandon under his wing when he wanted to quit. I'd asked Henry to encourage Bran to stay and he said he'd found someone to mentor him, like a big brother."

Because he wasn't getting any mentoring from his real big sister. Tears welled up again and Zanna took a deep breath. Surely these emotional episodes weren't going to continue through her whole pregnancy!

"Brandon really liked him," Jane said as they walked to her car. "I must thank him the next time I see him."

"Which won't be any time too soon," Zanna muttered.

"How so?"

"Dominic's home on leave from the navy. I imagine he'll be returning to his ship any day now."

"Oh. Well, please pass on my gratitude to him, if you see him tomorrow."

"Um, sure. Though I might be too busy to see him anyway. I forgot the memorial committee is meeting in the morning."

"Oh? I was hoping to come to one of those meetings."

"You will, Mom, when we're working on the final details. I'll let you know."

There was a flash of disappointment in her mother's face and Zanna bit her lip. She didn't want to exclude her mother from planning the memorial for Brandon, but her instinct was to protect her from any more pain. Jane had been through enough after Brandon's drowning, with her marriage falling apart and her daughter's return to college.

They rounded the corner onto Main Street, and Zanna said, "Don't worry. When we have a solid plan, we will for sure get you to help." Jane nodded but Zanna saw the doubt in her face. "I promise, Mom." She gave her a quick hug and her mother got into her car.

Jane was fastening her seat belt when Zanna poked her head through the open window to kiss her on the cheek. "Drive safely and text when you get home."

"How did this reversal happen, dear? You being the mother and me the daughter?"

You being the mother... Zanna felt a lump in her throat. "It's the cycle of life, isn't it, Mom? The adult children becoming parents to their parents?"

"You can joke all you want but I'm not relinquishing my title of Mother and all it means just yet!"

Zanna laughed. "Please don't!"

"I'll let you know when I'm home. And thank you for brunch and...and especially your lovely words." Jane pushed the ignition button and the engine's revving saved Zanna a reply. There'd been enough emotion that morning.

She waved goodbye until the car disappeared around the corner. Zanna felt a stab of guilt at keeping secrets from her mother, especially one that would be life-changing for both of them. Right now though, she had a more pressing matter on her mind—*confronting Dominic Kennedy with her news.*

DOM LOGGED OUT of his work email after reading the latest message from Personnel. His interview for Lieutenant Commander was scheduled for three weeks from tomorrow. He could return to his apartment on base in Norfolk in the meantime to prepare, but his mother had been so happy when he'd told her he'd be home for at least two weeks. He hated to disappoint her. She'd been a good sport over the years about his frequent absences and last-minute cancellations of trips home and deserved to have him around as long as possible. Even more so now. If he got the promotion, the new post would take him farther away, possibly to the West Coast. He'd decided not to tell her about that unless it was going to become a reality.

He went on to read the most recent email from his CO, John Reid, suggesting he could extend his two weeks' leave right up to his interview date if he wished. *Take the extra time to bone up for the interview and reflect on your long-term goals in the navy.* Dom's stomach lurched, and not from the huge omelet he'd devoured at brunch. He was grateful for his boss's relatively easygoing manner and especially his mentoring over the past few years, but Dom understood the implied message.

Their relationship had been tested during a search-and-rescue training session three weeks ago. Dom had disagreed with Reid about going ahead with the training on that stormy day. When the decision to cancel had proven to be the right one, Reid had acknowledged Dom's insight about one of his crew, who'd had a panic attack. But in the debrief afterward, Reid had also pointed out the exercise might have been okay, because the weather eventually improved. The incident taught Dom a couple of valuable lessons: put the safety of crew first and don't be afraid to question an order.

His mother walked into the living room as he logged out and must have noticed his expression. "Is there a problem, honey?"

He knew from her voice that she was steeling herself for disappointing news. "Not at all, Mom. It looks like I'll be hanging around to bother you for the next two weeks or maybe a bit longer." Her relief made up for his immediate realization that extending his stay could also mean ongoing encounters with Zanna, whose welcome had been far from warm.

"Lovely!" Marie exclaimed. "I have so many new recipes I've been wanting to try."

"I'm all yours," he said.

"This is the best Mother's Day gift, Dom. I'm going to dig out my recipe file right now."

"Um, don't forget that rather large brunch we've just had. Maybe soup tonight?"

"No way. You can eat all the soup you want when you're back on base." She waved a dismissive hand and bustled off to the kitchen.

At least there's something positive coming out of this possible delay, he thought. His cell phone pinged. The text was disappointingly not from Zanna, but from her cousin, Ben.

Hey Dom, if you're going to be around for the next couple of weeks, I wonder if you can do me a favor? I'm heading out for an early dinner with my folks right now but give me a call later this evening. Thx.

Dom's interest was piqued. He liked the idea of a project while he was stuck in town and after bumping into Zanna that morning at Mabel's, his fantasy of spending more time with her was fading. Her pretense that she'd forgotten they'd arranged to meet up today had been galling, though he'd tried his best to be nonchalant. He sighed. *She's simply not interested, pal. Best accept that and move on.*

Despite its size, the Cove did offer escapes from meeting people. The hotel probably kept Zanna busy enough and he'd inferred from their conversation months ago that her social life was a blank canvas. *Like mine*, he thought, giving in to another sigh. So whatever Ben had in mind for him would be a welcome diversion. That hope vanished when he listened with mounting trepidation to what Ben told him later that night.

"The thing is, Grace is on her two-week honeymoon and in all the wedding hoopla, she forgot to ask me to sit in for her on the memorial committee. I'm tied up in a new project myself and there's no way I can spare the time. Grace will be back by the time you have to return to base so I was wondering if you could stand in for her—well, I guess for me. Maybe even just for this one meeting?"

"What memorial committee?" Dom asked.

"It's for my cousin, Brandon. Zanna's younger brother."

Dom remembered his mother mentioning months ago something about plans for a memorial for Brandon. "Oh, right."

"It's only a committee of three and I'm sure the others won't expect you to get too involved but a new voice with different ideas might be helpful."

"Who are the other members?" Dom closed his eyes, predicting the name of at least one of the two.

"Henry Jenkins—you remember him surely—and Zanna, of course."

Of course. So much for avoiding her.

"Ten o'clock tomorrow morning," Ben went on to say, "at—"

"The hotel," Dom interjected weakly.

"Right you are! Really appreciate it, Dom, and let's get together before you head back to base."

Dom sat staring at his phone for a long moment after the call ended. So much for intentions. Still, a pesky inner voice whispered that maybe this was a second chance to get to really know Zanna and find out why she seemed to want nothing to do with him.

However things turned out, he'd be leaving the Cove in a couple of weeks anyway, perhaps for a very long time.

His next thought was a tad more worrisome. *Did Zanna know about his replacing Grace on the committee?*

CHAPTER THREE

ZANNA'S FACE TURNED as white as the blouse she was wearing when he walked into her small one-bedroom apartment behind the hotel office. "Dom?"

So she hadn't known he was coming. He looked around. The only change in the place from New Year's was the absence of the tiny Christmas tree. And Zanna's expression was definitely not as friendly as it had been at New Year's either.

Henry Jenkins pivoted around from where he was sitting and smiled broadly. "By golly, Dominic Kennedy! I heard you were in town and was hoping you'd drop by to see me before you left. What a great surprise." He lumbered to his feet to shake hands, grasping Dom by a shoulder and clapping him on the back at the same time.

Henry had white hair now and was thinner and more stooped than Dom remembered, but he was still the warm, avuncular man who'd led the Lighthouse Cove Scout pack. He'd steered Dom through the dark days after his father died until he felt like a normal teen again, one whose main challenge was getting good grades—along with snagging the attention of Zanna Winters.

"Good to see you, too, Scouter Jenkins."

"It's just Henry now." The man released Dom from his bear hug. "We're all long past those days, aren't we?" He glanced round at Zanna. "Did you know…?"

"No!"

Henry's brow furled at her tone. "I'm guessing Ben couldn't make it today, am I right?" He smiled at Dominic.

"Yes, sir. He called last night to ask me to fill in for him—well, for Grace." He silently cursed Ben for not giving them a heads-up.

"Take a seat, laddie." Henry gestured to the chair next to Zanna as he sat down with a slight groan. "Getting old," he muttered. "All right, then. Good to have another point of view, right, Zanna?"

She shrugged. "Sure."

"Why don't you fill Dominic in on where we are in the planning stages for Brandon's memorial," Henry went on, unfazed by Zanna's cool welcome.

Dom noted her tight mouth. If she wanted nothing to do with him, well, so be it. But wasn't the plan to get together today anyway? To "go over ground rules" as she'd said the other night.

She peered down at the notebook in her lap a moment before looking up at Dom. "We… uh…we've set the date for the dedication ceremony for the Memorial Day weekend. That gives us about three weeks. I know that day of remembrance is for the military, but Grace and I thought it would be appropriate. The lighthouse restoration will be finished and the ceremony could have a dual purpose."

"Okay."

"We ordered a bronze plaque which arrived a few weeks ago, and now we have to decide two things: where the plaque will be installed and what will be written on it."

"Is your mom involved at all?"

There was a swift glance between Henry and Zanna. "Mom will be involved soon."

"For the wording on the plaque," Henry added.

"The problem is we have a deadline of

sorts," Zanna went on. "Grace won't be back for two weeks and that means we'll have to decide on the wording so we can get the plaque etched and installed in time for the ceremony."

"I'm not sure I can offer much insight into what the plaque should say, but maybe I can help with where it should go. Though it's been years since I've been up to the lighthouse. I don't have a mental picture of what the site looks like now."

"So why don't you take him up there, Zanna?" Henry suggested. "Refresh his memory. We can reconvene in a couple of days—with your mother then, too."

Dom saw right away that was the last thing she'd planned, much less wanted, for the day and was about to bow out when she muttered, "Okay. But we'd have to go now because I'll need to cover Rohan for his lunch break."

This whole discussion was feeling awkward. "I'm sure I can manage to find my own way up to the lighthouse."

"No, no. She'll need to show you some of the places we're considering for the plaque." Henry slowly got out of his chair, reaching for his cane as he stood up. "And maybe pass some ideas by you for the ceremony. What do you think, Zanna?"

She took her time answering, busily putting away her notebook. "Okay," she mumbled and strode ahead to deposit the mugs in the kitchenette.

Oblivious to her lack of enthusiasm, Henry led the way through the apartment, past the office where Dom could see a young man sitting behind the desk.

"That's Rohan Lim, her assistant," Henry explained as they walked through to the deserted hotel lobby. "Looks like another quiet day here."

"Is it slow because it's a Monday?"

"The place was pretty empty on the weekend, too. Or so I heard." Henry shook his head. "Poor Zanna, she's tried her best to make a go of this place."

Dom glanced around, taking in the mix of old and newer chairs scattered about the lobby and the lackluster wainscoting below walls in need of a coat of paint. The last time he'd been in the hotel he'd had eyes only for Zanna. "The few times I've been home I got the feeling tourism had dropped in town. Is that the reason?"

"The main one, though the hotel has had trouble for years, starting from Fred's lack of interest after Brandon died." He looked at Dom. "Zanna's father. A sad story for the whole family." He seemed about to say something more but stopped as Zanna approached.

She was slipping on a bulky cardigan over the blouse and black skirt. Her business uniform, Dom figured. His gaze dropped to the floor where he noticed she'd exchanged the small heels she'd been wearing for sneakers. The look made her seem younger, though different from the teenaged version of Zanna Winters he'd been fascinated by, and he felt an unexpected twinge of regret that he'd never had the courage to say more than a mumbled hello to her back then.

They walked together across the white marbled lobby floor out into the sunny spring day. A brisk wind whipped up from the sea below and Dom zipped up his jacket.

"All right, you two," Henry said. "I'm heading this way—" he pointed up the street "—to meet with a councillor about snagging library space for the Historical Society."

Dom had a vague memory of his mother joining the Cove Historical Society and wondered if she still belonged. He would have to find out. "There's a library in town?" he asked.

Henry nodded. "It's in progress but well underway. Where the old cinema was, across from Town Hall. Remember that?"

"I do but didn't notice it last time I was home, around New Year's." It was an effort not to glance at Zanna when he mentioned that night.

"We're hoping we can use one of the community rooms that'll be available when the place is finished."

"Are you still involved with the Scout troop?"

Henry's guffaw rolled down the quiet street. "Too old and decrepit for that I'm afraid. One of Ben's employees is running the group, along with a friend. They're also looking for space, so I thought I'd be sneaky and get to town council first, though I imagine there's some kind of a waiting list already.

"Right now, the troop's dividing their time between St. Pat's basement and the school gym. When those places are booked, they might have to consider going to Portland, and that's not a good option, especially in winter."

"Must be a bigger troop than when I was a member."

"It is, thanks to the new subdivision up by the highway. The Cove has become what you call a satellite community." Henry shook his head. "The problem is it's all happened too fast, and the town doesn't have the necessary supports."

"The infrastructure of a regular community, you mean?"

"Right." Henry glanced at Zanna. "Okay then, we can carry on this conversation another time, Dominic. Come see me before you go back to base, if time permits. Off you both go!" He waved a hand and began the walk further uphill to the center of town.

Dom turned to Zanna, who was now peering at her watch. "Are you sure you have time for this? I can go up to the lighthouse on my own."

She managed a wan smile. "It's okay. I... uh... I need to talk to you about something anyway."

The ground rules, he figured, though her serious expression was concerning. He was both intrigued and apprehensive. When she silently turned around and headed down Main

Street, he tagged behind, feeling once again like that hapless teenager at Portland High.

He caught up to her when they reached the steps leading down to the boardwalk fronting the harbor. "Let's take this route," he suggested. Her shrug annoyed him. Connecting this Zanna with the one he'd met at New Year's was a challenge. He'd been naive to think that encounter had had a special meaning for her, as it had for him.

The few shops on the boardwalk were just beginning to open up, and as they passed a man setting up a signboard for the harbor boat cruise, Dom thought of yesterday, when he and his mother had strolled by after their brunch. "Ever been on one of those?" he impulsively asked Zanna.

She turned around, noticing the sign. "Um, once when I was a teen. Reluctantly," she added with a small laugh.

The way her face lit up, even briefly, warmed him. It was a fleeting glimpse of the Zanna from months ago. "How about you?" she asked.

"No, but the cruise became kind of a family story," he said, suddenly wanting to share it with her.

"How so?"

"I think I was about nine and already into my obsession with all kinds of boats, so one Sunday morning I suggested the cruise and my father said no, he spent all day every day out on Casco Bay and had no desire to spend his day off out there." When she frowned, he quickly explained, "He was a lobster fisherman. My mother promised to take me another time, but it never happened. When we came by here after Mother's Day brunch, I asked her if she'd like to go but the line was too long. We did have a bit of a laugh though, about Dad's stubborn refusal to get on that boat." After a second, he filled in the gap of silence. "I guess the point I'm making is that Mom and I were able to share a memory about him without feeling his loss."

Her expression softened. "Yeah, I can relate to that." Then, "We should get going," and she continued walking.

Back to business, Dom thought, but that quick glimpse of the Zanna he remembered from New Year's Eve was reassuring. She was still there, wrapped up in her hotel manager's outfit.

They reached the end of the boardwalk and

headed up the stairs to the beach road. The lighthouse loomed ahead, its white tower encircled by a single red band, gleaming in the morning sun. Despite the mid-May chill, there were a few hardy people—dogwalkers and parents with small children—strolling along the stony beach. The surf was up, pounding against the shore, and Dom wondered if the tide was coming in or going out. He shivered, thinking unexpectedly of the reason why they were about to climb up to the lighthouse. *Brandon.*

She led the way, mounting the dune easily in her sneakers while Dom lagged behind, his impractical loafers fighting the sandy surface. He finally joined her where she stood at the top, surveying the view of the town below and the glittering waters of Casco Bay. His breath caught, and he was about to say that he hadn't been up at the lighthouse since... no. Best to let her mention that—the reason why there was a memorial ceremony at all.

"The lighthouse looks good," he commented. "New paint, I guess?"

Zanna turned his way. "Yes, and some brickwork was replaced near the base." She pointed to the tower's base. "Those steps are new as well. Grace's fiancé—well, husband now—is going to get the beacon working again."

Dom stared at the three short steps leading down from the cement base. A mental image of Brandon trapped inside the tower as the tide rose around it overwhelmed him and he looked away, fixing his gaze on the long ridge of dune behind them. "I'm glad this side of the highway hasn't been developed," he said, observing the subdivision on the far side, beyond the dunes.

"The dunes are protected under some natural resources agency, which is why we can't erect anything here. Hence the idea of a plaque. The lighthouse was decommissioned last summer, and the town owns it now. The beacon will be operational, but it won't serve any purpose other than as a tourist draw."

"I remember my mother telling me a bit about the fundraising," Dom said. He'd also heard the story that shook the town for several days last summer—Grace Winters's confession about her small part in the prank that had led indirectly to Brandon's death.

"People really got on board with the project and there's still some money left for general maintenance. Henry and his friends at the Historical Society have volunteered to do that, along with Grace's husband, Drew. Anyway—" she took a big breath and shifted her attention back to the lighthouse "—as we said this morning, the plaque will be installed either on the tower itself or maybe in the concrete base next to the door."

Dom heard the tremble in her voice. After a moment he asked, "Where would *you* like to put it?"

She didn't answer for a long time. When she looked at him again, her eyes were damp. "I didn't want a memorial here at all. No plaque is going to bring back my brother, but I went along with it because my mother agreed with Grace that there should be something on this site as a reminder to people in town that as beautiful as the place is, there are clear dangers here." Her mouth tightened. "I've wished hundreds of times that I'd been home that summer. I might have noticed Brandon was struggling to fit into the teen scene. That day, he got a note he thought was from Ella Jacobs—one of the most popular girls in town—asking him to be her date to a bonfire. I could have told him she wouldn't have sent a note like that. She was dating Ben!" She shook her head. "I don't know what Bran was thinking. Especially when he found out that it was just a prank. He got upset and ran away. But I always wondered… *What made him go to the lighthouse?*"

Her plaintive cry rose into the air. Dom knew she wasn't expecting an answer. He guessed she and her family—maybe everyone in the Cove—had asked that same question many times. He had to tell her about his own small part that night, even at risk of breaking this fragile thread between them.

"I knew he was going to the bonfire."

"Who, Brandon? When was this?"

"I happened to bump into him that day. I'd been at Henry's to say goodbye before leaving for college on Labor Day Monday. Bran was coming out of the house where your family lived back then, and I was about to wish him a good year at school and try to give him some advice about sticking with the Scout troop. That sort of thing. But he was super excited because your mom had given him permission to go to the bonfire. It was a first for him and apparently some other kids from Scouts were going."

"Mom told me that last July when the whole story blew up again. Family confession time."

"I wanted to suggest maybe he wait another year. I knew from experience that anything could happen at the last-night-of-summer celebration. It used to be just for the graduating class, but then younger teens started going. And Brandon was younger than his years. Know what I mean?"

"Yes." Her voice was so low he barely heard her.

"The thing is," he pressed on, "I hated to ruin his excitement. He looked so happy. I just told him to have fun." He looked across the bay, far below. The water was calm and shimmering, the kind of sea he used to enjoy long ago, taking the wooden sea kayak he and his father had built out for a paddle. "It seems a lot of us let Brandon down."

"I wasn't here that summer because I was still angry at my mother," Zanna said.

Dom turned her way. Her face was as still as Casco Bay, but her eyes probed dark places of the past. He waited for her to go on.

"When I left for Augusta and college the year before Bran died, Mom told me she had something important to say. I thought she was going to warn me about the social scene I'd probably encounter there." She snorted. "As if. I was looking forward to that part of college! Instead, she told me I was adopted."

Dom blinked. That was the last thing he was expecting her to say. Questions filled his head, but he waited.

"She and my father had been trying to have a baby without any luck. Then some friend gave them a tip about a private agency in Bangor where they might not have to wait as long. And they were lucky because shortly after they applied, I came up for adoption. Mom didn't know anything about the…*my*… birth mother."

"Why wait so long to tell you?"

"That was the first thing I asked her."

"And?"

"My father wanted me to feel I was a real part of the Winters clan. He thought when I was a teenager I'd have enough to deal with— you know, the isolation and alienation some kids feel. Ironically, I always felt like that anyway. I never looked like a Winters, with their dark hair and eyes. Mom's hair was more reddish-blond though, so I always assumed I resembled her side of the family."

"How did you feel?"

"I was blindsided. My mind was a swirl of anger and self-pity. It wasn't the adoption part so much as the secret. And why tell me then, on the eve of my great adventure into the world beyond the Cove?"

She stopped suddenly. Catching her breath, Dom figured. After a moment he asked, "Is that why you stayed away the next summer, when it happened?"

Zanna nodded. "I purposely got a job in Bangor so I wouldn't have to come back home. I stayed with Mom's parents, which made it difficult for my folks to insist I return to the Cove. But then I did come home, when…"

She didn't have to finish. Dom knew what came next.

"I already thanked you for the hug at Bran's funeral. Mom told me later that your father was buried in the same cemetery so it must have been hard for you to…you know…not think about him at the same time."

But I had, Dom thought. *I was wishing I'd done more for Brandon and at the same time, remembering Dad and wishing I…*

"Are you okay?" Zanna was staring at him.

"Just thinking about everything back then."

"It's hard not to. But maybe now is a good time to plan something for the future, like the plaque. I was thinking somewhere on the lighthouse itself. Over time, the base and steps might need replacing but the lighthouse has been here a hundred years already so it should be okay for a long time to come."

"And it's a good symbol, too," Dom added.

"Will you be here for the ceremony?"

"Um, maybe." *That depends on seeing you again*, he wanted to add.

"It's just that, I…well… I have something to tell you."

"Okay." He waited but when she didn't speak right away, he prompted, "Go ahead. Better tell me now." He aimed for an encouraging smile despite the butterflies in his stomach.

He saw her take a deep breath. This seemed serious.

"I'm pregnant."

Dom stared, hearing what she was saying but not comprehending.

"I'm having our baby, Dominic. In September."

He saw the rise of color in her face and heard the pitch in her voice but when he moved his lips, nothing emerged, as if he were in the depths of Casco Bay, struggling to surface.

"It's okay," she snapped. "I'm not expecting a lot from you, but it would be nice if our child had a father to connect with. That's all I'm asking."

"Zanna…" His voice broke, and he inhaled, calming himself. "I…uh…"

She held up a palm. "Don't say anything. We'll talk later." Then she spun around and ran back along the grassy ridge, sliding down the sandy dune bank to the beach below.

"Zanna! Wait!" He watched her land, almost losing her balance, and continuing down the road to town. Never looking back.

A cloud passed across the sun, darkening the waters of the bay and chilling the air. Dom wiped a hand across his face, waking himself up to what had just happened. He had a sickening feeling he hadn't measured up. That he'd let Zanna down.

CHAPTER FOUR

ZANNA TURNED OFF her phone. Alex Corelli from Gateway Living had just informed her that representatives were coming tomorrow morning to view the hotel to survey its *viability*, as he'd said. She hadn't expected such a prompt callback since their phone conversation during Grace's wedding, but considering yesterday's visit to the lighthouse with Dom, maybe sooner was better than later.

She needed to sort out her future, especially after his reaction to her news. The dismay in his face had been bad enough but the fact that he hadn't uttered a word was worse. As far as she was concerned, Dominic Kennedy was a disappointment and Zanna had no place in her life for people who didn't come through for her.

"Zanna?" Rohan stuck his head through the open office door.

"Hmm?"

"Lisa just called in sick, but I can do the rooms today. There are two check-outs and one reservation. Two other rooms are occupied until tomorrow."

Zanna bit back a curse. Someone was sick and no one was to blame. "Do you mind? I have an important meeting early tomorrow that I need to prep for. It's okay, nothing serious," she quickly added, seeing his frown, though she knew the meeting could inevitably have an impact on Rohan's employment. That detail, along with many others, would be managed in time.

"Okay. Then I'll take a later lunch break."

"Fine, and thanks, Rohan. Did Lisa say whether she'd make it in tomorrow or not?"

"No. Should I give Cheryl a call just in case—give her a heads-up?" Cheryl worked part-time at the hotel and also as a receptionist at the town's newspaper, *The Beacon*.

"Please." Zanna held up two crossed fingers, hoping the single mother would be available. After Rohan left, she got up, smoothed out her skirt, picked up the laptop, and headed out to take over at reception. Rohan was just stepping into the elevator.

The young man had proven to be not only

a valued employee but a friend who'd tolerated some dark moods after her marriage fell apart. Even so, she knew very little about his personal life. She'd hired him right after his high school graduation two years ago. Recently his questions about the hotel management program she'd taken after college graduation indicated he might soon be leaving. While she was thrilled that he was continuing his education, he'd be hard to replace. This was another tick on the increasingly longer "sell" column.

Deciding whether to leave the Cove might not weigh upon her so much if Dom's response yesterday had been different. She could be making plans right now, working out some kind of visitation schedule for him, instead of staring into the dark abyss of the future. Well, there was nothing to be gained by feeling sorry for herself. At least selling the hotel would bankroll that future, whatever it entailed. When she was still married, she and her ex traveled across the States working in a variety of hotels, from five-star luxury to funky boutique ones. She'd built a network of contacts in the industry and childcare facilities were always better in cities. She could get a job running a hotel in some big city, a more exciting prospect than struggling to make ends meet in Lighthouse Cove. Lots of options, she told herself.

She thought of Cheryl, working two part-time jobs that probably barely covered her son's daycare, unless he had a grandparent available. That made her think of her mother. Jane would be disappointed, if not hurt, if Zanna left the Cove with her first and likely only grandchild. There was Dom's mother to consider, too.

Zanna felt a headache coming on. Everything was suddenly very complicated. If only Dominic had been more receptive to her news, she'd at least be feeling some optimism about the months ahead. Now she foresaw an ongoing struggle, one that she worried about managing on her own. *No*, she told herself. *You can do it, with or without Dominic Kennedy*.

HE HAD TO see her, tell her he was sorry for not hiding his shock better. Three cups of coffee that morning—drawing a raised eyebrow from his mother—had provided the adrenaline Dom needed. He stared at his reflection in the bathroom mirror while shaving. The puffiness under eyes that verged on blood-shot told the story of how he'd spent the night, though he'd deserved every second of the tossing and turning.

He sighed as he shaved the other side of his face. Hopefully he'd be able to come up with an explanation for his reaction yesterday that didn't sound too underwhelming. She'd been living with this situation for weeks, he reminded himself. *Alone.* He wondered if she'd confided in anyone but then dismissed the thought. Not Zanna Winters. He figured she'd been handling things all by herself. The one time he'd ever seen her vulnerable was that moment years ago at Brandon's funeral. He paused shaving for another face-to-face with himself. *Maybe if you'd called her after New Year's, she wouldn't have had to go through the last few months on her own. Sure, she'd insisted the night was a onetime thing. No expectations or obligations. Still, if you'd cared enough...*

But he *had* cared. That had been the crux of what kept him from picking up his cell phone after that night. He'd feared hearing a lack of interest in her voice or some hint that meeting him at New Year's hadn't been a big deal for her, not as monumental as it had been for him. The idea that she might not care for him as much as he did for her had kept him from calling.

He swore at his reflection. Knowing that he'd behaved poorly then and again yesterday didn't sit well with Dominic. There was no other option. He had to apologize. Be honest. Make her believe he'd do the right thing despite what she'd shouted at the lighthouse— that she wasn't expecting a lot from him, except to connect in some way with their baby.

The concept of fatherhood, much less marriage, had never really crossed his mind. He'd known since he was a kid listening to his Uncle George's stories that he was going to be a career navy man, but he'd kept the fantasy a secret because he'd also known that his father expected him to be a lobster fisherman, take over their family boat and maybe earn enough between the two of them to buy another. To build a real business.

But his father's dream and Dom's secret vanished the moment that boat had capsized in a storm when Dom was seventeen. A year later, when he was graduating from high school, his mother supported his application to military college and the navy. She didn't want to lose her only child to the waters off Casco Bay and she sold the family's lobstering assets. Dom got to realize his dream, but at a great cost.

He had plenty of money to support a child, but the problem was he had no time. And the promotion he sought—the one he wanted more than anything—would give him less time. Might even move him to the other side of the country. He'd wrestled with that possibility as well as being a father through the long sleepless night while the words Zanna had hurled at him spooled round and round in his head. *I'm not expecting a lot from you.*

Wow. What did that say about the connection they'd made months ago and again yesterday, at the lighthouse? Was she actually listening when he confided his regret about how he'd dismissed Brandon's decision to go to the bonfire that night? That he'd had a bad feeling about the idea, but didn't speak up? What hurt most of all was her lack of expectation of *him*. Did she even believe he could be a good father? That thought especially saddened him. Somehow, he had to convince her he could.

ZANNA'S HEART SANK when she saw Dominic striding across the hotel lobby to the reception counter. She guessed why he'd come—to make amends for his behavior yesterday—but it was the worst possible time and place. Rohan was upstairs cleaning rooms and although the morning was slow as usual, she knew there was a reservation due to come in. She wondered briefly if the man heading her way could get anything right, especially after he'd fumbled his response to her news. Then she immediately felt bad for the thought. He was the father of her baby after all, and she shouldn't give up on him.

"Have you got a minute?" he asked when he reached the counter.

His hoarse voice and the pouches beneath his bleary eyes touched her enough to soften her reply. "Rohan is upstairs cleaning rooms and there's no one else to take over."

He glanced around the deserted lobby. "Well, maybe we can have a short talk right here?"

Short talk? "We can try," she mumbled.

He took a visible breath and the fact that he was nervous was both pleasing and troubling. Maybe there wasn't going to be an apology after all, much less a discussion. Maybe there was simply going to be a good-bye. But no, she thought. He was a better man than that. She had no doubts about his basic character—only his plans.

"I'm sorry I wasn't more receptive yesterday when you told me you were pregnant. It was a shock…as it must have been for you, too, when you found out. To be honest, I never thought about being a father or even a husband. The navy has been my family and I've never considered any other life. I…uh…spent a lot of last night coming to grips with the idea of fatherhood and by morning, I realized—" he paused to clear his throat "—this might be a chance for me to…prove myself. To do my best for someone."

Like a challenge? Well, parenting definitely would be that, but this wasn't what she wanted to hear. She'd hoped deep down that he might mention the possibility of the baby uniting them in a more meaningful way than basic co-parenting. That some part of the

Dominic Kennedy she'd seen at New Year's might emerge. Disappointment swept through her, and she averted her gaze from his, pulling her cell phone from her skirt pocket, pretending to check a message.

When she looked up, she saw that his face was pink, either with frustration or annoyance. "Sorry," she said. "I'm expecting a check-in."

"I should have called to arrange a time for this."

"Look, why don't we meet up when Rohan can take over for me? Maybe later today or tomorrow?"

"Sure. Whenever. The sooner the better."

He was right on with that, she thought. "We could…go somewhere out of town." She cringed inwardly at the nuance of a secret tryst in the suggestion, but he seemed to get her gist.

"Some place private would be good. I mean, where no one here would see us together. Small town," he added, his face reddening even more.

"Exactly. I have a meeting tomorrow so I'll text you when I'm finished."

"Okay." He sounded unconvinced.

"I'm not putting you off," she was quick to explain. "It's just that this isn't the best time. I'll think of a place to go."

He gave a curt nod and without another word, marched off across the lobby. She watched his stiff back and guessed he was ticked off. But she also knew she had to take charge.

He pushed through the door and held it for a diminutive woman pulling a rolling suitcase behind her and carrying a small crate. Without looking back, he stepped out onto the sidewalk. Zanna closed her eyes. She was committed to the next day and wherever it led.

A cheerful voice brought her back to reality.

"Good afternoon. Oh, I love this hotel already! I'm Cora Stanfield and I have a reservation." The woman paused to set down the crate and smiled at the small fluffy white dog inside it. "I also hope you don't mind animals. This little fellow—Mo—is very docile. Also extremely well-trained. He won't be a bother to anyone, I assure you."

This was a first, Zanna thought. But the woman's enthusiastic greeting and the sweet expression on Mo's face—not to mention the hard fact that she needed the booking—persuaded her. "Welcome to the Lighthouse Hotel, Ms. Stanfield…and Mo." Zanna felt a small burst of pleasure as the woman beamed.

She opened up the reservations file on her laptop and, because there were so few on the page, found the booking right away. "You've asked for a suite on the waterfront side?"

"Please."

"What floor would you like?" At the woman's thoughtful expression, Zanna explained, "There are four floors, and some harbor view suites are currently available. Obviously, you'd get a better view from the top floor, but then you'd have to use the elevator and there's only one I'm afraid." She pointed to the far left of the reception counter where the elevator was tucked behind the staircase.

Cora Stanfield looked in that direction and then around the empty lobby. "Is the elevator usually very busy? I mean, I can manage the stairs down but going up, especially with Mo here, might be more challenging."

"Oh, the elevator isn't busy."

"All right. Top floor then. Be nice to see across the bay." Another glance around the lobby. "I suppose tourist season hasn't picked up yet."

"True. How long are you anticipating staying?" She looked up from the computer. The woman seemed to be staring at her ID tag swinging from the lanyard around her neck, but then she blinked and said,

"Oh, sorry. My mind was elsewhere. Um, I'd like to leave my visit open-ended. Is that okay?"

It was a surprise, but definitely okay. "Wonderful! You'll enjoy the town much more without a lot of tourists, anyway." Zanna retrieved a card key from a drawer, scanned it and handed it over. "There you go. Top floor, Room 410. Right next to the elevator."

"That'll be handy for when I take Mo out for his necessary walks."

"Oh, right." She'd forgotten about the dog, sitting so quietly in his crate. "My assistant, Rohan, might be able to help with that occasionally. He's very amenable." Zanna mentally crossed her fingers, hoping Rohan liked dogs.

"That would be wonderful, but I wouldn't want to take him away from his work."

"I'm sure he'd be available once in a while.

Right now, he's busy upstairs but I can help you with your things."

"I wouldn't dream of taking you away from the desk. I can manage."

"Not at all," Zanna assured her. She logged out of the computer and walked around to the other side of the counter. Standing next to Cora Stanfield made Zanna feel like a giant. As a teen, she'd felt self-conscious about her height, tending to slouch, especially when around boys. But her mother's incessant urging to carry her height proudly had eventually broken through her insecurity.

"I'll carry Mo. Cute name." Zanna grasped the handle of the crate.

"Yes, Mo for Maurice. After my late husband. Sadly, he never got to meet Mo, but I know he'd love him as much as I do."

After her husband. Zanna was beginning to think Cora Stanfield had an eccentric side. She liked that. Cora caught up to her as the elevator door opened and Rohan stepped out.

"Oh, it's small!" Cora exclaimed.

"You're not claustrophobic I hope?" Zanna asked.

"No, though if I were a larger person, I might hesitate going in there."

Zanna smiled. There was something engaging about the woman, she thought as she introduced Cora to Rohan.

"Want me to take Mrs. Stanfield up?" he asked.

Zanna shook her head. "Thanks, but I won't be long." She ushered Cora inside. As the elevator creaked slowly up to the fourth floor, the thought that Gateway Living would definitely have to replace the aging contraption flashed through Zanna's mind. But then she supposed the whole hotel would be renovated anyway. Or perhaps torn down. She shied away from that possibility, picturing Uncle Charles's face at the idea.

Cora broke into her thoughts. "How old is the hotel? I imagine this elevator is a relatively modern addition."

"Relatively is the right word, Mrs. Stanfield. The hotel was built in the late 1800s by my great-grandfather and I believe the elevator wasn't installed until my father was a boy. Maybe in the early sixties?"

"I was going to ask if you were related to the family—the Winters?"

"Yes. My grandfather left the hotel to my father."

There was a brief silence. "How long have you been running it?"

"Not quite three years, but I inherited it when my father passed away." The elevator jerked to a stop, and Zanna stepped onto the carpeted hallway, leading the way along the hall to the front of the hotel.

"Oh, I'm sorry to hear that. When—"

"Several years ago," Zanna said. The string of personal questions was tiring, especially when the woman could be asking about tourist attractions. But maybe she was one of those people who liked to make personal connections. "He was ill the last few years of his life and had hired someone to manage the hotel. After I graduated from college, I had no desire to come back to the Cove to take over the helm, so to speak." She arrived at the room and unlocked the door using her master key card.

Cora walked ahead of Zanna, exclaiming, "My heavens! What a view!"

Zanna smiled. This *was* the best view of Casco Bay and the lighthouse, and if she ever came into enough money, she'd definitely upgrade the waterfront rooms. If she were keeping the hotel.

As it was, perhaps the scenery would distract from the heavy velveteen drapes and the faded chenille bedspread. Many of the rooms had been updated with new linens but not the suites, which were seldom occupied. "The bathroom is right here," she said, turning on the light and trying not to focus on the avocado green sink, toilet and bathtub. At least the shower curtain was new and the towels. She was about to apologize for the deficits when Cora pivoted around from the large bay window.

"This is perfect. I love it!" She bent down to open the dog's crate. "Come on, Mo, look at where we're living for the next while."

The ball of white fluff yipped excitedly, running around in circles and then leaping up into Cora's arms. Zanna managed a smile but hoped the dog wouldn't be as active for the whole stay.

"He's just happy to be out of that crate. Don't worry," Cora said right away. "Despite his appearance, he's not a pup anymore. Getting old, like me." She looked from Mo to Zanna.

The woman's warm laugh, her short dark hair and smooth complexion gave no sign of age. Zanna figured she was younger than she implied. Definitely younger than her mother, Jane. "When you've settled in, come down to the desk. I'll put together some pamphlets along with suggestions of things to see and places to dine."

"Sounds good to me. And thank you, Ms. Winters—"

"Please—Zanna."

Cora nodded. "Zanna. Thank you for your assistance and I'd be grateful for some tourist ideas. I've done a bit of research on the internet about Lighthouse Cove, but I look forward to hearing about it from you. Someone who grew up here."

Zanna smiled. "My pleasure. See you shortly."

As she descended the stairs to the lobby, she decided to do as much as possible to ensure that Cora Stanfield had an enjoyable visit in the Cove and began making a mental list of places to see. Perhaps even introduce her to someone like Henry Jenkins. His enthusiasm and knowledge of the town's history might appeal to Cora. By the time she reached the lobby, she had some ideas and hoped the woman would be around long enough to make use of them.

She felt energized about the hotel but guessed it wouldn't last. Taking over had been a challenge, one that was exacerbated by her failing marriage and the family turmoil following Grace's confession. The potential hotel sale would give her options about staying or leaving. Of course, those options were subject to change now that Dominic Kennedy was back in her life.

CHAPTER FIVE

AFTER A LONG night working on his interview material, Dom had needed to get out of the house. He gazed across the bay from the boardwalk. The morning was warming up, but in spite of the promise of a spring day, Dom shivered. Tendrils of mist hovered above the cooler sea water. He knew the sea could be deceptive and worse, unpredictable.

Taking a deep breath, he reminded himself that delving into the past wasn't going to help his mood. There were plenty of new problems to deal with. Right now, he was glad he'd decided to get back into a regimen of exercise, given another couple of weeks' leave in the Cove. His mother was an excellent cook who was making good use of those extra days.

She didn't know yet about the news he was still processing—that he was going to be a father. Although the idea had terrified him at first, now he was beginning to think this might be a chance for him to prove he was made of the right stuff. His father had been a calm yet instructional parent, even when hauling up lobster pots in rough seas with waves crashing over the bow of their boat. From the time Dom was twelve, he often went lobstering on weekends, along with his father's partner, and gradually got used to the unexpected weather shifts a day could bring—calm and sunny to stormy in a matter of hours.

Dom had always loved the mystery of deep water, the air's salty tang and seabirds sweeping overhead. Yet he'd never wanted to be a lobsterman, as locals called the founders of the Cove and their descendants. His gaze had traveled further out to sea, to battleships, frigates and submarines. He had Uncle George, his mother's older brother, to thank for that.

Reaching the end of the boardwalk, he bounded up the steps two at a time where he paused, jogging on the spot as he decided which route to take. Straight ahead would take him past the section of cottages and bungalows fronting the beach to the long peninsula marking the end of the cove. The lighthouse beckoned, or he could tackle the long set of stairs leading from the beach up to the Winterses' big house, the turreted mansion overlooking the town. There was a public side road at the top so he wouldn't have to worry about landing on private property. From there his mother's bungalow was a ten-minute jog down the public road into the older area of town around Town Square. He didn't feel ready to go back home yet. *The lighthouse it is*, he decided.

He'd only run ten yards or so when he noticed a woman ahead bending over a small animal. As he got closer, she suddenly rose up, crying out as the animal—a dog?—dashed across the beach road toward the enclave on the opposite side. All Dom saw was a flash of white as the dog darted around parked cars and people heading for the beach. Reaching the woman, Dom saw that she was trying to play down her distress.

"He's so darn annoying. I should have taken him to obedience school." Her voice trembled. She held up a dog leash. "I was trying to unravel this and unclipped it for barely a second when he—"

"Made a run for it?"

She pursed her lips and nodded. Dom noticed her glistening eyes. She seemed vaguely familiar, but he couldn't quite place her. "Why don't I see if I can catch up to him?"

"Oh, would you? I mean, he's not a pup. He's sure to run out of steam soon."

Dom caught sight of the dog, trotting now up the side street leading behind the cottages into the newer area where Henry Jenkins lived. "I can try. What's his name?"

"Mo. But he only comes when he feels like it—just as stubborn as his namesake."

Dom took off. The road was quiet this early, but the weekday commuter traffic would be picking up. He dodged a pickup truck turning out of the side street and spotted the dog sniffing around the base of a lamppost. Dom slowed down. When he was about six feet away, he called out, "Here Mo!"

Startled, Mo looked up, waited long enough for Dom to get closer and then took off. Dom swore. His Good Samaritan act might prove to be an embarrassing failure. On the plus side, he was getting more of a run now. Mo made a right turn at the corner and as Dom followed, the front door of a small house about twenty feet ahead opened.

Was that Henry's house? It had been years

since he'd last been there and the place looked fresher, spruced up. What Dom failed to notice until too late was the gray-and-white cat strolling out onto the porch. Mo, however, noticed. He swerved left, up the sidewalk, barking furiously. The cat was clever enough to leap onto the porch railing where he sat, calmly oblivious to the drama beneath. By the time Dom had slowed down in front of the porch, the door was opening again. Henry Jenkins stood there, looking from the cat to the barking dog to Dom and smiled. "Well, what a surprise."

Dom lunged for Mo and picked him up before he could take off again.

"Your dog?" Henry's eyes twinkled.

"Hah! No. He escaped from his owner down by the beach. I was out jogging."

"I see." Henry's gaze shifted from Dom to the road. "And that would be the owner, I'm guessing."

The woman marching toward them waved and soon was up on the porch. Dom noted her red face and shortness of breath. Henry must have, too, for he quickly said, "Please, have a seat," gesturing to one of the two wicker chairs in front of the bungalow's picture window.

She sank into a chair and after a brief pause to catch her breath, smiled at both Dom and Henry before frowning at her dog. "Bad Mo," she scolded.

Mo's ears flattened but the moment Dom handed him over to her, the dog was wriggling to get off her lap and have another go at the cat. Henry chuckled. "Best if I put Felix inside." He scooped up the cat and set him down on the other side of the door, then asked, "Would you like a glass of water?"

"Oh, no, but thank you. I'm quite all right. Just a bit out of shape I'm afraid. And thank you for catching Mo for me," she said, turning to Dom.

"Feel free to rest as long as you like," Henry offered. "I'm Henry, by the way, and this young fellow is Dominic."

"Lovely to meet you both. I'm Cora. Is everyone in Lighthouse Cove as friendly and helpful as you two?"

"Depends who you're asking I suppose, but having spent all of my seventy years here, I can safely say I've run across very few cantankerous folks, even of my generation. And Dom here, whom I've known forever it seems, is a fine representative of the younger generation. I think it's rare you'll encounter anyone in the Cove who *isn't* welcoming."

"Well, I certainly haven't yet. I'm staying in the hotel down the road and have no complaints at all so far."

Dom remembered now that he'd held the door for her yesterday, when he'd been angry at Zanna. "The owner will be happy to hear that," he said. "How long will you be in town?"

"I'm not sure. That's the bonus of retirement, right?" She laughed. "Do you know the hotel's owner? Suzanna Winters?"

"We were at the same high school."

"Ah. I suppose in a town this size, everyone knows each other…and their business, too?"

Despite her smile, there was an inflection in her voice that was more serious.

"The Cove is much bigger nowadays," Henry said.

"I guess my comment reinforced a stereotype of small towns, didn't it? My apologies."

Henry waved a hand. "Not at all. Those stereotypes came from somewhere at some point in time. I'm guessing you didn't grow up in a small town?"

That brought a tinkling laugh. "Ironically, I did. I currently live in a suburb of Chicago, but I grew up here in Maine, in a small town near Bangor, which I left many years ago." She stood up, clutching the struggling dog to her bosom. "I must finish my walk with this naughty dog. Perhaps we'll meet each other again."

"No doubt. If you're here for a bit, ask Zanna for some tourism suggestions."

"She's already given me a list of places to see and where to eat. I'm going to try Mabel's for lunch, though I wonder if dogs are allowed?"

"Can't hurt to ask," Henry said.

Cora bent to link the leash through Mo's collar. "Thanks again, gentlemen." She waved a small hand and carefully headed down the steps to the sidewalk where she waved once more and headed to the beach road.

"Nice lady," Henry murmured.

"Yes," Dom agreed. "Maybe if she likes the town enough, she'll recommend the place to her friends."

"Back in Chicago?" Henry sounded doubtful.

"She said she was from Maine originally. Maybe she's visiting family."

Henry shrugged. "Maybe. And since you're

here now, care for a cup of coffee? Have that catch-up we talked about?"

Dom saw his plan for an extended run disappear. On the other hand, he was happy to spend time with Henry. As he followed his former mentor inside, he remembered that he and Zanna were supposed to meet to discuss the future. Two days ago, that future had been all mapped out and now…?

He took his cell phone from his sweatshirt pocket to check for messages and found one from Zanna.

Business meeting this afternoon. Can we get together tomorrow instead? 9 a.m. here? Wear casual clothes.

THEY TOOK THEIR time crossing the lobby, looking around them with interest. Zanna noted there were only two—a man and a woman—rather than the team Alex had mentioned. Although she'd spoken to Corelli on the phone a couple of times, she'd never met him. Perhaps he was strolling her way this very moment. She moved from behind the counter and met them halfway, extending her right arm and offering a large smile. "Zanna Winters," she said.

"Jason Broderick, and this is Kathleen Connor."

"Welcome to The Lighthouse Hotel," she said after the handshaking. "Would you like the tour first?"

"Sure," said Jason, taking the lead. "Then a talk?"

"My thoughts exactly. So, obviously, this is the lobby," she began.

The woman pulled a cell phone out of her shoulder bag. "Okay if I record as we go?" she asked Zanna.

"Of course. I have a handout of information in my office to give you. Some history of the hotel and so on."

Kathleen gave a vague nod and began speaking in a low voice on her phone. Already onto business, Zanna thought. Despite the pleasantries, this wasn't a social meeting, and she wanted them to have the best possible impression of the hotel and how it could fit into the Gateway Living model.

"I'll start with the treasure hidden at the end of this lobby," she said, leading them to the ballroom. Kathleen recorded some video.

Half an hour later they were sitting in her office, drinking the sparkling mineral water that Rohan had thoughtfully placed on her desk.

While Kathleen had been taking photos and videos and recording notes on her phone, Jason had asked only a few questions throughout the tour. Except for their enthusiastic response to the size of the ballroom, both of them had remained fairly impassive, their faces showing little reaction to what they were seeing. Zanna had no idea what they were thinking but guessed from her limited experience this was how negotiations started. Still, she refused to let their lack of enthusiasm dampen her spirits.

"Thanks for this," Jason said, folding the handout from Zanna and passing it to Kathleen, who tucked it into her shoulder bag. "Alex will be contacting you after the team has had a chance to go through our findings. That could take a week or so because we're also looking at another property. Just to let you know."

Reality was sinking in for Zanna, who'd been imagining an early decision. But she hid her disappointment. "Thanks, Jason, and

I'm hoping for a good result for all of us." She followed them out the office door where they paused to shake hands again.

"Nice meeting you, Zanna," Jason said, before following Kathleen, who was already crossing the lobby.

She watched them leave, then turned around to see Rohan standing behind the counter.

"Good meeting?" he asked.

The question sounded casual, but Zanna knew he wanted information. He deserved to find out her plans, even if they came to nothing. "There's something I need to tell you. I'm—"

The front door swooshed open, catching their attention. Cora Stanfield breezed into the lobby, led by an eager Mo. When she was a few feet away from the counter, she said, "I've just been to Mabel's and they allow therapy dogs and occasionally, small, quiet ones. As much as Mo provided lots of therapy for me when I got him as a puppy after my husband died, he doesn't really qualify as a therapy dog and I'm worried he might be too excitable." She looked expectantly from Rohan to Zanna, her gaze settling on Rohan. "Would you mind?"

Rohan took hold of the leash and started toward the front door when Cora blurted,

"Oh, I meant could you take him up to my room and put him in his crate. He's tuckered out from our walk and won't resist going into it for a nap." She laughed. "And after my late lunch, I'll be joining him. It's just that this saves me a trip upstairs and back down again."

Rohan gave a thumbs-up and headed for the stairs. Thinking the climb would tire the dog even more, Zanna wondered, hiding a smile.

"Would you care to join me for lunch?" Cora asked.

The unexpected invite surprised Zanna, who'd resolved long ago to avoid overly social interactions with guests, but she hesitated for a second. The woman was so warm and friendly, she was tempted. "Thanks, Mrs. Stanfield, but Rohan will be leaving soon, and I have some work to finish up." *Like brainstorming ideas for my future.*

"Oh, too bad." The flash of disappointment shifted to a smile. "Another time then."

Watching her head for the door, Zanna thought she was such an enthusiastic and charming woman that maybe she could bend her longtime rule and even show her a bit of the town. The check-in information had indicated a home address in Chicago and Zanna bet that Cora Stanfield would love to know more about Lighthouse Cove.

CHAPTER SIX

ZANNA WASN'T SURE if the butterflies in her stomach were due to her guilt leaving Rohan again or the sight of Dominic Kennedy in jeans and a crisp, sky-blue Polo T-shirt that brought out the cobalt flecks in his eyes. He clutched a windbreaker in one hand and a ball cap in the other and strolled casually across the lobby, a smile lighting up his face when he spotted her. She hadn't told him anything about her plans for the day—a trip to Peaks Island in Casco Bay—but from his air of anticipation, he was clearly expecting something slightly different from what she really had in mind—a fact-finding mission to learn what kind of man he was and what kind of father he would be.

"I'm mystified by what we could possibly be up to today," he said as he drew up to the counter where she was standing. "At least casual clothes are my go-to style when I'm not in uniform."

He was teasing her about her text. "I have a tendency to over-organize. Sorry about that."

"That's something we have in common then."

Off to a good start, Zanna thought, adding a mental check to the plus side of her pro and con list of shared traits she hoped to complete that day.

Rohan came through the office door and noticing Dominic, cast a questioning look Zanna's way. She realized he hadn't been officially introduced. "Rohan, this is Dominic, a…um…an old high school friend." She saw a glint of amusement in Dom's eyes as the two shook hands.

There was a slight pause until Rohan spoke. "Lisa's done the fourth floor and she'll probably finish early. Should I keep her around or send her home?"

It was a valid question, because Zanna was paying her an hourly wage. At the same time, she knew Lisa had lost a day's pay when she was off sick. "Um, sure. Maybe let her go after lunch if there are no check-ins. But if she wants to make up for her lost day's wages, she could do some general housekeeping." She might be paying Lisa for unnecessary work, but she felt bad that she couldn't offer any sick benefits.

He nodded. "And by the way, she told me the little dog chewed up a washcloth. Mrs. Stanfield insists on paying for it but Lisa told her not to worry. Okay with that?"

Zanna stifled a sigh. "Yeah, that was an okay call. I hope it wasn't one of the new ones though."

Rohan shrugged. "Don't know."

"Are you sure you'll be all right?" She'd asked him that question almost half a dozen times since yesterday when she'd decided to take Dominic on a short road trip. Well, ferry trip. "Text if you're feeling overwhelmed."

"Not too worried about that."

Zanna noted Dom's slight frown. Picking up the implication of slow business in Rohan's remark? Well, he'd find out soon enough. "All right, shall we go?" She grabbed her shoulder bag and lightweight jacket from the reception counter.

"An old high school friend?" Dom teased when they were out on the sidewalk.

Zanna ignored his grin. "It sounded better than old acquaintance." And she definitely wasn't about to introduce Dom as the father of her expected child! Fortunately, he dropped the matter as she led him to her car.

"Is this a mystery tour?" Dom asked as they rounded the corner of Main Street.

"You'll see." Her car's headlights came to life as she clicked the fob.

"Okay. We're driving somewhere."

"And boating. Well, ferrying."

"In that case, I'm guessing our first destination is Portland." He climbed into the passenger seat and, fastening his seat belt, added, "Just to warn you, I may find the ferry ride a bit tame compared to what I'm used to."

She smiled. "I'm sure you will. But you won't be on it long enough to get bored."

"Now I'm really curious, but considering we're getting the ferry in Portland, the destination must be an island in Casco Bay."

"Come on! You're spoiling the surprise. I don't want you to be disappointed."

There was a moment's silence. Zanna felt his eyes on her as she drove along Main Street to the highway. "I'd never be disappointed being with you," he finally said, his voice low.

"If I weren't driving, I'd have to make you

pinky swear to that," she joked. No way did she want the talk to turn serious so soon.

"I'd do it," he murmured.

Her face heated up. She kept her eyes on the road ahead and after a minute felt him shift his gaze from her to his window.

"I still can't believe how big the Cove has gotten," he said.

Braking at the stop sign where Main Street joined the highway, Zanna pointed to the new subdivision on their right. "Uncle Charles started building there about five years ago, but Ben's company has pushed further north and east."

"I'd heard he'd taken over the business. Guess he's doing well for himself."

"He is. Maybe you've noticed the new condos in progress on the other side of town, adjacent to the dunes and the lighthouse?"

"Yeah, I walked up there when I first got home. They look really nice. I mentioned them to my mother, in case she ever wanted to move out of her house, which is kind of big for one person."

"And?"

"She almost threw a dish towel at me." He laughed.

"Not a fan of condos?"

"A move in general. They looked too modern for her tastes anyway."

Zanna immediately thought of Gateway Living and their retirement apartments but kept quiet. That option was too far into the future.

He switched topics suddenly. "The dog that chewed the washcloth. Was that the little white one? Mo?"

"How do you know Mo?"

"I met his owner yesterday while I was jogging on the beach road. The dog got loose somehow and ran away so I offered to chase after him. He ended up on Henry's front porch because Henry's cat came out of the house at exactly the right—or wrong—time." Dom laughed. "There was a flurry of barking, but that cat was totally oblivious."

"Felix," Zanna said. "He's a character all right. Then you met Cora Stanfield?"

"Yeah. Very nice lady."

Zanna turned to look at him. "Apparently, Mo is named after her deceased husband."

"Makes sense. She seemed a tad eccentric, but in a sweet way." He paused to ask, "Think the dog will be a problem?"

"He might be if there were a lot of guests to complain but as it is…"

"I take it business is slow."

How much to reveal? Spill it all out now or save the whole story for later, when she hears from Gateway? Keeping her eyes on the road, she said, "Yeah, kinda."

"Maybe when tourist season kicks in? When's that, June?"

"Yeah. Fingers crossed. Rohan and I plan to brainstorm some ideas for the tourist season, like discounted getaways packaged with vouchers for a local restaurant or tour. Anyway, today is all about getting away from the job."

"Sounds like a good plan," he commented.

Zanna hoped the end result would be good—a clear picture of her future prospects with Dom Kennedy.

The outskirts of Portland loomed and Zanna slowed down to merge with the flow of traffic.

Several minutes later she'd found the Casco Bay Lines terminal and its parking area.

"Not taking the car on?" he asked as she drove into the lot.

"I read that parking is limited on the island so I figured this would be easier. Plus, it'll be fun to be a walk-on passenger, don't you think?"

"My guess is we're going to Peaks Island."

She gave him a playful punch on his shoulder as they unfastened their seat belts. "You're spoiling the surprise! What was the giveaway?"

His grin was sheepish. "Not many car-carrying ferries going out into the bay. But it's still a surprise, 'cause I've never been."

"Never?"

"Nope. How about you?"

"Once, on a field trip in elementary school, but I'm guessing it'll have changed a lot since then."

"Funny that we never noticed each other in elementary," he said, getting out of the car.

"As a preteen I was definitely not into no-ticing boys, and you were in a grade below me."

"True. Lighthouse Elementary was a small school, but I wasn't paying much attention to girls in those days." He paused. "Is the school still in operation?"

"It is but I heard it needs to be extended due to the influx of kids coming from the subdivision. Either that or the school board will need to get funds to build a whole new school."

They'd reached the ferry piers and Zanna stopped, looking about for the one to Peaks Island.

"Shouldn't we get in line?" Dom was pointing to the ticket offices.

Zanna held up her phone. "Got ours already. Just need to find the right pier."

By the time they reached it, the ferry was loading the last car. They sprinted to join the end of the walk-on passenger queue as the ferry's stern ramp was being raised.

"That was close," Zana laughed. "Though they're pretty regular so we wouldn't have had to wait too long for the next one. Where to? Up top?"

"Oh, definitely!"

The line to get to the preferred upper deck was long and Zanna doubted they'd find a seat, but as they navigated around the other passengers, she spotted an elderly couple who must have decided to go below, out of the stiff breeze. She made a dash and plopped down in the vacant pair of seats, followed closely by Dom, who was laughing.

"I'm surprised you didn't push them out of the way in your rush to grab their seats."

Zanna batted her eyelashes. "Who, me?"

His scoff at her fake act disappeared but he held her eyes with his, sending a sudden charge of heat through her. She looked to her right as the ferry pulled away from the pier, slowly leaving the city wharves and the sky-scrapers of Portland behind. A gust of wind whipped across the deck, and Zanna pushed aside strands of hair that were swept across her forehead. She reached for her jacket and saw Dom putting on his, too.

"Something to be said for sitting below," she said as she zipped the coat up. She'd for-gotten temperatures were always lower on the water, and she tucked her hands into her jacket pockets, wishing she'd brought gloves and a hat.

"This is nothing…a little breeze. Real wind is out there, in the open sea, when a boat's rolling from side to side or cresting six-foot waves."

"Um, no, thanks. I'm happy to restrict my wave experience to the inner harbor and the Bay."

"Fair enough. So what's the day's agenda?"

he asked. "Or is that going to be a surprise, too?"

The way he arched one eyebrow made him look like a twelve-year-old, and Zanna unexpectedly wished she *had* known him in elementary school or that she'd made some effort to get to know him in high school. Even after that day at Brandon's funeral when he'd comforted her. If their lives had connected in a more meaningful way before the New Year's Eve party, she might not be sitting here feeling this angst about him, about what he thought of her and especially, about what kind of father he'd be. She felt a rush of self-pity and averted her gaze from his happy face.

"You okay?"

When she turned around, he was frowning. She nodded but pretended to shiver so she wouldn't have to speak.

"Come on, get warm." He wrapped an arm around her, pulling her close.

She pressed her cheek against his jacket, catching a faint salty and musty scent and thinking this must be something he'd been wearing on his ship. She tried to imagine him onboard a big ship or boat or whatever it was called, realizing she knew nothing about his life outside the Cove. *Or even in the Cove.* But right then, she was content to be warm and to feel the close physical presence of her baby's father.

The arrival at Peaks Island, a mere half hour later, came all too soon for Zanna, who was beginning to like snuggling against Dom. When she pulled away as the ferry's horn sounded its arrival, she heard his exaggerated sigh of disappointment. "I could have sat here another half hour at least," he said. "Will the rest of the day be as nice as this?"

"I hope so," she said, locking eyes with his long enough to sense the color rising into her face again. That quick connection disappeared as the passengers around them began to gather their belongings. Working their way through the disembarking crowd, Zanna was grateful she'd chosen a weekday for the trip. She noticed a full parking lot adjacent to the ferry wharf as the cars onboard inched forward, clearly scouting for parking.

"Glad we left the car on the other side," Dom commented.

"Yes. There's only one main road that loops all around the island and even though it's midweek and not high season yet, the place is busier than I expected."

"What's the circumference of the island? Are we walking it?"

"We could. It's only four miles but there are off-road trails, so I have something else in mind. Follow me." She grinned as he gave a thumbs-up and led him out of the ferry wharf. She stopped to check her cell phone for directions and then proceeded to the center of the village area.

"All right!" Dom enthused when she stopped in front of the island bicycle rental. "It's been a while, but I think I remember how to do it."

"Like riding a horse?" she quipped.

"Never done that."

"Maybe another time."

"I hope so," he murmured.

Why did she say that? If he failed today's test, she doubted there'd be another time. Zanna evaded the serious expression in his face by pulling open the shop door and minutes later they were on the main road, fastening up their rented bike helmets.

"Sure we need these?" Dom asked. "I doubt I'll be speeding."

His helmet was perched atop his head like a

beanie and she tried not to grin. "Not a good fit I see, but the guy said there'll be car traffic since this is the one main road."

He sighed, readjusting his helmet strap. "Okay, I get it. Where to? Just pick a direction and go?"

"I think so. My research said there's a World War II relic called Battery Steele that was installed to protect the harbor. And a museum run by veterans of the local military regiment, with a Civil War memorial."

"I'm detecting a military theme today, which I'm excited about. Especially the historical aspect."

"There's also wildlife, beaches and eateries."

"Eateries?" He was grinning. "I hope they include an ice cream shop."

"After our hard work." Zanna straddled her bike and started pedaling. Cycling through the island's center and passing pretty wood frame houses and cottages took no time at all. Though she had had the lead on Dominic, he soon sped past, giving a teasing wave. When she caught up to him, he was off his bike and reading the sign at an off-road trail—Welcome to Battery Steele Conservation Area.

They walked their bikes along a narrow sandy trail toward the bunker, set amidst thickets of wild vegetation. The concrete structure had an open tunnel or walk-through, but Zanna came to a stop at the entrance, put off by the large puddles of water inside. Swirls of multi-colored graffiti patterns decorated the walls.

"Is any place safe from vandals?" Dom grumbled.

"Probably not. My father once told me that an old school friend of his toured some tombs in Egypt and saw graffiti that had been done thousands of years ago."

"Sort of an 'I was here' kind of thing."

"I don't like it either, but I can relate to why people want to leave something behind." Like a child, she suddenly thought and quickly looked away. This wasn't the time or place for a serious talk. But then where *was* the right place or time?

He seemed unaware of her shift in mood. "Let's head to that memorial you were mentioning." Turning his bike around, he headed back to the road.

Two hours later they were leaving the quaint wooden building housing the museum attached to the Eighth Maine Regiment Memorial. "I'm ready to wheel my bike back to the rental place," she told Dom. "Don't know about you but I'm aching all over."

"Nothing that a good massage won't fix, I bet," he said. His face flushed as he realized how she might interpret that and he quickly clarified, "Well, um, I'm sure even the Cove has a massage therapist now or maybe one of those spa places…you know."

Zanna felt a small heart-lurch at his boyish embarrassment. "Maybe lunch will fix the problem instead." They'd reached the bike rental and after checking the bikes in, Zanna said, "We could get a take-out sandwich from a café or eat inside. What's your preference?"

"You choose, but this is my treat."

She shook her head. "No way. Today is on me, remember? But I'm leaning toward the takeout. We could find a quiet place near the water to enjoy the scenery without a bunch of tourists around."

A whole range of expressions flitted across his face but the one Zanna identified was trepidation. She guessed he was concluding a waterside location could also be a private one, perfect for a serious talk. *And he was absolutely right.*

They were devouring the last of their take-out sandwiches, enjoying the sea view from a bench by the ferry dock, when Zanna asked, "What did you think of the regiment museum? I noticed that you were a bit quiet as we walked through the exhibit."

"It was great." His voice was subdued, as if his mind was elsewhere.

"The collection was modest and I'm sure you've seen other Civil War museums."

"Yeah, for sure, but there was something moving about the place. Maybe its humble displays—a reminder of the ordinary men who served in the regiment but who never got the fame and hoopla their commanders received."

Zanna studied the concentration in his face. He seemed to be making a connection to some memory, which intrigued her. "Isn't that always the case in any kind of military undertaking? The ordinary men and women who serve with trust and loyalty are often un-named or unacknowledged?"

"That's it exactly. You've said it much better than I could." His eyes fixed on hers as if he were seeing something in them he hadn't before.

"What made you join the navy?"

"I spent most of my childhood and teen years on the water, working with my dad on his lobster trawler. I grew to love the sea, like he did. It was my Uncle George, Mom's older brother and a career navy man, who fostered my interest in the navy. He was a noncom but worked his way up through the ranks. Whenever he came to the Cove for a visit—which wasn't often—he'd tell me all about his adventures. I loved those stories!"

Zanna liked the way his face lit up. "Was he the reason you applied to the ROTC program?"

"Sort of. He was definitely an influence. But that was also the only way I could afford to go to college. My marks weren't good enough for a scholarship. It didn't matter. I was always going to enlist." He waited a moment before saying, "I let my father down, I think. I knew he was expecting me to work with him, to expand our very small family business, but I never wanted that. Even though I never told him my dream, I think he suspected." He shifted his gaze to the small harbor.

She heard the regret in his voice and wanted to wrap her arms around him and hold him close. But they weren't a couple. "I can relate to that," she eventually said.

He turned her way, a question in his face.

"I always wanted to leave the Cove, to find the adventures that I knew for sure were out there. Even after I inherited the hotel, I refused to come back and run it. My mother was upset but Uncle Charles and Aunt Evelyn convinced her to keep on the man who'd been managing it at the time. They'd patched up the broken pieces of my small family after Brandon died and then later, my dad."

"And then you came home a few years ago?"

"Yes, with high but unrealistic expectations."

"How so?"

"I thought managing the hotel would save my marriage. Fresh start and all." She cringed inwardly at the bitterness in her voice and ducked her head as she crumpled up her sandwich wrapper. "Now I'm not so sure exactly how I feel. The hotel just doesn't have the same hold on me that it does for some of my family."

"It seems the Cove has some kind of magnetic pull on both of us, despite our desire to escape it," he finally observed.

"Not so much anymore for me."

"What do you mean?"

"The escape part. This last year I've made some new friends and reconnected with old ones. Even with the Winters clan, despite my tendency to avoid family gatherings as much as possible." She laughed at the admission. "Although I feel more a part of the community now, I sometimes still have those yearnings for adventure. New places and experiences." When he didn't speak, she added, "All of that is up in the air right now, though."

"Because?"

Zanna turned his way, stifling the rise of annoyance. Couldn't he figure that out?

His face reddened. "Oh. Right." His tone was flat. "I know we need to talk about the next few months and after. Do you want to do that now…and here?"

He had a point. The day was meant to be fun but also a way to find out more about him. Or so she'd kept telling herself but now Zanna wasn't so certain. Had she unconsciously set him up to fail with her secret agenda? She glanced around at the families and couples enjoying the sunny day and wondered why she tended to sabotage opportunities for happiness.

"No," she finally said, keeping her eyes on the scene around them.

"Okay. Then how about when we get back to the Cove? Or do you have to get back for Rohan?"

Here was an excuse to put off the inevitable for another day. But no, she thought. Time was running out. "He's not expecting me to."

"Fine. When's the next ferry?"

Zanna pulled her cell phone out of her windbreaker pocket, her fingers shaking as she searched the ferry schedule. "It's arriving in ten minutes." She stood up and shaded her eyes to look across Casco Bay. "I can just see it now."

The outing to Peaks Island was wrapping up, she thought as she kept her gaze on the distant ferry. Had it been fun? Yes. Had she learned anything about Dominic Kennedy? Yes. But what the day meant and how it might affect the outcome of their talk, she had no idea. She sneaked a glance at Dom, his outstretched legs and the way he was resting his head against the back of the bench. His eyes were closed, his face a blank canvas revealing nothing of the man or the father-to-be.

Zanna did not have a good feeling about the impending conversation.

CHAPTER SEVEN

DOM NEVER EXPECTED to be grateful to share space with a class of rowdy elementary students, but he was. Their antics on the ferry trip back to Portland were a happy distraction from the silence between him and Zanna. There was no such relief on the drive back to the Cove, which seemed to take twice as long as usual.

When she turned off the highway into town, Zanna asked, "Where to?"

"Your choice."

She continued driving along Main Street, through the heart of town and toward the beach, pulling into a parking spot just past the harbor.

"Let's walk from here." Dom stifled a sigh. He wished he'd directed her to some neutral place. The lighthouse on the peninsula at the end of the beach held emotional memories for both of them.

As he followed her down to the water, Dom

was thinking back to the day's outing, searching for the point the trip had taken a wrong turn. Zanna's mood had shifted and the carefree, fun person cycling next to him had been replaced by a grim-faced woman bent on serious business.

"Here," he said, throwing his windbreaker onto the compact sand, "sit on this." He grasped her elbow to help but she brushed his hand aside.

"I'm fine." Sitting down, she added, "But thanks. Maybe in another few months I'll need help."

Her smile eased the tension, but Dom was struck by what she said. Would he be around to help in another few months? That was the purpose of the talk they were about to have and to be honest, he had no idea what to say. What he did know in his heart was that he'd make sure wherever he was, he'd be available in some way for their child. He hoped he'd be able to convince Zanna of that because so far, he hadn't been very successful.

"I'm sure you'll want to help support our child financially and I want to assure you I won't expect anything more than that," Zanna abruptly announced.

Dom felt a surge of frustration. Her assumption hurt and for a moment he couldn't perceive any way out of this pattern of "act-react" they'd fallen into. Unless he changed it.

"I know I've been sending mixed messages about being a father and yes, I was stunned when you told me. I didn't handle that well and I ought to have. My response was counter to everything I've learned in the navy and as an officer. I'm sorry for that. But I assure you, from the bottom of my heart, that I will always be there for our child and not because it's my duty—" he paused, stressing that last word "—but because I *want* to be. And I will always be there for you, too. If you'll let me."

He saw the shine of tears in her eyes before she looked across the bay. "Thanks for that, Dom. I…um… I don't know what the future holds for us other than the fact we will be sharing a child. I've seen the passion in your face when you talk about the navy and what it means to you, so I'm not expecting you to make too many life changes for the baby… or for me."

He gently turned her face his way. "No assumptions, Zan. We've only begun to know one another. Let's go forward with that. Let's trust that we will find a way to be together for him or her."

"I call him or her my little bean."

"Little bean." He nodded. "Yeah, I like that." He pulled his knees up to his chest, wrapping his arms around them and stared out across the water. His mind swirled with thoughts and questions. "Getting his focus on" was what he'd always called his strategy for coping with problems large or small, another navy lesson. It was a skill that seemed to have deserted him since his return to the Cove and he was determined not to allow that to happen again.

"How big is this bean of ours?"

She held up a hand, spreading her fingers apart. "About this big."

The mental image stunned him. "So definitely not a bean."

"Not anymore. More like an avocado, or so I've read."

"Can you feel it? The bean?"

"Not yet, but soon."

"And how are you? I mean, are you in good health?"

There was amusement in her face, but her voice was almost tender when she answered. "Very good health, Dom, and…and thank you for asking."

He'd been remiss in that, too, he thought. "When are you due?"

"The end of September."

He tried not to think where he'd be then. Did it matter anyway, as long as he was available? That's what she wanted, wasn't it? "Okay, so let's work with that. Tell me what you'd like me to do for you, while I'm home." She blinked, taking in the full meaning of his words and Dom knew he'd messed up again. "I mean, in the interim. Until we've sorted everything out," he clarified.

"How long will you be in town?"

"My leave is officially up in a bit more than two weeks. Then I report to base."

"Where's base? There's so much I don't know about you."

He understood her frustration. "And likewise, Zanna, so, let's do something about that. Who's first? Me or you?"

"You."

"Okay. I'm based in Norfolk, Virginia. Ask away."

"Are you a career navy man, like your uncle?"

He took a moment, wanting to find the right words. "The navy is the only life I've known since leaving the Cove. Except for my mother, the men and women I've met and gotten to know are my family." An unexpected wave of emotion swept over him as he thought about the friends he'd be leaving if he got his promotion. They'd all been so supportive, emailing with him to give him tips about his promotion interview. *And not only the friends. People here, in the Cove.* A sideways glance at Zanna told him she was seriously pondering that last part. "But I have room in my life for more family. Please believe that."

She was nodding but not looking his way. He waited for her to speak, hoping she understood that he might not be around physically but would be in every other way. Yet when she eventually responded, he knew he should have been more transparent.

"I do believe you, Dominic. I know you'll do what's right for...for the little bean." She stood up then, dusting off the sand from her jeans and handing him his windbreaker. "I guess I should go relieve Rohan. And yes," she added with a smile, "we're not finished with the catch-up, but can we continue maybe tomorrow sometime? Dinner somewhere?"

Dom clumsily got to his feet, startled by her sudden move. He suspected he might have revealed more than she wanted to hear right then. "Uh, dinner sounds good, but maybe Saturday? I've promised Henry to go to a Scout meeting tomorrow night."

The change in topic was a positive one. "Oh, that's great! How nice for the kids—and you, too."

"It might involve a basketball game, I'm afraid. It's been a while."

"I have complete faith in you."

He knew she was teasing but couldn't help wondering—did she really? "I'll walk you to your car."

"You're not coming with me? I can drop you off wherever you'd like."

"Thanks, but I think I'll head up through town, check out any new places."

"Sure, though the library is the only new thing here and it's not expected to officially open until next month." She began walking toward the road.

"I remember the days when we had to be driven to Portland to take out library books."

Zanna dug into her shoulder bag and pulled out her car fob as they reached the road. "True, though the elementary school had a good library. Plus, there was always Henry's bookstore. Well, Grace's bookstore now," she added.

"Books were never at the top of my list when it came to spending my allowance."

"Not a reader?"

He shrugged. "There always seemed to be other things to do, especially when I was a teen. Now I seldom have the time or the opportunity."

"Your work duties? I suppose being an officer you have a lot of responsibilities."

It wasn't a question, so he simply nodded while she unlocked her car. She was about to climb in when he caught her hand. "Zanna, thanks for today. I really liked the island and especially the regimental museum."

"Thanks. It was fun. Well, most of it." A pause. "Sorry for the drama. I have a habit of rushing into things. Asking questions at inopportune times and basically coming across as an impatient, demanding person."

Dom pulled her close, pleased when she settled readily into his arms. He tucked her head against his chest and stroked her hair. He closed his eyes, shutting out everything but the warmth of Zanna, in his arms.

"I should go," she murmured against his T-shirt.

But she didn't move, and he held on as long as he could, until she stepped back.

"I'll call you tomorrow." Before she could close the car door, he blurted, "You're not that person, Zanna. The type you've just described, demanding and so on. Don't be hard on yourself. We're in this together. You and me…and Little Bean."

Her quick nod didn't convince Dom that she believed him. He watched her make a U-turn up to Main Street, then, slinging his windbreaker over a shoulder, he strolled along the beach road to the very end where it connected with the harbor boardwalk.

Dom knew he had a way to go before he could convince Zanna he was in her life now—for good. Except for a couple of general comments, she hadn't spoken about the hotel, but he guessed she had only the young fellow, Rohan, to help out. How would she manage once Little Bean appeared? And who would look after the baby? He knew her mother lived in Bangor, so she wouldn't be regularly available. He thought of his own mother, who didn't know yet that she was going to be a grandmother. He'd put off telling her because he wanted to sort things out with Zanna first. He shook his head, disappointed in himself. When had he become this man avoiding settling problems?

His mind was buzzing with all the decisions he had to make. Especially those that involved people who depended on him—now Zanna and ultimately, Little Bean. When he looked up, he realized too late he was about to collide with a man setting up a signboard. Fortunately, the other man had noticed Dom and had managed to sidestep to ward off a more serious impact.

"Whoa!" The man was laughing. "That was close. We both might have ended up in the water."

Dom blinked as he realized what had almost occurred. Then he focused on the man standing in front of him. Ted Nakamura, Ben's best friend in high school and owner of The Daily Catch. Heat rose up in his face as he watched Ted pick up the sign that had toppled over. "Sorry. I wasn't looking where I was going."

"No worries." Ted straightened up and frowned, pointing his index finger at Dom. "You're a friend of Ben's, right?"

"Yeah. Dominic Kennedy. Dom." He shook hands with Ted.

"Of course. I think you were at my New Year's event. The place was pretty hectic that night so…"

"Yep. I was there. Great party."

"Frankly, I was too busy to enjoy it myself. If I remember correctly, after high school you ended up in…um…"

"The navy."

Ted smiled. "Right. So, are you here on vacation or something?"

"A couple of weeks' leave."

Ted was nodding thoughtfully. Dom was surprised Ted hadn't already known he was back home. The smallness of the Cove always surfaced this way, reminding him why he'd been so desperate to leave. "Anyway, nice to see you," he said, "and thanks for saving me from catapulting both of us into the harbor."

They both glanced at the murky water. "Yeah, not a place I'd want to explore. Least not here. Come by for a meal while you're in town." Ted jerked his thumb behind him to the opened restaurant door.

"For sure," Dom replied and, as he continued on, thought this might be a good place for dinner with Zanna. Then he stopped. Maybe too much of a reminder of New Year's Eve? There was simply no getting around the ever-constant reminders of the past—recent and distant—here in Lighthouse Cove. His sigh was loud enough to catch the attention of a harbor cat strolling by.

"It's okay," he said to the cat, which had stopped to sit on its haunches, staring up at him. "I'll figure things out…eventually." He peered around the now deserted boardwalk, gave a quick wave to the cat and continued on up through town.

ZANNA READ DOM'S text message Friday morning one more time.

Dinner at The Daily Catch Saturday? I can meet you there or pick you up. Say 6:30?

Of all places, she silently moaned, thinking of New Year's Eve. Yet the more she thought about it, the more she realized going back to where it all started—she and Dominic Kennedy—could set the right mood for the intended talk that always seemed to be beginning but never quite ending.

That was the purpose of the dinner, to finish the talk. *It wasn't a date.* Though for a brief moment on the beach yesterday when he'd held her in his arms, she'd had a fleeting thought that even if they weren't a couple right now, perhaps they could be. Of course, that fantasy drifted away the minute she'd arrived back at the hotel.

She set her phone onto the reception counter and logged into the computer to check the day's agenda. A couple who'd stayed at the hotel at Christmas were due back—the Pattersons. Zanna was pleased that they'd liked the hotel enough for a return visit. She was grateful for their ongoing patronage, but they were from New Jersey and their visits to family in the new subdivision were sporadic. Occasional patrons couldn't save the hotel.

Her phone pinged again, and she saw an email from Alex Corelli at Gateway Living.

Initial survey looks good so now on to second stage—sending an engineer, architect and electrician/plumbing team. Thinking 9 a.m. Monday. Let me know if there's a problem with that. Alex.

She hadn't been expecting a report so quickly and realized Gateway must be seriously considering the hotel. Things were moving at a pace she hadn't anticipated and Zanna realized she still hadn't told anyone in the family—even her mother—about her plans.

The elevator door swished open and Rohan

headed her way, carrying a bucket with cleaning supplies.

"What's up?" she asked. "Is Lisa off today?"

"No, she's doing the rooms on first. This was an emergency trip up to fourth."

Zanna rolled her eyes. There was only one occupied room on that floor. "Don't tell me."

"A small accident." He gestured to wads of paper towel in the bucket. "But profuse apologies."

"Not from Mo, I'm guessing."

Rohan laughed. "No. But it's hard to be annoyed, honestly. They're both so charming."

"You have the makings of a great hospitality host, Rohan. Patience and tolerance."

"Thanks, and um, speaking of that, have you got a minute?"

Her stomach clenched at the change in his face. She had a bad feeling about what he might tell her. "Sure."

"I've had some good news." His face lit up. "I've been accepted into the Tourism and Hospitality Program at the University of Southern Maine, starting in September."

Zanna struggled to hide her dismay. "Oh Rohan, that's fabulous." She impulsively wrapped her arms around him, hoping he hadn't heard the catch in her voice.

"My parents are super happy," he said as she pulled back. "Plus, I can still live at home, save some money."

"That's so wonderful. Are you planning a celebration this weekend?"

"Already had a small one, when I found out a couple of days ago. I would have told you sooner, but we always seem to be just crossing paths here."

The innocent comment brought home how she'd overlooked the social side of work. Her next thought was more selfish. *How would she manage without him?*

"I have a big favor to ask," Rohan went on. "Could I pick up more hours over the next few months? I'd like to save as much money as possible before starting school in the fall. And…uh…just to let you know I'll be looking for some part-time work in Portland then. Save myself a commute."

She could tell from his flushed face that he was uncomfortable asking. He knew as well as she did that the hotel was currently operating at twenty percent capacity and she doubted that number would even double once the warm weather appeared, bringing more tourists. He'd be difficult to replace, and he deserved so much more than she could afford to give him. On the positive side, this was an opportunity to spend more time with Dom. Perhaps he might come to appreciate the community side of small-town life.

"Of course, Rohan! I'd love some 'me' time, especially now that spring is officially here."

"Are you sure?"

She was touched by his hesitation. "Absolutely. And let's start today." She scanned the day's schedule. "The businessman on three is leaving and a couple are checking in this afternoon. They've asked for a waterfront room on four so maybe ask them if they might be bothered by—"

"A little dog?"

"He does bark, doesn't he?"

"Mainly when someone knocks on the door or walks down the hall."

"I think the couple—the Pattersons—will be out most of the day visiting their family so that may not be a problem."

"Speaking of Mo, the only glitch I can see with me manning the desk is that I won't be available to walk him."

"Okay, well, Mrs. Stanfield will have to adjust her routine. Or I can help out, if necessary."

Rohan's laugh suggested otherwise.

"Seriously, I can do dogs. Especially little ones. How about taking later this afternoon, from four to five?" She thought of Saturday's dinner with Dominic. Six thirty, he'd said. "And can you do tomorrow evening, say about six? I won't be late. It's a…a business meeting." How pathetic she thought. As if I need to explain why I'm taking a rare night off.

"Fill me into the schedule wherever you like," Rohan said.

"For sure." She suddenly remembered the Gateway team coming next week. If an offer to buy rose out of their inspection, Rohan's job, along with hers, would be gone.

CHAPTER EIGHT

AFTER ZANNA ARRANGED the free afternoon with Rohan, she realized she had no plans. She could visit her mother in Bangor to tell her the news, but knowing her mother's love of questions, hesitated to do that until she'd firmed things up with Dom tomorrow. She could drive to Portland and check out the malls. *Seriously? You hate shopping.*

Yet shopping was in her future. She hadn't purchased a single item for the baby, despite entering her fifth month. Many women in her condition would have been organizing and planning for weeks by now while she plodded on with her daily routines, seemingly unaware of the life-changing event ahead. *Not thinking about something doesn't make it go away, Zanna.* She ought to know that by now. There had been plenty of clues about her ex's infidelities, but she'd opted to ignore them.

As for Dom, she'd overlooked certain clues

about the chances of some kind of relationship with him for the sake of their baby until yesterday's talk on Peaks Island and later at the beach, had revealed facts she could no longer ignore. He was a career navy man; his work could take him anywhere at any time. He wasn't going to be living in the Cove, probably not even close to it. She had to accept that. Her goal for Saturday night was to plan accordingly. As much as she wanted to postpone decisions, time was catching up to her.

She logged out of her office computer and headed into her apartment. Rohan was on the front counter already, waiting for the Pattersons to check in. Zanna decided some exercise would be a good way to clear her head and quickly changed into jeans and a sweatshirt. She tucked her cell phone into a back pocket as she closed the door behind her.

"Have fun," Rohan said as she walked past him.

"I've got my cell in case you get busy."

"Ha! Yeah, right." He grinned.

The elevator swooshed open and Cora, in slacks, sweater and sturdy walking shoes and led by Mo on a leash, strolled into the lobby. "Good afternoon, everyone!"

"Hello," Zanna said. "I hope all is well with you—and Mo." She was tempted to ask how much longer the woman would be staying but realized that might prompt Cora into making a decision right then and really, the longer she stayed the better for the hotel. Despite the unpredictable Mo.

"All is good," Cora said, as she drew near. "Mo and I are getting into a routine that suits us both."

A routine? That sounded promising for a longer stay.

Cora took in Zanna's casual clothes and smiled. "Day off?"

"For a couple of hours."

"Any plans?"

Zanna hesitated. She had a feeling where the talk was headed. "Um, some exercise I think."

"Mind if I join you?"

There was no way Zanna could ignore the expectation in the woman's face. "Not at all. Are you up for a walk?"

"I am, and are you up for Mo coming with us?" There was an impish twinkle in Cora's eyes.

Irresistible, as Rohan had said. "For sure."

As they walked toward the front door, Zanna turned around to wave goodbye. Rohan gave a thumbs-up and grinned.

"Anywhere in particular?" Zanna asked when they were outside.

"Well, I've been up to Town Square, which is very interesting. Some people were playing chess on those concrete table things. I saw the statue of the town founder—Hiram Winters." Cora peered up at Zanna. "I suppose he's a relative?"

"My father's grandfather. Care for a walk along the beach, since we have warmer weather today? Never know what it'll be like tomorrow."

"I recall that about Maine's weather. The coastal currents bring lots of fluctuating temperatures."

"I take it you're familiar with Maine?" Zanna turned onto Main Street toward the harbor.

"Grew up in a small place near Bangor, but I've spent the last thirty years in Chicago."

They took the stairs down onto the boardwalk and Zanna slowed her pace, aware of some breathlessness in Cora. Mo had slowed, too, checking out the smells in the air and on the ground.

"The day I checked in you mentioned that you took over the hotel only a few years ago. How did you feel about coming back here, after all that time?"

The unexpected question gave Zanna pause. "Um, well, it was a challenge, but I had a strong personal reason." She pointed to the cruise kiosk. "Have you taken the Casco Bay cruise? It's very good and probably easy to get tickets now, before tourist season picks up."

Cora shook her head. "Not a fan of open water and boats."

"Okay. Well, have you checked out this restaurant yet?" Zanna stopped in front of The Daily Catch. "Terrific seafood."

Cora paused to look over the menu posted next to the door. "It does look good, and I love seafood. The problem is Mo." She gestured to the dog, sniffing around the signboard nearby.

"You could leave him in his crate, surely, just for a little bit."

"I could but he barks."

Zanna remembered the Pattersons, who'd be checking into their fourth-floor suite, probably right at that moment. "I suppose I could always have him in my apartment for a bit—if you want to dine here one night. Unfortunately, it's only open for dinner right now. No lunch service until mid-June when tourist season picks up."

"That's sweet of you and I may take you up on the offer."

"Anytime," Zanna said. They continued along the boardwalk, then ascended the stairs at its end to the beach road. The tide was out and Mo strained at his leash, eager to investigate all the treasures. Cora was pulled ahead, laughing, but Zanna noted her flushed face. "Here," she said, grasping hold of the strap, "let me take him now. Give you a break."

"Thank you. You have to watch him though. Not only does he smell everything, but he also wants to taste. And I see there's lots to sample here."

Small hermit crabs scuttled across the wet sand, which was littered with strands of drying seaweed and bits of plastic. Mo spotted a tide pool and raced for it before Zanna could restrain him. He yipped frantically at two sea stars trapped in the pool and tried to jump in.

"Maybe we should go farther away from

the beach," Zanna suggested. "There are some benches up by the road."

Cora needed no persuading and Zanna tugged Mo away from all the temptations. The beach was almost deserted and she aimed for a bench close to the end of the road, near the dunes leading up to the peninsula. As they sat down, pulling a reluctant Mo close to their feet, Zanna looked over at the lighthouse.

"I'd like to see that lighthouse close-up," Cora commented, following Zanna's gaze. "But I'd never make it up the dune." Her light laugh sounded a bit sad.

"There's a good path from the highway above us and a bit of a parking space. You could drive to it and walk from there." When Cora didn't reply, Zanna added, "Or I could drive you, too. I've been wanting to have a look at the new condo construction nearby."

Cora smiled. "Thank you for the offer. I'm curious to see the lighthouse up close. Years ago, Maurice and I explored part of Maine's coast and toured some lighthouses. I especially remember the Portland Head Light in Cape Elizabeth, but we never made it to Lighthouse Cove."

"What prompted you to come here, to the Cove? It's kind of out of the way."

Cora was patting Mo and didn't answer right away. "An impulse really. I noticed the sign on the highway—Welcome to Lighthouse Cove—with its illustration of the lighthouse and thought, why not?" She smiled at Zanna. "One of the perks of retirement. Spontaneity!"

"Ah. My cousin's new husband is in the coast guard and is in charge of maintenance for all the lighthouses in Maine. They're on a tour right now, as part of their honeymoon."

"That's a different kind of honeymoon," Cora remarked. "But I like the idea of it. So much more interesting than a resort or a trip to some big city." After a minute, she went on to say, "I happened to see an old copy of your town's newspaper—*The Beacon*—when I was having lunch at Mabel's Diner. There was a reminder in it that donations were still being accepted for the lighthouse restoration and also a mention of a Brandon Winters memorial."

Zanna took a quiet breath. There had been many comments, questions and opinions voiced over the last several months since the fundraising campaign last August. Some townspeople had no qualms about raising the topic of her brother's death while others were more discreet. But she was gradually learning to deal with it all—a necessary acceptance if she planned to spend the rest of her life in the Cove.

"Yes," she finally said, "Brandon was my brother and he drowned at the lighthouse almost eighteen years ago, when he got caught in high tide."

"Oh dear," Cora murmured, reaching to pat Zanna's hand, "I'm so sorry. How awful for you and your family."

"It basically triggered my parents' divorce, though as an adult I realized that had been inevitable anyway." The memory of those days rushed back. "My father was an alcoholic, even before Brandon died. That's why the family—well, my Uncle Charles—stepped in to take care of the hotel. He hired someone to manage the place."

"How old was your brother?"

"Fourteen."

Cora was shaking her head. "Can I ask what happened?"

Zanna bit her lip. "My younger cousin,

Grace, was involved in it, along with a friend of hers who had a crush on Ben, Grace's older brother. They were teenagers and obviously, kids with poor judgment. Grace and her friend sent fake letters to Brandon and a girl vacationing here, Ella Jacobs, who was dating Ben at the time." Zanna gave a loud sigh. "You know—teenagers and their crushes. It was meant to be a prank but had disastrous consequences."

"I can relate to the impulses of teenagers." Cora's low voice caught Zanna's attention. The woman was staring out across Casco Bay, lost in thought. When Cora didn't elaborate, Zanna went on. "Anyway, when Brandon found out he'd been tricked, he was embarrassed and ran away." She had to stop for a minute, her mind going back to a scene she'd imagined often over the years. "For some reason he went to the lighthouse, maybe to hide. In those days it wasn't locked. Maybe he fell asleep and didn't realize the tide was coming in. The coroner at the inquest thought Brandon might have tried to wade or swim from the lighthouse to the land. It's only a distance of a few feet, but difficult to master at high tide and in the dark." Cora patted her hand,

and Zanna added, "It's okay. It was hard when Grace revealed the whole story last summer. But her confession led to the idea of a memorial for Bran at the lighthouse."

"I'd like to make a donation to that cause."

"Oh, well, that's a lovely thought but—"

"I want to. Heavens, I've got plenty of money and little to spend it on."

Impulsively, Zanna said, "To be honest, I'm not sure if I want the type of memorial that we've planned. And I'm on the planning committee, so go figure." Her light laugh sounded a tad rueful, even to her own ears. "No one really goes up there anymore. Few tourists are interested in it because it's not as breathtaking or charming as most of the lighthouses along the coast. There's not much else to draw tourists here besides the beach, and there are plenty of nicer beaches along the coast."

"Is that why the hotel seems so…?"

"Empty?" Zanna pulled a face. "Yeah. People have to make a choice where to spend their money and unfortunately, Lighthouse Cove rarely makes the list of options. But I'm working on some ideas to address the situation."

"What made you come back then, to run the hotel? Could you have sold it?"

"My marriage was failing, and I foolishly thought the hotel would be a good project for my ex and me. We'd worked together at hotels all over the country, and I thought having something more permanent could save us." Zanna snorted. "Now I think my family, especially my Uncle Charles, would be upset if I sold it. Part of the Winters legacy and all that. But I may be wrong."

"You sound a bit cynical there," Cora observed.

The remark surprised Zanna, who'd been watching Cora scratching Mo behind the ears and offering him small treats from her cardigan pocket. Clearly, she was paying complete attention to what had become a long story.

"Not cynical so much as conflicted. I grew tired of all the lore about my family's ancestors. I'm sure your walks around town have spotlighted a lot about the Winters—the family legacy is everywhere." Zanna laughed at herself. "Okay, I'm exaggerating, but really… the hotel, the newspaper, the construction company that built the development up on the highway and is currently building the condos

I was telling you about. Plus, the bookstore, Novel Idea, and heaven knows how much property Uncle Charles has purchased over the years."

"It's a charming bookstore," Cora said. "The woman who's managing it was very helpful."

"That would be Grace's friend. Grace is the owner/manager, but—"

"On her honeymoon."

Zanna nodded. Cora had definitely taken in every word.

"But other than typical teenage angst perhaps, what led to your conflicted feelings about your family's history?"

Except for her best friend in college, her ex and Dominic, Zanna had never spoken to anyone about her adoption. But there was something about Cora Stanfield that invited soul-baring. "The September I left for college—a year before Brandon died—my mother told me I was adopted." Zanna turned away from Cora's serious face to look at the sea. The tide was slowly coming in and she was about to suggest they leave when Cora's next question stopped her.

"Have you ever thought about searching for your birth mother?"

She had occasionally, but more in that first year of finding out than later. Brandon's death and Jane's withdrawal afterward had deterred her. "Mom and I don't talk about it," was all she said.

Cora seemed to get the hint that Zanna was finished. She stared down at Mo, snoring softly at her feet, and after a while murmured, "I think it must be time for a cup of tea."

Zanna was grateful for the chance to leave the past behind. "Great idea. Mabel's?"

"Perfect," Cora slowly got to her feet. "And they do allow small, quiet pets."

"Well, let's hope Mo is feeling quiet." Sensing Cora was stiff from sitting so long, Zanna looped an arm through one of Cora's as they strolled back along the beach road and into the diner.

They found a table with a small banquette at the rear of the diner and to Zanna's relief, Mo made only a cursory glance around the room before he contentedly sank onto Cora's lap. "It'll be faster if I order at the counter. Tea, Cora?"

"Yes, please, Zanna, and some kind of muffin or scone will be lovely." She shifted Mo while she pulled her shoulder bag around to open it up.

Zanna shook her head. "My treat." She was giving their order when she heard a familiar voice from behind.

"Well, well. This is a rare sight. Zanna Winters in Mabel's in the middle of an afternoon."

She spun around, grinning. "You may be seeing more of me over the next few weeks, Henry. Are you staying or doing takeout?"

He scanned the room and frowned. "Hmm, maybe takeout. Looks pretty full, which is a good thing for Sam but unlucky for me."

"Come and join us." She pointed to the rear corner where Cora sat, facing them.

Henry narrowed his eyes. "I think I met that lady the other day. She's staying at the hotel, isn't she?"

"Yes, Dom told me about her dog running away from her and ending up on your porch, scaring Felix."

"Hah! I think it was the other way around. The doggie was barking, but I think he'd have hightailed it if Felix had actually jumped off his perch."

"Tell me what you want and I'll add it to my order," she said as she saw one of the young women behind the counter setting up a tray with mugs of tea and two muffins.

"If that's yours, I'll have the same."

"Okay. Then go sit down." Zanna watched him lumber across the room and pull out a chair opposite Cora, who looked up from Mo with a welcoming smile. She added his order and in less than five minutes was depositing the drinks and muffins on the table. The two were deep in conversation by the time Zanna was sitting on the bench next to Cora.

"Cora's interested in seeing where the Historical Society hangs out. Someone at Tourist Information sent her to Town Hall, only we've moved."

"You have?" Zanna sipped her tea and broke off a piece of muffin. She noticed that Mo was inching off Cora's lap and heading for hers.

"After New Year's.'"

Zanna frowned. "Okay, guess I've been out of touch with some things in town." Especially since New Year's Eve, she thought.

Henry nodded. "Anyway, we were only in the hall temporarily and now we're using a room in St. Pat's church basement. We were planning to move into the new library, but we've just heard we may not get space. There's a waiting list, for pity's sake!"

"How come there's no room in the library?" She surreptitiously passed a chunk of muffin to Mo while Cora was busy buttering half of hers.

"Too many groups need space. The Scout troop has asked, along with the Lighthouse Cove Book Club—"

"A book club?" Cora enthused. "Surely a book club should have space in a library."

Henry shrugged. "First come is the way it should go. Then there's the Philatelic Society—"

"The *what*?" Zanna asked.

"Stamp collectors," Henry and Cora answered together.

"Sheesh. Who knew there was even a club for that in the Cove? But won't there be enough space for everyone if they share? These groups will only use a room weekly or even only monthly."

Henry drank some tea before saying, "True, but now I've heard there's talk of a daycare taking over one of the large rooms in the basement, full-time. Not a sure thing yet, but…"

That definitely interested Zanna.

"Is there no community center in town?" Cora asked.

"Nope. Lighthouse Cove has never been big enough to warrant the cost of one, I guess," Henry put in.

"Not even with that big subdivision up on the highway?"

"Not so far. I assume people drive to Portland to use facilities there. We've talked about doing that if needs be, the Historical group. But many of us are getting on in years." He gave an exaggerated grimace. "And we hesitate to make a drive like that come winter." He finished the last of his tea and changed the topic. "How about if I take you to our current place tomorrow? One of our members plans to be on the premises to sort out what we need for the next few months of meetings."

"I'd love that! Thank you."

Henry stuffed his paper napkin into his empty tea mug and, pushing back his chair, used his cane to slowly get to his feet. He was about to pull a wallet out of his trouser pocket when Zanna stopped him.

"No, Henry. Your turn the next time."

"I look forward to that, Zanna. You need to get a break from the hotel more often. And by the way, do we still have a committee meeting this Monday?"

They hadn't discussed the follow-up meeting and Zanna wondered if Dom would be there again. "Sure. I guess we should if we're going ahead with the dedication in June. I can find out if Dom will still be here, unless Ben can make it."

Henry nodded. "Good. I'll leave you to it then. And Cora, I'll come to the hotel about ten tomorrow. Does that suit you?"

"Perfect." Once Henry had exited, pausing to speak to a couple of other patrons on his way out, she said, "He's quite lovely. Married? Divorced?"

"Yes, he's a wonderful and dear family friend," Zanna agreed. "And never married."

"Shame."

Zanna noted the thoughtful tone and inexplicably thought of her mother, who'd clearly enjoyed Henry's company at Grace's wedding. As she and Cora were leaving, she said, "Thanks for the company today, Cora. It was great to get away from the hotel."

"The pleasure was certainly all mine, dear." Cora placed a hand on Zanna's arm. "And thank you for telling me your story. I'm grateful for your trust in me and…well… I hope we can have another conversation again. Soon."

Zanna smiled but was puzzled at those last few words which sounded almost ominous. But by the time she and Cora were walking across the hotel lobby, her thoughts were on other matters, like Henry's mention of a possible daycare in town.

She waited while Cora and Mo were safely in the elevator and on their way up to the fourth floor, then headed for her own apartment to change. As she pulled off her jeans, her thoughts went back to the daycare and the library. Wouldn't a community center be a more appropriate place for small children? she wondered.

CHAPTER NINE

DOMINIC CARRIED THE last box up from the basement and plunked it on top of the stack of three in the front hallway. When he'd asked his mother if she needed help that morning, he'd expected to mow the lawn or wash windows, which she usually liked to do in early May. But she'd decided to declutter, and Dom didn't want to discourage her. The last time he'd been home at Christmas, he'd hinted that she might want to consider paring down the "collection of memorabilia," as he'd diplomatically called the boxes and plastic bags of possessions. She'd always been a packrat, as his father used to tease, and Dom knew she'd struggled to get rid of the things that reminded her of him, even after all this time.

He heard her puttering in the kitchen, guessing she didn't want to see the boxes leave the house. His plan was to drop them at a charity in Portland because she'd told him their church no longer had space to take and distribute household donations. While she was busy, he decided to go through his bedroom once more. The desk was tidier than it had been when he lived here, but the bulletin board above it still displayed the pennant that Portland High's basketball team won in his senior year. His teenaged nautical-themed bedspread had been replaced by one with red, white and blue stripes. Marie had proudly told him it reflected his service to his country and Dom had hidden the tears that welled up at that. Unfortunately, the mattress hadn't been upgraded at the same time, he thought, rubbing his lower back.

"Are you planning to get rid of anything in here?"

Dom spun around. His mother was standing in the doorway. "No, I think it was decluttered years ago, when I went off to college," he joked.

"I kept your room just as you left it for a long time, thinking you'd be back for summers. I couldn't bring myself to turn it into a den or a sewing room, which is what some of my friends did after their kids left home."

"Mom," he said, wrapping his arms around

her. "I'm glad you didn't. I've heard bad things about sofa beds."

She gave a small laugh and playfully pushed him away. "You're a tease, Dominic Kennedy."

"Seriously, I'm sorry about those summers. I hope someday I can make up for the lost time with you," he said, immediately thinking he could tell her right now, make her really happy. But then what if you had to let her down again? If Zanna wants to parent all on her own and only allows occasional visits? His heart sank at that possibility.

"As your father would have said, the past is past. I know summer jobs were easier to find in a college town like Orono, rather than the Cove, and later on you could hardly turn down the opportunities my brother provided you through his contacts. Don't feel guilty! I know you'll visit as often as you can."

"I will for sure," he said, hoping she didn't notice his lack of conviction.

"All right, now to more pressing matters. Will you be home for supper tonight?"

"If you don't mind, I think I'll pick up something later, after the Scout meeting."

"Oh yes, I'd forgotten. Are you looking forward to that?"

"I'm a bit nervous. You know I don't really have any experience working with teenagers. But their leader, Glen Kowalski, texted to tell me they've planned a basketball game."

"Perfect! You'll be great."

"It's been a while since I've played."

"You told me there were often games on base and even on ship."

"Yeah, but the last year or so I was too busy to participate in most of them."

"A shame, but as George would say, the price you pay for more duties."

"I remember him giving that excuse for missing some Christmases with us." Dom thought for a minute of his uncle's visits, always fun but also sporadic and unpredictable. Would that be him someday? He took a deep breath. If his thoughts wandered down this path any further today, he'd be useless at being a positive role model for the Scouts, not to mention a really bad basketball player. "I should take the boxes to Portland now," he said. "If I'm not home by the time you go to bed, you'll know I'm at the pub after the meeting."

Marie smiled. "I'm proud of you for helping out with the Scouts. Maybe some of them will have questions about the navy or adventures on the high seas. George always used to regale you with those tales."

"Maybe," Dom said, "though from what Glen has told me about them, I think they might be more interested in which team wins tonight. The losing team has to make cookies for the next meeting."

Marie laughed. "I like that." As they left Dom's bedroom, she said, "Text me if you're definitely going to the pub after."

"I will, Mom," he promised, hiding a grin.

DOM SET HIS cell phone back onto the table as the server deposited a pitcher of ale and glasses.

"Mom?" Glen teased.

Maybe he shouldn't have told Glen about his mother's request. He gave a sheepish shrug. "You know how it is."

"Kinda, but in my case it's a text to my wife. Moms aren't nearly as demanding."

That was a conversation topic Dom had no intention of following. He'd already sidestepped Glen's earlier questions about how long he'd be in town, what he'd been doing so far and what his plans were for the rest of his leave. Dom had guessed he was wondering about the next Scout meeting, which was in a week's time, and had quickly offered to participate.

Fortunately, another server brought their burgers just then. As they tucked in, Dom's thoughts went back to Zanna. What kind of day had she had and had she thought about him at all or their dinner plans tomorrow? Helping his mother, the Scout meeting and basketball game had all been welcome distractions from thinking about Zanna Winters. That worried him. If he was this preoccupied now, what was it going to be like when there'd be a third person—a baby!—to consider? How could he focus on his duties when he was back in Norfolk, miles from the Cove?

"Something wrong with your burger?"

"Hmm?"

"You looked lost in thought there. Not replaying the basketball game, are you?" Glen teased.

"Hah! If it wasn't for your team's free shot..."

"That's the way the cookie crumbles. And speaking of cookies, I hope you and your team come up with something more interesting than chocolate chip."

Dom groaned and took another swig of beer. "This is where moms come in handy."

"Not sure if that's in the rule book. Theoretically the team is supposed to bake, but maybe we can make an exception this time."

Dom gave a thumbs-up. "Speaking of the next meeting, will it be at the school again or in St. Pat's basement?"

Glen sighed. "We try to book the school gym for games or if we have a guest speaker, but if it's a regular meeting, we usually use the church, mainly because we don't have to book it so far in advance. Right now, the school wants groups to book space at least a week ahead."

Dom shook his head. "I don't remember problems like this back in the day. Didn't our troop always meet in the school?"

"Yeah, but the Cove has a bigger population now, with the newcomers up in the subdivision." He paused briefly. "Plus, the development isn't even finished yet. We've got enough land for another ten homes. Then there are the condo units farther down the highway."

"They're not likely to draw families, though," Dom pointed out.

"True enough, but they might draw seniors, who'll want community space, too, and won't want to drive to Portland."

"Seems like an impossible situation."

"We need a community center," Glen said, plunking his glass down for added emphasis.

"Did I hear the words *community center*?"

Dom and Glen turned as one to the man standing next to their table.

"Hey, Ben," Glen said. "Trust you to home in on a potential building project. What're you doing here?"

"Waiting for my fiancée. And poke fun as you will, a project means more business, which means more money in all our pockets. So, what are you two up to?"

"Unwinding from a hectic basketball game," Dom said.

"Seriously? Why didn't you let me know? I'd have loved the chance to take on you two in a pickup game."

Glen smirked. "Maybe so, but could you have taken on half a Scout troop?"

Ben laughed. "You've got me there. I assume this late meal is a reward for good playing then?"

"It is and a bit of a catch-up, too," Dom said.

"Speaking of that, thanks again for filling in for me on Monday. The memorial committee meeting?" he prompted at Dom's blank expression.

"I can't believe that was only Monday. Seems like weeks ago." Dom thought of all that had happened in five days, every one of which had been centered on Zanna…and their ongoing attempts at resolving the baby situation.

"Sign of aging, fella," Ben joked. "Anyway, Henry texted me that the next meeting is this Monday and…uh…"

"Want me to go for you?"

Ben gave a sheepish grin. "If you don't mind."

"It's all good," he said, though he wondered if that would be true after tomorrow night's dinner and co-parenting discussion. Would he be welcome at that meeting?

"Thanks, Dom, and tell Henry and Zan I'm happy to go along with whatever you guys decide." Ben suddenly looked across the room. "Oh, here comes Ella. Okay, you two… I'll leave you to your burgers and, Glen, if you can come in for a quick meeting at the site tomorrow, that'd be great. Nine?" He clapped

Glen on the shoulder and headed toward the front of the pub.

Watching him cross the room, waving here and there to people he knew, Dom said, "I don't remember Ben being such a go-getter."

Glen shook his head. "He definitely wasn't. That's what happens in your mid-thirties, maybe. Awareness of impending middle age or knowing it's time to settle down?"

Dom was the same age as Ben, yet these thoughts had never occurred to him. He knew Glen was married and the father of two girls, one just a baby. Impulsively, he asked, "What's it like being a dad?"

The transformation in Glen's face said it all. "Awesome and scary." He paused to think some more. "The best thing that ever happened to me."

Dom nodded. There wasn't much he could say to that, but he knew he'd be mulling over Glen's words all night long.

ZANNA PACED HER BEDROOM, which was even smaller than the sitting area in her apartment behind the hotel office. She recalled how impossibly suffocating the space had been while Mark was still hanging around, after knowing their marriage was over. He'd claimed he was changing, would never do it again. Blah blah blah. She'd listened and believed him too often and vowed never to be taken in by false promises again. She felt the whole Mark debacle had given her a special kind of radar for detecting fake assurances. But for some reason her instincts weren't functioning as clearly as usual when Dominic Kennedy was around. She'd have to be extra cautious.

She stopped pacing and checked herself in the mirror once more. Recently she'd noticed some roundness in her cheeks, which nowadays were pinker as well. She'd always been curvier than most of her friends, even as a teenager, and now those curves were more apparent than ever. The emerald green dress she'd worn to Grace's wedding would be going back into her closet for a long time after tonight. Zanna pursed her lips, studying her reflection, looking for obvious signs of Little Bean. *That slight swelling won't be disguised by loose clothing much longer. It's time to tell Mom.*

Rohan's jaw dropped when Zanna came up to the reception counter. "Wow! You look amazing!"

Aware that her cheeks were flaming by now, she quickly said, "Thank you and just a reminder that I won't be late. I also have my cell phone so—"

"Zanna, go and have a good time and forget about the hotel. You deserve the break."

Dom had wanted to pick her up at the hotel, but she'd insisted on meeting him at The Daily Catch. Having him escort her to the bistro would be too much like a date, and this was no date. Or so she reminded herself every time a zing of anticipation at seeing him caught her by surprise. She slipped into her all-weather coat and slung her purse over a shoulder, waving a final goodbye to Rohan as she went out the hotel door.

The temperature was already dropping and Zanna knew the waterfront would be even cooler. Most newcomers to Maine were surprised at the cool spring and summer weather and would show up at the beach expecting a day of tanning and swimming only to sit wrapped in blankets. If the town had other attractions than the beach, perhaps more tourists would visit. Zanna stopped walking to have a "wee chat" with herself, as her Granny Winters used to say.

This is your night off. Stop thinking about the hotel. You know what your future is definitely bringing and that's your focus for tonight. Yet she loved the shivery thrill from Dom's expression when she entered The Daily Catch, handed her coat to the hostess and walked toward their table.

He stood up and met her halfway, reached out to clasp her hand in his, his eyes shining as he murmured in her ear, "You look absolutely stunning!"

She felt heat rise in her face and let him lead her to her chair, which he pulled out for her. *Maybe tonight you can just be Zanna,* she told herself as she sat down, *enjoying an evening with an attractive man.* And yes, he was breathtakingly handsome in his powder blue shirt and crisp black jeans, though a tiny part of her yearned to see him in navy uniform.

"I've ordered a glass of wine for me and sparkling mineral water for you," he said, sitting across from her at their small table. "I assumed—"

"Correctly," she interjected. "Thanks. Have you had a look at tonight's menu? It's been a while since I've been here." She stopped herself, suddenly remembering when she'd last been at the bistro. Dom's arched eyebrow signaled he was thinking the same thing and she glanced away, scanning the room already full of diners.

"This is a good table," he said. "Corner by a window facing the harbor. Would be especially nice on a warm summer's evening, the window open to a soft sea breeze." Then noting her grin, he added, "What? You didn't know I could be romantic?"

"I'm up for more surprises, romantic-wise. Bring them on," she teased.

"I'll do my best. Bit rusty in that department but for you, Zanna Winters…" His eyes stayed on hers.

She peered down at the menu then. Had she actually been flirting with him? This wasn't an auspicious start to a night intended for business. The server brought their drinks and took their orders after a brief discussion about which appetizer and main course until they opted for clams to share and the flounder special.

"I'm going to miss this when I'm back on base," Dom said when the server left.

"No good seafood in Norfolk?"

He shrugged. "Fish and chips. I'm sure there

are good fish restaurants, but I haven't come across one as great as this."

"What's your life there like, when you're not at sea?"

"Pretty humdrum. I have admin work to do, some training until we go back to sea."

"Do you like that best? Going to sea?"

"I do. Despite the occasional glitch in on-board routines or stormy weather, being out on the water is the best."

Zanna forced a smile at the passion in his face, wondering if she or Little Bean could generate such enjoyment. There was a lull then, and she stared at the flickering tealights on the table, hiding her thoughts.

"Zanna?"

She looked up and saw his frown.

"You okay?"

She could get serious now, but there was a meal to look forward to and the room sparkled with candlelight. "I'm fine, Dom. Just realizing how much I've missed nights out like this." She gestured toward the room.

"Same here."

"Are you a workaholic, too?"

"Kind of. I mean, I have a social network in Norfolk—a small one." He gave a light laugh.

"But I've always been a bit of a loner, happily doing my own thing."

"Me, too." She smiled and thought back to that moment years ago at Brandon's funeral, when he'd known instinctively what she needed more than anything in the world right then was a hug.

He seemed about to speak when their clam appetizer arrived, along with a basket of bread. Zanna was about to reach for a piece of baguette when Dom suddenly caught hold of her hand. "Let's stop denying the connection between us, Zan. It's there—I know you feel it and I do, too. Let's see where this goes, for our sake and for…for Little Bean's."

A lump rose in Zanna's throat. She nodded, afraid to talk, and was about to withdraw her hand from his when a hearty voice next to her said, "Well, what a small world!" Ben Winters beamed.

Standing next to him was his fiancée, Ella. Dom cast a rueful glance at Zanna as he released her hand and got to his feet. After Ben introduced Ella to Dom, there was an awkward silence. Zanna was grateful for their small table and hoped Ben wouldn't suggest moving to one for four.

Instead, he looked quickly from Dom to her,

sizing up the scene. Then he asked, "Clams good?"

She hadn't tried one yet but said, "Delicious! Oh, and, Ben, Henry suggested another committee meeting on Monday."

"Yeah, he texted me but I can't make it. Dom has agreed to fill in for me again."

She glanced quickly at Dom, who shrugged. "Sure, fine by me," she said. "I can catch you up after, if you like."

"Okay, thanks," Ben said. His eyes flicked from her to Dom again.

"Ben," Ella prompted, tugging on his hand. She locked eyes with Zanna and winked.

"Okay. Enjoy...you two," Ben said as Ella pulled him off to the rear of the room.

"She seems nice," Dom commented as the pair walked off. Then he grinned. "So, the clams are good, are they?"

Zanna laughed and reached for a piece of baguette.

CHAPTER TEN

IT WAS DARK when they left the bistro. Dom paused outside the door to breathe in the crisp air, coming to his senses, despite his effort to hold on to the magic of the night and the woman whose hand was clasped in his. She'd been quiet after he'd paid the bill, reminding her that the dinner was meant to be his treat. He guessed she'd remembered then that the main purpose of the evening had been to have a discussion about their future. Perhaps she didn't want to have that talk now any more than he did.

"Go for a walk?" he asked and when she nodded, he led her along the boardwalk. "Where to? Beach? Town?" His laugh was sheepish. "I feel like a teenager with nowhere to go after a date except home."

"Never a big problem for me. I seldom dated."

"Same here. I acted as if I wasn't interested in a social life, but truth was I didn't have one." When she smiled his heart gave a small flip-flop. "So, where to?"

After a moment she said, "Beach? More privacy."

Her smile was gone. Back to business. "Okay." He could already feel the light inside dim and he let go of her hand once they mounted the steps up to the road. "How about there?" He pointed to a bench several feet beyond. Except for a late dogwalker, the area was empty. Saturday night, and people were either cozy at home or enjoying some nightlife—not having serious conversations on a lonely bench. He let a wave of self-pity flow through him.

"Are you warm enough? Sure you want to be out here?"

"I'm fine."

"This doesn't have to be difficult, Zanna. We're both adults. We know what we need to do, and I have faith that we can discuss everything without...without..." He didn't want to say *arguing* but the word popped into his head.

"Getting emotional?" she asked, a tinge of sarcasm in her tone.

"I wasn't going to say that, but emotion is okay. Look, let me make this easier for both of us." He reached for her hands, folding them into his. "In a few months you're going to have our baby. I'm happy and excited about that." He paused a beat. "Scared, too. I want to be a good father and I want to be part of Little Bean's life. I promise to do my best for both of you. I've said that before and you have to believe me."

"I want to, Dom. I really do. It's just that… I'm scared, too. About being a good mother. About supporting a child when I can barely make ends meet with the hotel. About being—"

"Alone?" She didn't answer but he saw her trembling lips. "You won't be alone, Zan. That's what I'm trying to say. Norfolk isn't that far by air. If I'm not physically here, I'll be a phone call away. And I plan to get leave for…you know…when the baby comes." He pulled her closer. "As for the financial support, you know that will never be an issue." Her hands slipped from his and he stifled a sigh. Would she ever trust him?

"I know you'll help out as much as possible, but…there are complications."

"Such as?"

She looked out across the dark water. "I'm thinking of selling the hotel."

That single sentence took ages to register,

all of its ramifications swirling in his mind. After a moment, he asked, "Is business that bad?" When she faced him again, he saw that her eyes were damp.

"I've only a few bookings so far for the Memorial Day holiday and it's less than three weeks away. Rohan is leaving to go to college in September and I doubt I'll find someone else as wonderful as he is. My part-time room attendant wants more hours, which I can't afford to give her. I'm using up most of my savings to keep the place running, pay the basic bills—"

Dom drew her into his arms. He felt her shiver. "Want to go somewhere warmer?"

"No. I should let Rohan have what's left of a Saturday night."

"We'll figure things out, Zan. Together. You're not on your own here—about anything." A tear fell onto her cheek and he stroked it away, using the same finger to tilt her chin up. Without a thought, he lowered his mouth to hers. There was a hint of caramel on her lips—the dessert they'd shared?—and she reached up to pull him closer, her mouth on his and her fingers clutching the back of his head. Her body swayed against his and a tiny part of him whispered *we shouldn't be doing this*. But he didn't care. The quiet night wrapped around them, and Dom knew he'd never want to let go of her.

FOR THE FIRST time in months, Zanna slept in. Sunlight streamed through the small bedroom window, and she yawned, stretching out her legs and luxuriating in the novelty of awakening well past daybreak. Last night Rohan had offered to come in for the morning shift and she hadn't hesitated to accept. She placed her hands across her belly, cupping the bump that was Little Bean. Then her cell phone buzzed from her bedside table. She reached for it, hoping it might be Dominic, but it was her mother and Zanna bit back her disappointment as she said hello.

"I'm coming to the Cove, darling, and wonder if you're free for lunch?"

"Today?"

There was a slight pause. "Is that a problem? Can you get Rohan to cover for you?"

"Um, no it's not a problem, Mom. I'm just surprised because you were just here a week ago and—"

"Yes, but there's something I want to talk to you about and it's best done in person."

"Is everything okay?"

"Goodness yes. Not to worry. What time shall we meet up?"

Zanna's mind raced. She and Dom hadn't arranged to meet today but she thought they might, especially after the way they'd parted last night. Mentally reliving the kiss, she missed Jane's repeated question. "Zanna? Are you still there?"

"Sorry, Mom. Yes, no problem. What time are you planning to get here?"

"One o'clock, okay?"

"Yes. I'll speak to Rohan right away."

"I'll meet you at Mabel's."

"You're not coming to the hotel first?"

"No, I'll meet you there. See you soon, sweetie."

Zanna stared at her phone a few seconds after her mother disconnected. Why wasn't her mother meeting her here, where she usually stayed when she visited the Cove? It was only after she'd showered that she realized her mother had used one of Henry's favorite expressions. *Not to worry.* Well, of course she wouldn't worry, but the phone call was odd.

Then her mind leaped to more important matters, like Dominic and the way she'd felt when he'd kissed her. During that kiss, she could believe that the connection between them at New Year's had been real after all, and not merely the headiness of a big party night. There'd been the same sense of comfort in his arms, the same passion in his lips. After he'd walked her back to the hotel, they'd lingered outside holding hands and staring silently into each other's eyes. A new hope for the future—hers and Little Bean's—had stayed with her all through the night.

As she got dressed, she thought that whatever her mother had to say couldn't possibly diminish her glow. And now it was time to tell Jane she was going to be a grandmother.

But Zanna's plans swerved off course right after she and her mother gave their lunch order at Mabel's. She watched her mother nervously fiddling with her napkin. "The reason I'm not staying in my usual room at the hotel," Jane began, "is because I'm staying with Henry."

"Okay," she said slowly, unsure of the import of that statement. Henry had been a family friend to all the Winterses as long as she remembered. "Well, that's nice for you. More comfortable than staying in a hotel room."

Jane smiled. "I mean I'm staying with him because we're a couple."

Zanna's mouth gaped.

Her mother's smile grew bigger. "Is it that much of a shock, dear?"

Zanna reached for her glass of water and sipped, needing the few seconds to come up with a reply that didn't include any condescending phrases like *at your age*? She set her glass down. "Not a shock, Mom, but definitely a surprise. How long…?"

"Since Christmas, but basically—for Henry—since I first met him." Jane leaned across the table and lowered her voice. "He told me he's been smitten with me since your father's and my engagement party."

"But that's—"

"Thirty-nine years ago."

Zanna did the math. "Let me get this straight. Are you telling me that Henry has had a…a 'thing' for you since you first met? Thirty-nine years ago?" She chewed a bite of sandwich, fixing her eyes on Jane, who was nodding. "How do you feel about all this?"

"Almost like a teenager. You know, that giddiness of finding out someone has a crush on you."

Zanna nodded, thinking of her own giddiness last night.

"Other times I'm in disbelief that something like this can happen at my age." Her eyes were shining.

"Sixty-four isn't old, Mom. Well, I'm happy for both of you. And I'm resisting asking parental-style questions like what the long-term plans are." She picked up her water glass. "Cheers!"

"Thanks, dear. I was hoping you'd be amenable."

"Why wouldn't I be?"

"In case you were worried about...you know...how it might go."

"Are *you* worried about that?"

"Not at all. Granted, I've been slow to realize my own feelings for Henry, but looking back over the years, I see now there were signs I simply chose to ignore. I have complete faith in him—and in us."

Zanna peered down at her lunch, tears stinging her eyes. Her mother's admission struck too close to home. Had she been ignoring feelings for Dominic? Finally, she asked, "Plans?"

"I'm going to sell the house in Bangor and move back to the Cove. Maybe stay at the hotel for a bit or just move in with Henry right away. Whatever works best."

This was the moment for Zanna to make

her own confessions. But which one first? Impulsively, she blurted, "Speaking of the hotel."

"Hmm?" Jane looked up from cutting apart one of her English muffins.

"I'm thinking of selling it."

Her mother set her knife and fork onto her plate. "Oh heavens, Zanna! Why?"

"You know why, Mom. Nothing has changed since our last discussion about it a week ago." Zanna was wishing she'd gone with her other, happier, piece of news first. "But it's only a thought right now," she quickly said, "nothing definite." She dismissed the stab of guilt at misleading her mother because at the moment, a sale was realistically more than an idea. At her mother's frown she quickly said, "But I have other more definite news." She glanced around, noting the table closest to theirs was vacant now. "You're going to be a grandmother." She tried not to giggle at her mother's own jaw-drop. "I'm having a baby."

Jane's frown deepened. "Is this an intention or…or a fact?"

"I'm pregnant." Zanna's nervousness returned. Jane wasn't responding the way she'd imagined.

Jane was shaking her head. "I'm having

trouble taking this in. You've been alone since Mark left, almost a year ago. Who…?"

"Dominic Kennedy." Zanna waited for her mother to register the name.

"The man we met here on Mother's Day? Who mentored Brandon in Scouts?" Jane's voice rose and Zanna anxiously scanned the room. She was being paranoid, but this was the Cove after all, where news travelled quicker than lightning.

"Didn't he just arrive in town? From the navy or something?" Jane asked. "Henry mentioned he was filling in for Ben on the memorial committee."

Zanna sighed. *Yes, news really did travel that fast.* But she knew what her mother was asking. "We met up at New Year's." She wasn't going to spell it out for her. Jane was nodding though, making the calculations.

"I'm…I'm at a loss for words." She reached across the table to place her hand on Zanna's. "Of course, I'm thrilled at becoming a grandmother. It's something I've often fantasized about, but I didn't expect it to happen like… like this."

Me neither, Zanna was about to quip when Jane added, "But the timing. Oh, Zanna. The timing isn't good, is it? I mean, with your idea to sell the hotel when you're about to become a mother." She hesitated, then asked, "What's the plan? Are you and Dominic getting together or will you be a single mother? If so, that's not ideal, considering selling the hotel will leave you without employment."

Zanna's head was spinning. She'd been filled with similar questions minutes ago after Jane's reveal and the irony of this turntable situation almost made her smile. *Almost.* What she'd anticipated as a celebratory end to lunch was rapidly fading. "Mom," she began, struggling to keep her voice level. "I don't know yet what will happen between Dom and me. He wants to be part of our baby's life in every way. Including financially. But we're still working things out."

"When are you due?"

"The end of September."

Jane pursed her lips. "Not much time left to work things out."

Zanna felt herself getting pulled into their old roles. She took a calming breath. "None of us are teenagers, Mom. Not Dom and me nor you and Henry." Jane flushed and Zanna knew her message had hit home.

"You're absolutely right, dear, and if I sound like the mother of a sixteen-year-old again, it's only because I'm worried." Jane paused to dab at her eyes with her napkin. "Parents never stop worrying, even when their children are adults." She managed a quick smile. "You will learn that in time. If there's anything you need me to do for you—a loan or whatever—I'm always here for you."

Zanna fought back tears. Dom had promised much the same thing last night and she was suddenly overcome by the realization that love—and hope—were irrevocably linked. "Thanks, Mom."

The serious talk was set aside by silent agreement it seemed to Zanna. They finished their lunch and soon were hugging goodbye outside Mabel's.

"I guess we both have a lot to think about," Jane said.

"And plans to make," Zanna put in.

Her mother nodded. "Yes. All right then, dear. I'll be going back to Bangor in a couple of days to get a start on my own plans." She began to walk off when she stopped to turn around. "Zanna, take care of yourself." Then she blew her a kiss and headed down to Main Street.

Zanna watched until Jane descended to the boardwalk and out of sight, likely going to Henry's house. She decided to go for a walk herself rather than return to the hotel. There was much to process. The one person she longed to see and confide in was Dominic, but after the almost painful talk with her mother, she was beginning to feel doubts creep in. Her vagueness to Jane about a future with Dominic was because she knew there was no solid plan yet. Promises weren't plans.

She shoved her hands in her coat pockets and trudged up the street toward Town Square. Exercise and a change of scenery would help, but her thoughts shifted unexpectedly to Henry and his thirty-nine years of unrequited love. However things turned out for her and Dominic, she knew she did not want a life like that.

CHAPTER ELEVEN

"How was your dinner last night?"

"Hmm?" Dom looked up from the article he was reading in the *Maine Sunday Telegram*. His mother was pouring the rest of the soup they'd had for lunch into plastic containers for the freezer.

"Didn't you say you were going to The Daily Catch? How was it?"

"Oh, great. Delicious. I'll take you there before I go back to base." He smiled and resumed reading.

"And did you and Suzanna meet up with anyone else?"

"Um, no, but her cousin, Ben—remember him?—was there with his fiancée."

"Of course I remember Ben Winters, from your basketball days." Marie frowned. "I think his fiancée is the new editor of *The Beacon*."

Dom raised his head again. "Is she?"

"Yes, and she was the one who was blamed

for that awful business years ago, with young Brandon Winters. But she was a victim herself. Very sad situation."

"I remember you telling me about it all at Christmas."

There was a pause while Marie ran water into the now empty soup pot. "So…was your dinner with Suzanna a date?"

Dom hid his smile. He figured his mother would get around to the question she'd been itching to ask since he left to meet Zanna at the bistro. "Mom, I'm helping her and Henry Jenkins organize the memorial ceremony for her brother. I told you that."

"Dominic Kennedy," Marie said, walking over to where he sat at the kitchen table. "Your face is a dead giveaway. I've always been able to tell when you're trying to pull the wool over my eyes, as your father used to say." She stroked the top of his head before going back to the sink.

Dom sighed. His mom still treated him like an adolescent sometimes during his visits home. Still, this was the perfect moment to tell her about the baby.

He thought back to Zanna's reveal about selling the hotel. That meant there could be another option than co-parenting from a distance. If she was no longer tied to the hotel, she'd be free to leave the Cove. Perhaps follow him wherever the new job took him.

Then there was the kiss. He'd fallen asleep floating on that kiss. There was no denying the attraction between them and neither distance nor time had affected it. Their connection went deeper than attraction, too. But was it love?

His sigh drew his mother's attention again. "I'm not prying, Dom. I'm happy that you're getting out and meeting up with old friends from high school. I realize you probably have a busy social life in Norfolk when you're not at sea and I hope you meet somebody special, if you haven't already. That's what parents want—to see their children happy with someone to love." She looked at him, her eyes shining, and he was about to confide in her when she unexpectedly added, "Why don't you invite Suzanna to dinner here? Maybe tomorrow or Tuesday. Whichever works for both of you."

"Okay, Mom, I will. And now, please let me finish this article."

She waved a dismissive hand and he grinned.

After a few minutes, he folded up the newspaper. "I think I'll get some exercise. Is there anything you'd like me to do before I head out?"

Marie tucked the last container in the freezer. "No. Can't think of anything. Will you be home for dinner?"

Mealtimes, when his mother cooked all his childhood favorites or the new recipes she liked to try out on him, were the highlights of his visits home. The real possibility of his relocation to the West Coast made him blurt, "Hey, why don't I get tickets for one of those harbor cruises? For this afternoon, if possible?"

Her face lit up. "Lovely!"

"I'll text you if I get tickets. We could meet at the pier, depending on the time." He put his arm across her shoulder and kissed her on the cheek.

While he rummaged through the hall closet for his hooded all-weather jacket, he noticed his father's old navy-blue pea jacket stowed at the back, behind the collection of outdoor wear belonging to him and his mother. His father had loved that coat, wearing it even to church despite Marie's protests. Yet she hadn't been able to pack it up with the clothing and other items Dom had taken to Portland. He stroked the lapels and thought what a wonderful grandfather Jerry Kennedy would have made.

The idea of grandfathers was still in his mind as he walked through the neighborhood toward Town Square. He realized Little Bean would have grandmothers—and doting ones—but no grandfather. There was Uncle George, who might be persuaded to be a substitute. That had been a bit like his role to Dom, growing up, for there were no grandparents on either his mother's or his father's side. The problem was his uncle was happily ensconced in his retirement compound in Florida. Dom couldn't remember the last time he'd seen him—just holiday cards and occasionally, texts, were exchanged. Zanna only had her mother, but the extended Winters family would be available for support. *Would she want to leave that network, to go with him wherever he was posted?* A hearty voice suddenly roused him from that worrisome thought.

"Dominic! The very man on my mind!"

Dom stopped and turned to see Henry Jenkins walking his way with the small white dog from the hotel on a leash. "Does Felix know about this?"

Henry's booming laugh drew the attention of two men playing at one of the square's concrete chess tables and he nodded a hello to them as he caught up to Dom. "Nope and no telling, either." He winked. "Ben says you're still sitting in for him on the memorial committee. Did he let you know we're meeting at noon tomorrow instead of nine? Zanna has an early appointment."

Dom frowned. She hadn't mentioned a word about that last night. Zanna Winters kept information close. "No, he didn't, but thanks for letting me know." He gestured to the dog. "Have you been conscripted into the Mo walking club?"

"Hah! I suppose I have. I just met Cora as I was coming up here to the Square and she looked a bit tired, so I suggested she go back to the hotel for a rest and I'd bring Mo later."

"Still doing good deeds," Dom said, grinning.

Henry shrugged. "Once a Scout, always a Scout." He squinted against the sunlight, studying Dom. "Say, how's your mother doing? I haven't seen her at the Historical Society for a bit."

"Oh, she's fine." But was she, Dom suddenly wondered? "Um, maybe she's been busy?"

"Well, give her my regards. Our next meeting is coming up and we'll be having a heated discussion about where to locate when we leave the church. I think I have her email address, so I'll let her know." He clapped Dom on the shoulder. "See you tomorrow."

Questions swirled in Dom's mind as he watched Henry lead Mo over to the chess players. *Why had his mother stopped going to the Society's meetings? And what was this appointment Zanna had? Something to do with the baby? If so, why had she left him out?*

Head bent in thought, he continued on down to the harbor, where he managed to buy two tickets for the next cruise, and he texted his mother to meet him there. When Dom saw her beaming face as she rushed along the boardwalk toward the dock, he knew at least he'd gotten one thing right that day.

ZANNA READ DOM'S text again. Henry told me the meeting today changed to noon. Everything OK? Word always got around fast here, she thought as she quickly answered. All good. See you then.

She'd actually forgotten about the Gateway Living team's arrival until midafternoon yesterday. Her mind had been elsewhere since lunch with her mother. The likelihood of Jane moving back to the Cove had complicated her own half-formed ideas for the future.

If she sold the hotel, she'd be all right financially for the short term, once all the bills were paid. There'd be family support for her as a single mother, with Jane back in town. But without the hotel, Zanna was also free to move elsewhere, and how would Jane feel if she moved away with her only grandchild? Zanna knew if she had a close friend in town to whom she could confide her frustrations or fears, her stresses could be eased. Her relationships with her cousins were friendly, but not close enough for confidences. Ironically, the one person who probably would understand how she felt right now was Dominic.

The phone on her desk buzzed. "The people are here for your meeting, Zanna," Rohan said from the reception counter.

She grabbed a notebook and pen, pocketed her cell phone, smoothed out her blouse and left her office. Three men and two women in business attire smiled politely as she greeted them and introduced themselves. They included an architect, an engineer and an electrician/plumbing team as Alex had mentioned plus the addition of a marketing officer.

"Alex sends his regards," the architect explained, "and sorry he couldn't make it today, but he'll be in touch as soon as he gets our report."

She'd been hoping to finally meet Alex Corelli, thinking that she'd be able to get a sense of the company's intentions from a face-to-face talk. Her hotel experience had honed her ability to read people from body language and facial expressions.

"Okay with you if we take a floor plan and just wander? We all have different areas we need to explore independently," the man continued.

"Of course, and my assistant will give you master card keys and will also print out a list of occupied rooms." She glanced at Rohan and saw he was already on the computer. *I will miss this young man so much*, she thought as she ducked back into her office for the floor plans she'd printed out last night.

She'd expected to accompany them, which was why she'd postponed the committee meeting, but now realized how difficult that would be, considering the five were wandering on their own. Once she'd made copies of the plans for everyone, she returned to the front counter.

"How about we start in the ballroom," the architect suggested, looking up from his copy.

Zanna said, "Let me know when you're about to finish and I'll arrange for coffee."

The architect paused. "Thanks, Ms. Winters, but no need. We don't want to bother you any more than necessary." He flashed a big smile.

She watched them stroll across the lobby, glancing briefly at the motley collection of small tables and chairs on their way. One of the women—the engineer?—split off to check out the elevator.

Zanna looked at Rohan and sighed heavily.

He grinned. "So, are you going to tell me who these people are, Zanna?"

She had yet to tell him about Gateway Living. Now that he was leaving the hotel anyway, the possible sale wouldn't affect him unless it happened before the end of the summer.

"What will you do if you sell it?" he asked as she wound up her summary. "I've seen how much you like this work and how good you are at it. Will you leave the Cove to find work in another hotel? For someone else?"

His voice pitched in disbelief, mirroring Zanna's own thoughts. Working for someone else, likely a huge corporation, would be a real challenge after managing a hotel on her own. The investment she'd made here—personal and financial—was huge. Could she blithely walk away from it all, go work for a faceless employer, one of a cast of thousands? Her stomach churned at the idea. On the other hand, she'd be free of the constant worry about bankruptcy.

"I'm trying not to get ahead of myself," she mumbled, knowing that was the very thing she'd been guilty of since Dom's arrival in town. "Do you mind hanging around till they're finished? In case they need to consult with me on something?"

"Nope. Except for a dog-walking appointment at ten I'm available all day."

"I'm guessing Mo?" she smiled.

"Mrs. Stanfield says she's feeling a bit tired

today. I popped out an hour ago to pick up coffee and a muffin for her."

"What?"

Rohan shrugged. "Not a problem. Oh, and by the way, the Pattersons are checking out this afternoon instead of tomorrow. Plus, that businessman from Augusta on three? He's decided to check out this morning."

Zanna's head was spinning. How had she lost track of what was happening in the hotel, with her guests and probably her staff, too? The answer came almost immediately. Dominic Kennedy—the man she couldn't get off her mind no matter how hard she tried.

When the Gateway team returned their card keys, Zanna scrutinized their faces for any hint of their reactions. But the architect merely smiled and promised Alex would be in touch once they'd made their reports.

"When will that be?"

"We'll move as quickly as we can," he said cryptically, perhaps noticing her flushed face. As she watched them file out the door, she wanted to scream. How much longer could her life be on hold?

Rohan took in her red face and discreetly peered down at his cell phone as she strode past him into her office, closing the door behind her. She plunked onto her chair and tried to calm herself with deep breaths. She had to get her emotions under control. This negative energy couldn't be good for Little Bean. There was almost an hour before the committee meeting and she knew an early lunch and a lie-down were exactly what she needed.

"ZANNA?"

The soft voice broke into a dream that Zanna forgot as soon as she opened her eyes and saw her mother hovering over her. She sat up, the duvet slipping off her onto the floor.

"Mom? What're you doing here?"

Jane smiled and backed away as Zanna swung her legs over the side of the bed and rubbed her face. "We're here for the committee meeting, dear, and Rohan told us you might be having a nap, which is so unlike you! You must be feeling your pregnancy." She patted Zanna's cheek. "The men are waiting in the lobby. Refresh yourself and meet us out there."

By the time she spotted them sitting at one of the larger tables on the far side of the lobby, Zanna felt more like her usual self. The shakiness had gone as well as the queasiness in her stomach, which she knew had been from stress. The three smiled as she walked their way but the only face she focused on was Dominic's. He was still substituting for Ben and that made her happy, but when she saw his concerned expression, she guessed her mother had told them she'd been napping. Well, she was entitled, wasn't she? A busy, pregnant woman?

"I've invited your mother to this meeting, Zanna," Henry quickly said, "because I knew you'd want her to be part of the discussion about the wording on Brandon's plaque and how the ceremony will go."

Zanna noticed her mother nervously tapping a pen on a notebook and sensed something was up with her. "A good idea, Henry." She decided to let him chair the meeting and asked, "What should we start with?"

Henry said, "The plaque, I think."

Immediately Jane blurted, "I know that the plaque has always been part of Grace's plan for Brandon's memorial, but I have conflicting feelings about it."

This was the first time Jane had expressed an opinion on a plan that had been in the works for months and Zanna was startled. Why hadn't Jane spoken up weeks ago? The family had agreed to a memorial ceremony at Christmas. Then she realized she'd made some assumptions about her mother—that her silence meant agreement when it actually might have meant something entirely different. Had Jane taken a back seat to avoid disagreeing with her?

"What *are* your feelings?" she asked. The swift glance of surprise from Jane to Henry told Zanna she was right, and she turned away, pretending to check her cell phone. Then she felt the warm touch of a hand over hers.

Dom leaned toward her to whisper, "Zan, I think everything will work out. Don't get ahead of yourself here."

His words were so eerily similar to what she'd admitted to herself yesterday that she could only nod.

Henry winked and Zanna knew that these three people cared about her. When had she become this person, distrusting the people she loved? She took a deep breath. "Mom? You were saying?"

Jane set her pen onto the table. "This whole

idea, the memorial plaque and lighthouse restoration, came from Gracie. Although her intentions were admirable and sincere, I can't help but think her underlying hope was for some kind of atonement. For what she did." Jane looked directly at Zanna. "You and I forgave Grace last summer for what happened. She was only a young teen at the time with all the poor judgment that goes with that age. And after so many years she finally got up the courage to tell us what she'd done. What happened that night was a family tragedy, but not a public or community one."

She took a tissue out of her sweater pocket and blew her nose. "It was a terrible accident for the family and a reminder for the town of the dangers in our environment that we tend to overlook or minimize. Henry tells me few people go up there anymore and with the increased population in town from the new subdivision, even fewer people know anything about that night. Perhaps that's a good thing. Brandon's memory will always be here—" she tapped her chest "—and the people who knew and loved him won't need a plaque. I'd prefer a more meaningful memorial for my son. Something vital and useful to everyone in the Cove." She paused and locked eyes with Zanna. "That's my story," she said, with a sad laugh. Henry put his arm around her.

It was the longest and most heartfelt talk Jane had given on the subject, and Zanna realized she'd terribly underestimated her mother. Henry seemed about to speak when the elevator door opened and a small white furball propelled itself toward them. Mo tore across the lobby floor, followed by Cora, apologizing the instant she stepped off the elevator. The dog leaped onto Jane's lap and began licking her hands and face. Jane giggled, ducking her head from side to side to evade Mo's kisses.

"Oh dear, sorry for interrupting your meeting, Zanna. I'm Cora," the small woman announced to Jane as she reached their table. "And I see you've already met Mo."

"I'm Jane, Zanna's mother, and he's delightful."

"Yes, but naughty, too."

Cora glanced at the others. "Sorry, again." She scooped Mo from Jane's lap and fastened his leash.

Zanna saw Jane's quick look at Henry, who

said, "I think we're just wrapping up, aren't we?"

They hadn't decided anything about the plaque, but a wave of exhaustion swept over Zanna, and she immediately chimed in, "Yes!" She remained sitting as Henry and her mother got up to leave.

Jane gathered her things and said, "I'll call you before heading back to Bangor, dear."

Zanna nodded. There were things she wanted to say to her mother, but not at that moment. She watched the three stroll toward the hotel door—Henry's shining white head and lanky outline; Jane, tall with strawberry-blond hair streaked with silver; Cora, petite and dark-haired—and was about to remark on their differences to Dom when he leaned over to murmur, "Before I forget, my mother has invited you to dinner. Tonight, or tomorrow."

She was about to reply when she saw Rohan coming her way-not with good news, she concluded from his frown.

CHAPTER TWELVE

THE MEETING AT the hotel had occupied much of Dom's thoughts after he'd watched Henry, Jane and Cora walk out of the hotel together like old friends. He was about to talk more with Zanna about Jane's thoughts on the memorial when Rohan approached. Her frown as she heard that one of the housekeepers had called in sick deterred him, though. He'd been watching Zanna's face while her mother spoke, noticing a whole range of emotions in it, and couldn't decide if she was for or against Jane's comments about the plaque. There was some unfinished business between mother and daughter and Dom hoped for Zanna's sake that it could be aired and resolved well before the end of September, when Little Bean was due.

Little Bean. He felt a rush of warmth at the nickname and tried to imagine what that Little Bean would look like. But he couldn't, any more than he could imagine a life without ever knowing. Which was why he had to convince Zanna to consider the possibility of a life together. The first step would be to tell her about his promotion interview. Now that he knew she might sell the hotel, he had to convince her he could give her more than financial support.

From the clatter of pots in the kitchen Dom figured his mother was already getting dinner organized and he hesitated to dampen her enthusiasm. But he needed to tell her about his possible promotion before he told Zanna. He headed into the kitchen.

"Mom? Have you got a minute?"

She was washing lettuce leaves at the sink, her back to him. "What is it?"

"I need to talk to you about something."

The tone of his voice was enough to get her to drop the lettuce and turn around. She picked up a tea towel to dry her hands, a small frown creasing her forehead.

"Let's sit." He motioned to the table.

"Is this about whatever's been on your mind these past few days?" she asked, settling beside him. "And don't look so surprised. When you haven't been staring off into space you've been constantly sighing and rubbing your face as if you're trying to wake yourself up from a bad dream."

Dom shook his head and sighed, proving his mother right.

"See?" She smiled. "I'm guessing you're either in trouble or in love. Which is it?"

Both, he wanted to cry, but instead managed a light laugh. "Something else. I've got an interview in about ten days or so, for a promotion." He reached across the table for her hand. "Lieutenant Commander. I'd have my own ship."

Her mouth tightened. "You've talked about that. Do you feel you've got a good chance at it?"

"I do."

"And are you happy about the possibility?"

Was he? He peered down at their two hands folded together on the table. If only he could say for sure. He was about to tell her about the baby—some good news to temper the not-so-good, at least from her perspective—when he realized he didn't know if Zanna had told her own mother. Best to wait and besides, there was only so much emotional information a person could process at one time. That was definitely his take on the past week.

"I have conflicting feelings, to be honest. It's a huge boost to my career but at the same time, the responsibilities involved are—"

"Scary?"

She knew him so well! He shrugged, unable to speak.

"I've never known you to back away from a difficult decision or challenge, Dominic, and I'm guessing this means you'll be transferred somewhere else."

"'Fraid so."

She squeezed his hand. "I'll be fine, Dom. You can rest easy about that."

"Thanks, Mom," was all he could say.

ZANNA WAITED OUTSIDE the door a moment before pressing the bell. She shifted the wrapped bunch of flowers to her other hand to tuck the few strands of hair that the wind had ruffled back into the bun at the nape of her neck. Then she smoothed the fabric of her loose-fitting dress across her hips, wishing she'd worn her more comfortable work shoes instead. Her feet were pinched in the low heels she'd worn at Grace's wedding a mere week ago, leading her to suspect she was retaining fluids, and all she needed right then was something else to worry about. She could have driven but had decided walking up through the midtown neighborhood would be a way to calm her mind and ease the jitters. She took a deep breath and pressed the bell.

The expression on Dom's face as he opened the door validated her decision to wear the dress. He pulled her close in a hug, then grasped her hand and led her inside. "Let me take your sweater. The oven's been on so you probably won't need it."

She handed him the flowers and slipped off her bulky cardigan, suddenly feeling exposed as his eyes skimmed over her. "You look beautiful," he whispered. "That blue…"

"Turquoise," she said. "And those are for your mother." She realized at once how abrupt she was sounding. "Sorry. I'm a bit nervous."

"Me, too." He reached for her hand again. "Mom will join us in the living room in a few minutes. Meanwhile, I'm to give you a tour of the house. It's not very big so…"

"Show me your bedroom." He raised his eyebrows and she giggled. "Will it tell me about the adolescent Dominic Kennedy?"

"I'm afraid so."

Holding her hand, he led her along the hallway, pointing to the small living room on one side and the dining room on the other. At the end of the hall, he opened a door boasting a hand-printed sign that read keep out. Zanna grinned.

"It seems my mother is unable to get rid of anything from those days."

"I think that's sweet. My mother wiped out all trace of me." Zanna paused. "I mean, after my parents divorced, they sold our house and she moved to Bangor. I never really had my own room in her new place, just the guest room. But that was okay with me. I didn't go home that often."

He pressed her hand and she silently cursed herself for steering the talk in such a pitiful direction. She let go of his hand and wandered over to his desk, gazing at the basketball ribbons and the pennant pinned to the bulletin board. She scanned the row of books on the shelf above the desk, noting that most of the titles related to military or naval history, then spotted the large poster of navy ships on the wall next to it. "I love this. Basketball and the navy. Your uncle's influence, I see. You were lucky to have the support of someone else besides your parents. There were bad feelings between my father and Uncle Charles, so we didn't socialize a lot with that side of the family."

"Has that changed? I mean, since…"

Zanna knew exactly what he was referring to—Grace's confession last summer. "We were stunned at first and it took us a while to accept what had happened. Mom's more comfortable around the rest of the Winters family now."

"And you?"

She pretended to examine the items on top of his desk. "It's taken me a bit longer," she eventually murmured. "For me, the forgiving part is easier than the forgetting." It was the first time she'd ever acknowledged that fact to herself, let alone another person.

"All of us have personal foibles or whatever you want to call them."

"Weaknesses?" She turned to face him.

"I wouldn't call them that. Just things in our character that challenge us. They make us what we are. But we have to rise above them, not let them control us."

She moved close enough to feel his body's warmth and detect the scent of citrus aftershave. Her face was inches from his, her eyes fixed on his lips. She raised her hands to cup his head and brought it down to hers, kissing him. He drew her in and Zanna held on, breathless, aware only of his heart beating against hers and his mouth on hers. Then Marie's voice called from somewhere in the house and they broke apart, gasping and grinning at the same time.

"Dinner's ready!"

"I feel like a teenager," she whispered.

"That moment right then was my dream as a teenager."

"What?"

"Kissing you."

Zanna wanted to kiss him again. "Dinner?" she murmured, giggling.

He heaved a sigh. "Yes. Are you ready for this?" He reached for her hand once more. "Coming, Mom," he called as they left his room.

"THAT WAS ABSOLUTELY DELICIOUS, Mrs. Kennedy," Zanna said, placing her fork and knife on her empty plate. "I can't remember the last time I had a home-cooked meal like that."

"Please, call me Marie. And thank you for

the compliment. It's such a pleasure to cook for someone who enjoys food, and I don't often get the chance. Only when Dominic is home."

She stood up to remove plates.

"Can I help?"

"No, no. Guests only help the second time they come. That's a house rule. You and Dom go relax in the living room. I thought we'd have coffee and dessert in there."

Zanna was tempted to sprawl on the sofa but was afraid she might fall asleep. She glanced across the room at Dom, her eyelids drooping in a post-dinner stupor, and let out a long, satisfied groan.

"Yeah," he said as he sank into an armchair. "If I thought I was going to be here much longer, I'd go for a run twice a day, instead of once."

Marie returned bearing a tray laden with coffee cups and plates. "The coffee's almost ready and there's apple pie. Would you like ice cream with yours, Zanna?"

"I shouldn't but...um...yes, please."

"And I have a nice bottle of sherry to go with our pie."

"Oh, no, thanks, I—"

"Zanna doesn't drink...uh...very much," Dom put in. "And can I help with the rest?"

"I'm fine, dear. You entertain Zanna.""

After she dashed back into the kitchen, he met Zanna's questioning look with a shrug. "Didn't mean to interrupt," he said.

She was about to ask if his mother knew about her pregnancy when Marie returned with the rest of the dessert course, and for the next several minutes Zanna's only focus was apple pie and ice cream.

"Another piece?" Marie prompted as Zanna set her fork down.

"I won't be able to eat another bite until tomorrow at least" she said, patting her stomach.

"I'm sure I could arrange for Dominic to take some over to the hotel." She smiled at Dom. Then her gaze skimmed across Zanna, resting—or so it seemed to Zanna—a second too long on her stomach.

"I'll take care of these dishes." Dom jumped to his feet.

After he left, Marie asked, "How do you like running the hotel?"

Zanna knew this wasn't the time for a serious conversation about how bad business was. "It can be tiring. You know, supporting staff and taking care of hotel guests."

"I can imagine—everyone wanting a bit of you every day."

Her insight warmed Zanna. "Exactly. Fortunately, I have a terrific assistant, though he's going to college in the fall."

"Oh dear, that's a shame. Hopefully you'll find someone else just as good."

Zanna smiled. "Fingers crossed."

"It's good that you're getting some free time now, before he leaves."

"Yes." She lapsed into silence then, listening to the sound of running water and clinking of cutlery from the kitchen. "Dom told me about the role your brother played in his joining the navy."

"George has been a wonderful uncle, both before, and especially after, my husband died. Dom's been obsessed with the navy since he was a boy. I guess you noticed the tattered old poster in his bedroom?"

"The poster was a giveaway for sure." Zanna laughed. "Especially the ratings he'd made beside each illustration."

Marie beamed. "I know. He gave each a score out of five, based on his favorites as well as the ones he'd hoped to command some day. And he'll probably get his wish, too."

"How so?"

"His interview, of course. Getting command of one of those ships would be part of his promotion." The pride in her announcement filled the room.

Dry-mouthed, Zanna asked, "Does that mean he'll be leaving the Cove sooner than planned?"

"The interview's about a week and a half away still. I'm very happy for him because this is something he's dreamed about for years. His own ship!" Then she added, "The downside, of course, is that I'll see even less of him."

"Why?" Zanna asked, but she was afraid she already knew the answer.

"Not just because of the extra responsibilities, but he says he'll be transferred out of Norfolk to another part of the country. I'm almost afraid to think where—maybe even the West Coast."

Her sigh was the only sound in the room, but it reverberated in Zanna's ears, along with the question *Why hadn't he said anything to*

her about a move that would take him away
from her...and Little Bean?

Minutes after Dom returned from the kitchen, Zanna said, "I should really get going, but this has been lovely, Marie. Thank you so much. As I said before, I seldom get to eat a home-cooked meal."

"My goodness, it was my pleasure and wonderful to get to know you a bit better. Please come back again, soon. We could have tea or another meal together. And Dominic doesn't have to be here for that either."

She smiled at her son as if expecting him to echo her invite, but Zanna saw his puzzled frown. When he insisted on walking her back to the hotel, she didn't argue, keeping silent until they were crossing Town Square where she stopped midway.

"Your mother told me you have an interview for a promotion that might take you anywhere in the country. Why didn't you tell me? Don't I have a right to know where you're going to be in the coming year?"

"Zanna, it's not what you're thinking. I wasn't keeping anything from you, and I just told my mother this afternoon. I was going to tell you on the walk to the hotel."

"Well, here we are."

He took a moment. "My application for this new rank has been in the works for a couple of months but the interview date was only set a week ago."

"So you've known for a week."

"Yes, but I didn't tell you about it because it seemed the least important matter amongst all the other bits."

"*Bits?* You mean the subject of our baby and your role as a father? How is the possibility of your being moved to some faraway part of the country not an important part of the discussions we've been having?"

"I might not get it anyway," he mumbled.

"Come on, Dominic. You can do better than that."

There was fire in his eyes now. "I admit I've been living in a dream world these last few days. Once I got used to the idea of being a father, I wanted to be more than that. I wanted to find out if you and I…if we could be parents together. If we could be a family."

Zanna looked away, tears blurring her vision of Town Hall at the other end of the square. "Families don't keep secrets, Dom. They talk, they air their differences and share their doubts." But as soon as the words tumbled out of her mouth, she knew that family portrait hadn't been hers.

"I think I've been in denial about the possibility that I'll be moving not only from Norfolk, but from you, Zanna. From you and Little Bean."

She turned at the break in his voice.

"And I'm torn, because this is what I've been working toward for a long time—commanding my own ship. To have the honor and privilege of working with my own crew, serving my country."

Despite her resolve not to give in, she was awed by his passion. If only she could summon a similar zeal for running a hotel. "You want the promotion," she said.

"I do, but—"

"That's okay." She raised a palm before he could go on. "Bean and I will manage."

"Zanna, you don't understand. *I want both.* I want to be with you and Bean, and I want this job."

Another thought occurred to her. "Does your mother know? About our baby?"

"I was going to tell her, but I thought I should wait to find out if your mother knew."

Zanna rolled her eyes. "Here we go again with feeble excuses. Listen, I want to go the rest of my way home alone. I need to think about all this when I'm not feeling so…so confused." She swung around to leave.

When he called out, "I love you!" she kept on walking.

CHAPTER THIRTEEN

DOM KNEW IT would take way more than a slice of apple pie to appease Zanna, but his mother had insisted.

"Back already?" she'd asked when he'd returned home after watching Zanna head to the hotel.

He'd slumped onto the armchair opposite his mother. "I think I messed up."

"Okay." She'd put aside the book she'd been reading. "Remember when I told you I'd noticed you've been preoccupied, and I said you must be either in trouble or in love? Is it the love part that worries you?"

"Kind of but it's not that simple."

"Love seldom is."

How had he gotten so lucky, to have her as a mother? "The problem isn't the love part… well, it is a bit because I don't have a clue what's going on in her mind…the problem is my promotion. My career."

"Career navy officers have wives and families, Dom."

"Yes, but I don't know if she'd want that. I don't even know exactly what she feels for me and…and she's going to have a baby. Mine. Well…ours." He'd stammered at her face. "You're going to be a grandmother." The silence that fell had reminded him of the time he'd been suspended from school for taking on the class bully at recess.

"Oh boy," was all she said before tearing up and crossing the room to hug him.

This morning she'd told him to make amends—"Tell her how you feel about her, Dominic, and don't forget the pie."

Now he was standing at the hotel reception counter holding a plastic-wrapped plate while Rohan went to get Zanna. She hadn't answered any of his phone calls last night after stomping away from him. He doubted she'd heard him call out after her, that he loved her. At least, that was the scenario he wanted to believe. He remembered what she'd admitted about being better at forgiving than forgetting. He hoped the two of them could start from there and maybe reach the forgetting part well before Little Bean arrived.

That hope wobbled a bit when he saw her face. The dark circles under her eyes and the straggly off-kilter ponytail told him her night had been as troubled as his. He held out the plate. "Peace offering?"

She pursed her lips, but her half smile was encouraging. "Not sure it counts unless you made it yourself."

"I've come to apologize and explain."

"Let's talk back here." She led him into her apartment. "Look, I'm sorry about last night. I didn't mean to offend your mother by rushing off like that." She sank onto the sofa.

She looked exhausted and he was tempted to take her into his arms, but this conversation had to run its course. "Mom was puzzled but definitely not offended, Zanna, and I should have told her about Little Bean sooner. I did when I got back home."

She raised her head from the back of the sofa. "Was she—"

"Thrilled? For sure…but a bit concerned, too, about the logistics." He leaned forward until their knees almost touched.

"Aren't we all?" she murmured, closing her eyes and laying her head back down. Then she shot up. "I didn't mean that to sound sarcastic. It's just that it seems we've been running in circles around the whole issue of what happens when the baby is here. Last night I found out you might be moving to some distant place to do a job you've always wanted."

"There's a big 'if' in that."

"I'm sure you'll get it, Dominic. What's to stop you?"

He was thinking of the botched search-and-rescue op and his CO's words afterward— *Although I pressured you to go ahead, you made the right call in the end.* Dom knew he'd been lucky to have the right kind of CO, one who wasn't afraid to admit he might have been wrong. He hoped he, too, was that kind of man. "I'm sure there are other applicants as well qualified, or even more qualified, than I. But that's not the issue here."

"What *is* the issue then? I've told you I want Beanie to have a father. How can that happen if you're hundreds—maybe thousands—of miles away?"

"You could come with me."

"As what? Your girlfriend? The mother of your child?"

"I want to be with you and Little Bean, Zanna. I don't know how you feel about me being permanently in your life, but I do know that the thought of you and Bean miles away from me is very…very heartbreaking." His breath caught on those last few words.

"Let me think about that," she eventually said, her voice low. "When I hear from the company that's interested in the hotel, I'll have a better idea of what my future looks like. For now, it would help if I knew what your schedule is for being here. I assume your interview will be in Norfolk…and then what?"

This is the all-business Zanna speaking. He felt like they were back at square one in the game of deciding their future. "I'll be reporting to duty after the interview, but my contract is up the first of September."

"Then what?"

"I either re-enlist or quit."

"Quit? Would you do that?"

Would he? The notion had never entered his mind and for a second he was worried she might consider it. "Zanna, we're both getting ahead of ourselves. There are too many 'what-ifs' at stake here. Let's see how my interview goes and take it from there. Meanwhile, let's plan for Little Bean's arrival. I'm sure there's a lot of organizing before a baby comes—you know, like buying things and so on." He was encouraged by her half smile. "And when you hear from that company about the hotel, we can make more plans."

"Sure."

"Do you want to go get some lunch? Maybe continue the discussion?"

"Rohan has an appointment so…"

"How about dinner? The Lobster Claw?"

"I'll let you know after I check with Rohan."

"Some time off would be good, Zanna." He hesitated to tell her she looked tired. They stared at one another a long uncomfortable moment. Dom knew there was still a whole lot more to say. "Okay then, I'll get in touch later this afternoon."

On his way out the door, she said, "Please thank your mother for the pie. I'm looking forward to it."

He went over the entire conversation along Main Street to Porter, where he turned to head up to Town Square. At least this time there'd been a bit more transparency, but they were still dodging the big question—*Will we be together as parents, or separate?* It seemed she was as uncertain about that as he was.

Yet with the possible sale of the hotel, there'd be no reason for her to stay in the Cove. She and Little Bean could be with him and if she wanted a union—like marriage—well, he knew he loved Zanna and that she cared for him. Was that enough for him, though? Caring as opposed to loving?

She'd witnessed her parents' marital breakdown after Brandon's death. Had that experience forged a wariness about marriage... about love? The possibility worried him. His parents had had a good marriage. Not perfect, but solidly based on trust, honesty and love. Could he and Zanna have something similar? Or would their different wants and needs make that impossible?

THE PIE WAS just as delicious the second day. Zanna washed the plate and took it with her to the front desk. Rohan was talking to someone on the hotel landline and from his expression, the news wasn't good. Zanna braced herself as he hung up.

"That was Cheryl. She...uh...she just gave her notice. But she's sending you an email to make it official."

Zanna shook her head in disbelief.

"She got a full-time offer from *The Beacon* and…you know…" he shrugged. "Are you okay?" He rolled the chair behind the counter toward her. "Here. Want some water?"

"No, no, I'm fine," she said, sitting down. "Just a bit dizzy. Pie for lunch today." She gestured to the plate on the countertop.

"Let me get you something from your fridge."

He was gone before Zanna could say a word. She rubbed her forehead, trying to focus on a next step. She ought to have seen this coming. Cheryl had applied unsuccessfully for a full-time job at the town's weekly newspaper a year ago and Zanna knew the better pay, plus possible benefits, was what a single mother would want. Until she could find a replacement for her, there'd only be Lisa to do all the housekeeping.

Rohan appeared with a plate of cheese and a couple of crackers. "After you eat this, why don't you take a walk? Maybe go do some food shopping. Not much in your fridge."

"Thanks, Rohan." She ate a piece of cheddar and nibbled on a cracker, mainly to show her appreciation for his kindness.

"Cheryl also said she'd stay for the two weeks unless you hire someone sooner."

Two weeks to find a room attendant, in the Cove, at minimum wage.

"Maybe between the two of us, we can cover her hours until high school finishes for the year. You'll probably be able to find a summer hire at least," Rohan suggested, reading her mind.

And in the fall, I'll be looking for a replacement for the student and you, too. But she kept that thought to herself. The dizziness had settled and Zanna stood up. "Okay, so she'll be in tomorrow as usual?"

Rohan nodded. "Sure you don't want to go lie down or something?" His brow wrinkled.

She was touched by his concern, knowing that as a twenty-something-year-old she'd been far more self-centered. He obviously had solid family influences and she thought unexpectedly of Little Bean. *That's what I want for my baby.*

"Can you manage on your own for a bit, Rohan? I mean, Lisa is here—somewhere—" she squeezed out a small laugh "—but instead of a nap I think a short walk will help clear my mind a bit."

"Good idea. I can eat my lunch right here, but…" His frown reappeared. "Are you sure you're all right?"

"Yes, the food helped so thanks for that." Then, impulsively, she blurted, "There's something you should know."

"The hotel?"

"No. I…um… I'm expecting a baby. In late September."

His wide eyes and jaw-drop would have prompted a giggle in someone else, Zanna thought.

"Uh, wow! I guess."

He was obviously searching for the correct response and Zanna helped him out. "Yeah, a surprise all round but a happy one." He was too polite to ask about a father, but she came to his aid there, too, because Dominic had been around the hotel a lot. "You know Dominic Kennedy—we…uh…we're working something out."

"Well, congratulations, Zanna. That's very cool." He seemed about to give her a hug but ended up shaking her hand.

She smiled, wishing the situation *was* cool. "Okay, then I'll take you up on your offer to man the desk."

HALF AN HOUR later Zanna was standing in the middle of Novel Idea, Grace's bookstore, staring at a shelf of books on child-rearing. Popping into the store had been an impulse. In fact, if Dom hadn't asked about baby preparations, she wouldn't be standing here, pondering the choices. His casual remark had reminded her she'd purchased nothing so far for Little Bean.

She found the section she wanted and scanned the shelf. A large hardcover titled *Everything You Need to Know About Child-Rearing: Infants to Teenagers* caught her eye. Go big, she decided. All the info she needed in a single book. She pulled it out and leafed through the first few pages, wondering if there was a chapter on fathers, until she found a couple of references in the appendix—*getting father involved* and *father substitutes*—that looked promising. She took the book to the cash counter.

Julie Porter, Grace's friend, glanced up from the computer, not immediately recognizing Zanna. "Oh! Hi, Zanna."

Julie stared down at the book. "This looks serious. *Everything You Need to Know...*" She looked up. "Do you know something I don't know?" She raised one teasing eyebrow.

Zanna squeezed out a smile. "I don't think so."

"Grace?" Julie prompted.

"Um, she's on her honeymoon, isn't she?"

"Still…" Julie shrugged.

Zanna sighed. This exchange was precisely why she'd left the Cove years ago. People wanting to know things you don't want them to. "For a friend," she lied. Besides, Dominic *was* a friend.

"Aw, nice." She rang up the bill and while Zanna was using her credit card, added, "Speaking of Grace, she'll be home this weekend."

"You're right. Heavens!" Zanna accepted the bagged book from Julie. On her way out, she counted the days. Four more till Saturday. In only two weeks, she'd been navigating a tenuous reunion with Dominic, met with potential buyers of her hotel, found out her mother and Henry Jenkins were moving in together and learned two employees were leaving. Not to mention the half-dozen or so emotional meltdowns she'd dealt with—both hers and her mother's.

She stood on the sidewalk outside for a second, unconsciously patting her abdomen while thinking surely life will settle down now. *How much more drama can I handle?* Checking the time, she saw that she still had more than an hour until she'd promised to relieve Rohan. She shifted her shoulder bag and felt the weight of Marie Kennedy's plate inside. Turning her back to the harbor, she strolled up through the square and into Dom's neighborhood. With any luck, he'd be out and she could hand over the plate, with her thanks.

When he answered the door, Zanna felt a quick rush of pleasure, despite her hope that he wouldn't be home. His beaming smile was an extra bonus.

"Hey, this is a nice surprise."

She held out the plate. "Thought I'd better return this before it got lost or forgotten in my kitchen cupboards."

"No chance! I've seen those cupboards and they're pretty empty, Zanna. Come on in."

"I don't want to disturb you and your mother. Besides, I have to take over for Rohan in an hour or so."

"Then you've got time for a cup of tea,

which is what Mom will want to offer." He took the plate and then her hand.

"Who is it, Dominic?" Marie came into the hallway from the kitchen. Noticing the plate, she said, "Oh goodness, you didn't have to come all this way just to bring that back. But thank you. I'll put the kettle on."

"I can't stay long, Mrs. Kennedy. Marie, I mean."

"Tea doesn't take long, dear. You and Dom go into the living room."

She returned to the kitchen and Zanna could hear water running seconds later. Dom grinned at Zanna. "One cup and a cookie or two and you're safely out of here," he teased, following her into the living room across the hall. Then he noticed the plastic bag in Zanna's other hand.

"Shopping?"

She'd have shown him the book but thought Marie might come back any minute and wasn't sure about pulling it out for discussion right then, so she placed it beside her on the sofa. Removing her vest, she saw Dom's eyes sweep over her, taking in the bump outlined by her blouse. When she noticed him looking at her, his face turned red.

"Sorry, I don't mean to stare but Little Bean seems to be making a star appearance today."

Zanna was giggling when Marie came into the room, carrying a tray of cups and saucers. "Did I miss something?" she asked, setting the tray down on the coffee table in front of Zanna.

"Not really, Mom." Dom winked at Zanna, then looked at the tray. "Cookies?"

"Oh, on the kitchen counter."

"I'll get them."

Marie watched him leave. "I want to tell you how thrilled I am at the news, and that I'm available for any kind of help at all."

"Thanks, Marie. I appreciate that."

Marie smiled and began pouring tea. "And you know you can rely on Dominic, too." She lowered her voice to say, "He sometimes gets caught up in his work responsibilities, but a gentle nudge will help with that."

"Help with what?" Dom asked, coming back with the cookies.

"Whatever Zanna needs," his mother replied.

To Zanna's relief, he just nodded, and they

drank tea in silence until she mentioned she was losing one of her staff.

"Oh no!" Marie exclaimed. "Will you be able to manage?"

"I'll have to until I can find a replacement. But it's okay," she quickly added when she saw their worried faces. "In a few weeks there'll be high school students looking for summer jobs."

"Well, I'm a pretty good housekeeper, as Dom can tell you."

"Mom definitely is," he said. "I can never find anything in my room after she's been in there."

They all laughed and soon were talking about events planned in town for the upcoming holiday weekend. When Zanna glanced down at her cell phone and saw the time, she said, "I have to get going."

She hoped Dom would walk her to the door but as she was pulling on her vest, his cell phone rang. He looked down at the screen, then up at Zanna.

"Got to get this," he said. "Are we still on for dinner tonight?"

Zanna frowned. Had they agreed on dinner? "Uh, sure."

He smiled. "Great. I'll call you in a bit." Then he left the room, his phone at his ear.

Marie was shaking her head. "There's always some work thing or whatever." She walked Zanna to the door and impulsively hugged her. "I'm so excited to be a grandmother."

Zanna nodded, tearing up now, too. "Little Bean is very lucky to have you."

"Little Bean? I like that." Marie pressed Zanna's hand. "Come anytime. Please."

After she said goodbye, Zanna paused on the front porch, comparing Marie's reaction about the baby to Jane's. Then she caught herself. That wasn't fair. Mothers and daughters have a completely different relationship and perspective—something she needed to remember, now that she, too, would be a mother.

On the walk back to the hotel, she remembered something else. The tone of surprise in Dom's greeting when he answered his phone. An old friend, perhaps? Or someone calling about his interview? She'd find out at dinner.

CHAPTER FOURTEEN

WATCHING DOMINIC STROLL across the lobby, Zanna was glad she hadn't cancelled their dinner plans. She'd been tempted to, asking herself if she could cope with another bout of unresolved issues. But the sight of his cheerful face set her heart racing, and his light gray suit with a crisp powder blue shirt indicated some effort had been made for the evening. She was glad she had, too.

Lisa was just leaving work for the day, and Zanna noticed her sneak a sidelong glance at Dom as she passed him on her way out. Her intention to keep things business-like vanished the minute he leaned over the counter and kissed her on the cheek.

"You look amazing," he murmured, "and you smell wonderful, too."

Her face was burning. Rohan was a mere five feet away. "You've seen this dress before."

"I'll never get tired of seeing you in it," he said, grinning.

Rohan coughed. "Say, I forgot to mention there's no need for you to come back early. I can easily bunk down in one of the empty rooms."

Zanna caught Dom's eye, noticing he was red-faced now. She stifled a giggle and was about to reply when the elevator door opened and Cora Stanfield rushed out.

"I've lost Mo!" she cried.

"Lost him where?" Zanna asked when Cora reached them.

"In the hotel!"

Dom met Zanna's gaze over the distraught woman's head. He was frowning and she immediately got his message. Cora's color was high and she was panting, as if she'd run down the stairs instead of taking the elevator. Rohan pulled over the chair for her.

"Cora, have a seat. He can't be far. Dominic and I will look for him," Zanna reassured her.

"What if he ran down the stairs and followed someone out the door?"

"I haven't noticed anyone leaving, except for Lisa," Rohan said.

"Let's assume he's still in the hotel," Dom

said. "Where and when did you last see him, Mrs. Stanfield?"

Her breathing had slowed but she still took a few seconds to answer. "I was getting ready to go to dinner at The Daily Catch and was halfway out the door when I remembered I needed to put him in his crate, so I went to get his treat. When I returned, he'd gone. My room door was ajar and he must have squeezed out."

"Dom and I will go up to the fourth floor and start there, Cora. You just sit. Rohan will get you a glass of water."

"I don't want to make a fuss," she protested.

When Rohan came back with the water, Dom said, "Zan, you take the elevator and I'll take the stairs, in case he comes down that way."

She didn't think it likely, given the closed fire doors on every floor leading to the main staircase. She grabbed a master key from the reception counter drawer.

"I can't believe I left my door open. I'm sorry to cause such inconvenience. I'm not usually this scatterbrained," she apologized, "but Mo means the world to me."

"Don't worry," Zanna said, patting her shoulder. Then she raised an eyebrow at Rohan, letting him know he needed to stay with Cora. As she headed for the elevator, she saw that Dom had already gone through the door leading off the stairs onto the first floor. She was exiting the elevator on four when she met Dom coming through the fire door. "That was fast!"

"Took the stairs two at a time. He wasn't going to be using them anyway."

"No." The door to Cora's room was partially open and Zanna gave it a light push. "Mo? Here, Mo!"

"He's not in there. Let's walk along the hall. Could he have gone into someone else's room? I mean, if someone left a door open?"

"No one else on this floor." She followed Dom past the elevator down the hallway to the rear of the hotel and together they called Mo's name.

"Wait!" Dom stopped abruptly and listened. Faint yips sounded from behind the housekeeping closet door. Zanna pulled her master key out of her dress pocket; the high-pitched yelping grew louder as she swiped her card and opened the door. The barking was frantic now, but no sign of Mo. Dom looked questioningly at Zanna.

"I think he's trapped behind the housekeeping cart."

Dom grasped hold of the cart handle and tugged hard. A white ball of fur shot past them, racing down the hall. Dom fell backward against Zanna, who could barely speak through her laughter. "He's gone to Cora's room," she blurted.

"Sorry if I stepped on your toes," Dom said as they hurried down the hall. "He took me by surprise."

Zanna didn't point out how small Mo was compared to Dom, afraid she'd start laughing again. When they reached Cora's room, Mo was running frantically in circles around the bed, into the bathroom and around the bed again. Then he dashed toward them, but instead of bolting out the door, leaped up onto Zanna. She wrapped her arms around him before he could escape, giggling and ducking her head as he licked her face and neck.

"He's happy to be out of there, for sure. What do you think happened?" Dom asked.

Zanna put her hand on of Mo's head to calm him. "He must have run down the hall and seen the open housekeeping door, went in to investigate and then Lisa pushed the cart in without realizing he was inside."

"Well, Cora will be happy."

"And hopefully feeling better." Zanna noticed the bedspread had slipped off onto the floor. "Can you pick that up, save Cora the effort? I don't want to let go of Mo and I don't see his leash anywhere."

"Sure." Dom went farther into the room and as he bent over to lift up the spread, he paused to look at something beneath it.

"What is it?" Zanna asked, tightening her grip on Mo, who was squirming to get down.

He picked up a file folder and some loose papers that had fallen out of it, placing them on top of the bed. "Oh, um, some papers."

"Coming?" she asked when he seemed to take his time. "Cora will be anxious."

"Oh, sure. Sorry." He left the papers on the bed and followed Zanna into the hallway, closing the door behind him. They got into the elevator and Mo, who must have sensed they were taking him to Cora, began yipping again. Zanna gently shushed him, stroking his head.

"He likes you. Did you have pets as a kid?"

"No. My brother had asthma. But we did

have an aquarium, briefly," she added with a light laugh. "Poor Brandon. He got into tropical fish for a month or so, but he really wanted some little furball—like Mo here—to cuddle."

"Yeah."

He didn't say anything more but from the corner of her eye she saw him nodding thoughtfully. "How about you?"

"My father wasn't a fan of pets."

"Likewise," Zanna murmured. "We have that in common."

"We do." His gaze lingered on her face. "Maybe more than that, too."

If she hadn't been holding Mo, Zanna guessed Dom might have kissed her. The elevator reached the ground floor with a soft thud—*like my heart*, she was thinking—and Mo made his escape as soon as the door opened. He jumped out of her arms and tore across the lobby and up onto Cora's lap.

"You naughty dog!" she exclaimed, but she was beaming.

"He'd been accidentally locked in the housekeeping closet," Zanna explained. "We closed your room door, Cora."

"Thank you so much," she enthused. Her eyes glistened. "I knew he'd be in the hotel somewhere and I'm sorry that I panicked. It's just that Mo is very special. I bought him a few months after Maurice, my husband, passed and I was so down in the dumps. Mo gave me something to live for. That's why I named him after Maurice."

Zanna felt her own eyes well up. "What time is your dinner reservation? Would you like me to call the restaurant and say you might be late?"

Cora shook her head. "I don't think I'd have the energy to go now. I just want to stay in my room with this rascal of a dog. But maybe you could phone and cancel for me, if it's not too late to do that?"

"Sure." Then Zanna had an idea. "The owner is a good friend of mine. Why don't I see if he could deliver something to the hotel? It'd be a shame to miss a meal from The Daily Catch."

"Goodness, do you think that would be possible?"

"I can try. Anything in particular you'd like to order?"

Cora shrugged. "I guess they'd have regular fish and chips? That would be plenty."

Zanna took out her cell phone and, walking a few feet away from the group, called Ted Nakamura's personal line. Less than a minute later she tucked her phone away and said, "He'll get someone to bring your meal over. Why don't you let Rohan help you get back upstairs with Mo and when the food is here, he'll bring it up to you."

Cora's voice wobbled as she said, "My dear, thank you ever so much. You're too kind." Then she looked at Dom and Rohan. "You've all been wonderful. I'm lucky to have found such a welcoming place to stay." She let Rohan take her by the elbow as they walked to the elevator.

After the door closed behind them, Dom grinned at Zanna. "Speaking of fish and chips…"

"Let's go!" As soon as Rohan returned, they left for The Lobster Claw, a bit later than planned but with bigger appetites. It was already dark as they strolled through the nearly empty streets toward the pub.

"That was a nice idea you had, getting delivery for her," Dom commented.

"I bet it was a first for Ted. I'd recommended the bistro days ago to Cora and hated for her to miss out."

"How long has she been here now?"

"It's been a while. At least a week?"

"Isn't that long compared to the usual length of stay for tourists?"

"I guess so. Frankly I've been involved in other matters and haven't really thought about it. Why?"

"It's nothing really, but when I picked up her bedspread off the floor, I noticed a folder and I wondered if she was doing some kind of research on the Cove."

"I saw you looking at something."

"They were articles from *The Beacon* and *The Portland Press Herald*—about the town. *And about your family.*"

"Probably research before she came here. You know, things to do and see."

"Some looked old."

"Maybe she's a writer, working on a novel."

Dom laughed. "About the Cove?"

"Or she could be a private eye!" She was laughing now, too.

"You're really getting into the mystery, I see," he teased. "And I think that term isn't used anymore."

"Yeah, I'm not into fiction these days, especially mysteries."

"No time for reading?"

"No time for make-believe," she muttered.

He reached for her hand, pressing it against his chest. "Maybe so, but tonight is all about make-believe. We're leaving real life back at the hotel. Okay?"

His eyes were shining, and in that moment Zanna knew she loved him. "Okay," she whispered, gazing into his dark, serious eyes.

Sighting the pub's neon sign, Zanna thought of her most recent visit there—the party after Grace's wedding. Reading her mind, Dom said, "Can you believe Grace's wedding was less than two weeks ago? Seems longer than that. Another lifetime almost." He stopped to look at her. "Does it feel like that for you, too? That we've lived years in only days?"

"Yes, it does. But in a good way."

"Likewise," he murmured, smiling. A small group of people jostled past them into the pub, breaking the spell. "Let's eat," Dom said, taking her hand and following the group inside. The place was crowded. "Busy tonight," Dom said in her ear, over the chatter.

Zanna peered around the room. "Especially for a Tuesday."

Dom went inside, approaching a server.

When he came back to her, he said, "There was a softball tournament and both teams are here. It'll be a wait for a table. What do you think?"

"Takeout from somewhere?"

He shrugged. As they were turning to leave, someone grasped Zanna by the shoulder. She wheeled about to see her cousin, Ben.

"Hey, you two! Ella and I have a table over there," he gestured to the far side of the room. "And it's a foursome. Come and join us."

Zana looked quickly at Dom. Their private dinner wouldn't be possible, but on the other hand, they'd get to eat, and she was starving.

Dom got the message. "Fantastic, Ben. You saved us from huddling on a park bench with takeout."

"Come on."

As they followed Ben past the bar, he halted a server with a tray of drinks. "Can we have more drinks at our table? In the far corner?" he pointed. "What'll you two have?"

"A pint of ale for me and sparkling mineral water for Zan," Dom said.

"Mineral water?"

Zanna gave a nervous laugh. "I need my wits about me tonight."

"Okay. We'll have to explore that topic further." He repeated their order to the server and led them around the tables to where Ella was sitting.

"This is a lovely surprise," Ella exclaimed, standing to greet them.

"Yes, and we're very grateful," Zanna said.

After they were sitting, Ben announced, "Ella and I have finally set a date for our wedding."

"That's wonderful! When and where?" Zanna asked.

"Undecided on the where, but—"

"The July Fourth weekend," Ella finished for him.

Zanna envied their mutual laugh. She remembered when Ella came back to the Cove just before Christmas, determined to set the record straight over the whole Brandon story. Those had been challenging days for the entire Winters family, but Ella's courage, plus her love for Ben and his for her, had inspired the reconciliation that followed.

"Well, congratulations, you two!" She was tempted to take a peek at Dom to see his reaction to the wedding news but was afraid he'd take that as some kind of hint. They'd only begun to negotiate their own plans for the future and marriage wasn't even on the agenda. She staved off an unexpected rush of sadness, focusing on her menu.

The server came with their drinks and took their orders. The talk drifted away from families to general life in the Cove while Zanna furtively read Rohan's text that Cora's meal had arrived. She almost missed Ben's remark to Dom, catching the words *Eagle Scouts.*

"Thursday night," Dom was saying. He noticed Zanna's interest and explained, "Glen Kowalski, the current Scout leader, called today. Invited me to give a talk to the older kids working toward Eagle Scout rank, along with my navy ROTC experience."

She mentally chastised herself. *So that was the phone call that you assumed had something to do with his promotion interview. More assumptions, Zanna Winters!* "That's great."

Dom smiled. "Yeah. I'm actually looking forward to it. I helped out with the troop once already, but I'm not sure how teenagers will respond to an old geezer like me."

Ben and Ella laughed but Zanna said, "You're definitely not that."

Dom's eyes met hers and there was a long

silence, which Ben finally broke. "I hear the Scouts are meeting in the school. Be weird for you, won't it? Walking around our old elementary school after all these years?"

"For sure. Plus, Glen said the gym wasn't available and it'll be in a classroom. I'm hoping there'll be at least a teacher's chair for me, so I won't have to squeeze into one of those desks!"

"No better place?" Ella asked.

"The *only* free place that night," Dom said. "Too many groups and clubs in town these days, I suppose."

"I've been hearing the same complaint from other people, too." She looked at Ben. "Your mother says the Historical Society is having a much-needed growth in membership but is running out of venues for meetings. And no one wants to drive to Portland."

"The Cove's population is a lot bigger, even since my return here just three years ago," Zanna said. "Seems like what the town needs is a community center."

"Yes." Ella looked across the table at Zanna. "Say, I need an editorial for Friday's issue of *The Beacon*."

"There you go!" Ben exclaimed. "Why don't

you two get together for some brainstorming? And now, how about some food?"

Zanna smiled at Ella. "Are you up for that?"

"Definitely. I'll text you tomorrow after I've checked my schedule."

By the time their orders came, Zanna's head was spinning with ideas. She thought how energizing it was to have something else on her mind besides Little Bean and how Dominic Kennedy would fit into their lives. One idea, germinating right then, was especially appealing.

CHAPTER FIFTEEN

DOM AND ZANNA watched Ben and Ella head down toward the harbor after the foursome said their goodbyes outside the pub.

"I didn't realize Ben has his own place now," Dom commented. "For some reason I just assumed he was still living in the Winters mansion up on the hill."

"He moved out after New Year's. He'd bought the old cottage that Ella's parents used to rent every summer and completely renovated it. It's quite beautiful now. A real, permanent family home."

Her wistful tone made him ask, "Would you like that?"

"What?"

"A permanent family home." She didn't answer right away, which worried him a bit. They'd been having a good time with Ben and Ella. Dom hated to break the spell, but he wanted to know how she felt about those three important words.

"Doesn't everyone, deep down inside?" she eventually replied.

"Sure, but I want to know how *you* feel."

She placed a hand on his jacket lapel and smiled. "I'm no different from anyone else, Dom."

He set his hand on top of hers. "I know, Zan. It's just that I...I care for you. Very much. And I know you have feelings for me—at least, I *think* you do."

She slipped her hand out from under his. "I care for you, and I want you to be in my life as...well...definitely as a father to Beanie."

"Is that all?"

"That's pretty important!"

"I know it is, but we can have more," he hastened to explain. "We can be together. If your plan to sell the hotel succeeds, you'll be free to come with me, wherever I go."

"Dominic, if I followed you to some distant place—assuming you get the promotion, which I'm positive you will—I'd want the arrangement to be permanent. I don't want any more disappointments. No more anxiety about being let down by people I love. Can you guarantee that?"

He was still sorting out his answer when she abruptly said, "We should go. It's late."

Dom shoved his hands into his suit jacket pockets and followed her down the dark street. He regretted raising the topic again, especially after such a pleasant evening. During dinner, he'd felt they were a couple in fact, and not merely in appearance. He'd even envisioned other nights like this one, with other couples, sharing meals and anecdotes about their lives.

By the time they reached the hotel, he knew what he wanted to say. "I'm not giving up on us, Zanna. I'm putting you on notice right now that I plan to spend the rest of my leave campaigning for a future together, however that may look."

"And I'm warning you that my obstinate side will resist." But she was smiling.

"I'm always up for a challenge, Zan." He leaned forward and sealed that promise with a quick kiss. "Maybe I'll see you tomorrow." He felt her eyes on him as he started up the street toward home, but he didn't look back.

His mother was watching television in the

den and Dom hoped he'd be able to ponder the end of what had been a great night in the privacy of his bedroom, but no such luck.

"Did you have fun?" she called out when she noticed him passing the open doorway.

Dom pictured his teenaged self calling out a simple *yeah* before closing his bedroom door. He changed direction and joined her, and she muted the TV as he sat in the reclining chair next to hers.

"Nice dinner? I haven't been to the Claw in years," she said. "Is the food still good?"

A stab of guilt struck. How many times could he have treated her to dinner out when, instead, he'd enjoyed a home-cooked meal? But she'd have insisted on cooking anyway, he told himself. Or maybe that was the story he'd been blithely telling himself all these years. If he won the promotion, there'd be fewer opportunities for talks with his mother.

He leaned back into the recliner and told Marie about meeting Ben and Ella at the pub. Then he thought of something. "Henry Jenkins told me the Historical Society is looking for a permanent place, too. But he also told me you haven't been attending meetings recently. How come? Is everything okay with you? Your health, I mean."

"I'm fine, Dominic. You don't need to worry about me."

"Of course I do! I'm your son. What is it? My absences?" He reached over and set his hand on top of hers.

"Not at all. When you signed up for the navy, I knew the chances of your being close to home would be slim. It's simply that when I went to the meetings, there was always a bit of a social thing first and everyone would talk about what they'd been doing and so on. I never had a lot to say. You know I'm an introvert. So, I just thought I'd take a break from the Society for a bit. That's all."

"Okay, but you'll let me know if you need me to come home, won't you? Because I will, anytime and from wherever I am. Promise you'll do that?"

"I promise, honey." She pressed gently on his hand before withdrawing hers. "Now, changing the subject, Zanna left something when she was here this afternoon." She reached down beside her chair to pick up a bag from the floor. "I was naughty and had a look inside, just in case she might need it right away."

She was grinning as he took the unexpectedly heavy bag. He pulled out a large book and stared at the cover—*Everything You Need to Know about Child-Rearing: Infants to Teenagers*.

"Do you think she left it behind on purpose for you to find? As a hint to...you know...*get with it*?"

Dom had to laugh. "Um, I'm not sure, but Zanna generally has a reason for all her actions, or so I'm learning."

"Well, I'm off to bed now." Marie got out of her chair and bent down to kiss his cheek. "Keep on learning, Dominic," she murmured before leaving the room.

He sat for a while, thinking about his promotion and of being miles away from the Cove, and from his mother. Then he opened up the book and began to leaf through it.

ZANNA TEXTED ELLA BACK, agreeing to meet for coffee at Mabel's that afternoon to discuss their community center idea. She'd spent a lot of time during yet another restless night thinking about the center and was excited to exchange some ideas with Ella. She'd no sooner sent the text than her phone rang.

"Ms. Winters? Alex Corelli here. Listen, we've gone over the reports from the team that visited the hotel on Monday."

"Already?"

"Yes, they were fast but thorough. As expected, most of the issues they noted are electrical and plumbing ones, but the rooms will all be gutted anyway. We're not sure yet how the available space will be configured but think the ballroom will serve nicely as a dining-recreation area. Anyway, there are lots of questions that need answering. Marketing and Finance are still reviewing the reports and everything looks good but our next steps are on hold for the moment. Are you okay with a longer wait?"

Did she have a choice? "Of course. No timeline yet, then?"

"Not really, but I assure you we're moving on this as quickly as possible."

"Thanks, Alex." Disconnecting, she leaned both elbows on the reception counter, resting her forehead in her cupped palms. She'd been hoping for an answer but realized that she'd been naive. Still, Alex had sounded optimistic, and she knew she ought to hold onto that rather than assume the worst, which is what she tended to do.

She immediately thought of Dom's suggestion, that she and Beanie follow him wherever he was sent. She'd wrestled with the possibility most of the night. If she sold the hotel, there was no specific reason why she couldn't go with him. They wouldn't have to live together. They could simply be near each other for their child. He'd been persuasive, but his plea had fallen short of something concrete—like a proposal. Not that she wanted one. She'd only been divorced for a year and wasn't ready for another run at marriage. Still, a sign of commitment on his part would have been reassuring.

The problem with his scenario was that she'd be leaving the Cove just when she'd adjusted to its small-town vibe. The thought of a community center had stuck in her mind all night. If the idea became a reality, she might not want to leave Lighthouse Cove at all. She might want to stay. *So many "ifs."*

Her phone rang again. This time the call was from her mother. "Morning, dear. I'm just calling to say I'm leaving for Bangor today but will be back on the weekend. Also, I'm getting the house ready to put up for sale and I think there may be some boxes that belong to you, in the attic. Shall I bring them with me?"

At least some things were happening, Zanna thought. "Are you sure about this, Mom? Selling and moving in with Henry? I mean, you won't regret giving up some of your independence, will you?"

"Yes, Zanna, I've thought everything through. As for independence, I've had that in buckets since your father and I divorced. It's been sixteen years. What you see as independence, at my age I see as loneliness."

There was nothing Zanna could reply to that. "Okay, Mom. I'll see you on the weekend. But before you hang up, I want to tell you that I'm meeting with Ella Jacobs today to brainstorm some ideas about petitioning for a community center here."

"Oh, just what we were talking about on Monday! That's terrific. Let me know how it goes."

After she disconnected, Zanna thought about her mother's comment about independence and loneliness. The spectre of single motherhood rose up as an inevitability for her. She knew she could handle it. But was that really what she wanted, when she could have some version of a family with Dom and Little Bean? *That was the crux of her dilemma.*

At the moment, there were real-life issues to deal with. Rohan was due at noon and Cheryl was finishing the rooms, having decided to stay on a further two weeks. Zanna and Rohan together could help Lisa until Zanna could hire one or two teens for the summer.

She logged into her bank account to check the hotel's financial outlook for the short term. The news wasn't any better since she last reviewed her accounts two weeks ago. Money would be coming from the salesman on the second floor, but he planned to check out on Friday. There were two other businesspeople who would also be leaving Friday. A couple of seniors on three were sightseeing along the coast and they hadn't specified when they'd be leaving, but they'd already toured Portland, taken the Casco Bay cruise and wandered around the Cove, so Zanna guessed their departure was imminent.

That left Cora as the hotel's longest staying

guest and she'd given no hint of when she'd be leaving. Although Zanna was grateful for her business, she was curious about the long stay. The woman seemed to have no other family than her little dog, which clearly allowed her flexibility of time. She was paying for a waterfront-view suite, so she also had money. Zanna remembered Dom's discovery yesterday of her news articles about the Cove. Despite their jokes about the find, she wondered if there was another reason for Cora's arrival, other than as part of visiting her hometown outside Bangor. The Cove was certainly not on that route!

She let that train of thought go as she stared bleakly at her accounts. She'd have to borrow from her personal savings again to make the wages for her staff. Her stomach clenched at the dwindling balance, and she knew she couldn't continue drawing on her own money much longer.

"Good morning!" Cora was standing in front of the counter, holding Mo in her arms.

Zanna's head shot up.

"Everything all right?" Cora's smile shifted to concern. "I didn't mean to startle you."

Zanna sensed her face was red. "Oh, that's okay, just deep in thought." She laughed.

Cora's smile reappeared. "I trust they were good thoughts then. I'm about to go for a walk but wanted to thank you again for all your help last night. Yours and Dominic's, too. Please pass that on to him. Unless I meet him again here, sometime."

"I hope your dinner lived up to your expectations."

"It was delicious! I gave Rohan cash, including a tip, to pass on to the person who delivered it."

Speaking of cash… "There's no rush for an answer, Cora, but do you have an idea how much longer you plan to stay?" Noticing the instant change in her expression, Zanna quickly added, "There's absolutely no deadline, I'm just going through the bookings."

"I…I'm not sure. But you know, visiting the Maine coast after all my years in Chicago was a dream. So—"

"We love having you. Please stay as long as you want and don't feel you have to have an end date," Zanna rushed to say, already regretting asking.

Cora stared thoughtfully at her. "Why don't

I pay you up to today, right now? Then I can budget better for the rest of my stay."

In spite of feeling she'd dug herself into an embarrassing hole, Zanna knew she could use the money. "That would be wonderful. Thanks, Cora."

Zanna was still feeling chagrin from this exchange on her way to meet Ella. She'd been unreasonably curious about Cora merely because of some newspaper articles when there was likely a simple explanation for her interest in the Cove. She decided to compensate for her guilty feeling by taking Cora for lunch one day. Perhaps here, she thought as she entered Mabel's and spotted Ella at a rear table.

"It was fun last night," Ella enthused as Zanna draped her cardigan on the back of her chair and sat down. "We should all get together again soon, before Dom goes back to base."

If Ella was curious about the relationship between Dom and Zanna, neither her voice nor her face gave her away. "That would be great," Zanna replied. "And I've made some notes already." She pulled a notepad and pen out of her handbag and set them on the table.

"Terrific! Then let's get to it. Oh, and I've ordered us tea and scones. That okay with you?"

Zanna could have hugged her. "You're a mind reader! Okay, my first thought is location. Where, do you think?"

Ella laughed. "I like how you get right to business, Zanna. I can see we're going to get along really well."

"What about the area up in the new subdivision? More room than down here."

Ella opened up her notebook. "Exactly my thinking."

For the next hour they exchanged ideas until Ella finally announced, after a second round of tea, "I've got more than enough for my Friday editorial. The biggest question is funding. What will that look like?"

"We could go to town council and see if they'll add this to their agenda for the next meeting."

"I'll find out when that will be," Ella said. "Ben's going to draw up some kind of a basic plan, have his engineers look at it and get his team to run some figures. We'll need that information before we even approach town council."

The logistics were daunting. Zanna had a

sudden realization of the immensity of the project. Her fingers wrapped around her pen trembled and she felt her heart rate pick up.

"Slowly, slowly. One step at a time, right?" Ella smiled.

Zanna nodded, too overwhelmed to speak.

"I thought we should start with a survey," Ella continued. "I'll get our tech person at *The Beacon* to set up an online one. The council will need to know about the community support. And as manager of the paper, I might need to distance myself a bit from it. For now, you and I are a committee of two, as private citizens."

Zanna said, "How does the *Brandon Winters Memorial Community Center Committee* sound?"

Ella gave big smile. "Lovely."

CHAPTER SIXTEEN

"YOU LOOK DIFFERENT TODAY," Rohan commented when he arrived for work the morning after Zanna's meeting with Ella. His brow furled in thought. "New hairdo?"

"You've seen me in a French braid before."

His frown deepened. "Okay. Just you seem—"

"Happy?"

He shifted uncomfortably. "Um, I wasn't going to say *that*. Maybe relaxed?"

"I had a good sleep last night, so maybe the bags under my eyes have gone."

"Okay," he said with a small shrug and proceeded into the office to hang up his jacket.

She *had* had a great sleep! For the first time in weeks, she awoke with a sense of purpose, focused on something positive. After her meeting with Ella, she'd rushed back to the hotel to jot down more ideas about the community center. It made sense that the center should be as large as possible, to accommodate the needs and wants of everyone in the community. Granted, the cost would determine the design, and she hoped that Ben would come up with an estimate soon.

Zanna realized she was getting ahead of herself, but she felt optimistic about the project. The center would be a fitting memorial to her brother—a place where kids of all ages could hang out, supervised and mentored by adults. Free to be themselves and safe from bullying. *If only Brandon had had such a haven.*

She was so excited about it that she decided to call her mother right away, rather than wait until the weekend when Jane planned to come back to the Cove. But her enthusiasm was challenged by a surprising silence after she outlined her idea.

At last, Jane said, "I really like the thought, honey, but are you up for such a big project right now?"

"I'm not going to be building it myself," Zanna joked.

"You know what I mean. Something like this will demand persistent campaigning to local politicians and if it got approved, overseeing all the details and coordinating with teams of people. Not to mention the time involved. Months and months."

"Ella and I will get volunteers. We'll figure it out."

"But you're having a baby in four months!"

Zanna fought back the urge to quip, *no kidding*. "I'm sure there'll be options available around dealing with a baby, too. Single working mothers manage. Why couldn't I?"

"I get your point but as a first-time mother-to-be, don't underestimate the demand on your body, mind and emotions from that small baby. That's all I'm saying."

Zanna bit the inside of her cheek. She refused to let her mother dampen her excitement. "Okay, Mom. We'll talk more about it when you're here."

"Have you spoken to Henry about this? Or Dominic?"

"I'll call Henry. Dominic was with me when the idea came up so he's on board."

"Are you sure about that?"

"Of course I am. Why wouldn't I be?" Zanna felt her blood pressure rise again.

"He's the father of your baby, Zanna. Won't he be worried about this commitment?"

Zanna rolled her eyes. "I have no doubts about his support, Mom. Oh, Rohan is beckoning me for something," she fibbed, "so I have to go. See you Saturday." She turned off her cell phone and placed it on the reception counter, wishing she hadn't called.

It always felt like she and Jane were miscommunicating. As a teenager Zanna had felt at odds with her mother, but she'd also heard similar complaints from her friends. Later, when she found out she'd been adopted, she sometimes wondered if she and her birth mother might have had a less oppositional relationship. She'd never felt the need to research her birth parents, though. Despite the shock, as far as she was concerned, Jane and Fred Winters were her parents and they'd given her a happy childhood. The years after Brandon's death were another matter.

Now that she was going to be a mother, she wondered if she ought to have tried to locate her birth parents, if only to learn about any genetic medical conditions.

She was about to phone Henry about the community center idea when she saw him ambling across the lobby. Rohan was in the office on his cell phone, and she signaled him that she was going to take five. Then she met Henry halfway.

"The very man I was about to call," she exclaimed.

He looked surprised. "It seems I'm popular these days."

"You're always popular here in the Cove, Henry. Come and sit." She gestured to a table and chair arrangement a few feet away.

Once seated, he said, "I was coming to speak to you, too, but you go first."

"Okay. I met with Ella Jacobs yesterday to discuss an idea for a community center, here in the Cove."

He leaned forward, resting his elbows on the table. "Hah! Some of us in town have been talking about that very thing. What's the plan?"

She liked how he got right to the point, rather than start off with a lot of questions. "Ella's writing an editorial in tomorrow's *Beacon* about the need for one and she'll include an online survey. After we've met with town council representatives she'll add a donation link—assuming we get the okay. Plus, Ella's going to have Ben and his team come up with a ballpark figure on costs. I know it'll take some time," she put in at his slight frown, "but it's a start, right?"

After a moment's thought, he said, "It's a grand idea and I'm happy you're working with Ella. She's a real go-getter, like you."

Zanna flushed at the compliment. "I'm hoping the center will be named after my brother."

"Do you now?"

"I do. I think it's a far more meaningful memorial than a plaque on the lighthouse door. It'll be a place for kids, families and groups in town that need space, like the Historical Society."

"But what about our plans for the lighthouse ceremony?"

She'd been thinking about that through the night, too. "Let's make the ceremony at the lighthouse just for family. We can still put up the plaque there, or even install it at the center when it's completed."

"These are good ideas, Zanna, and I agree that a family ceremony is best, but isn't a project like a community center an awful lot of work for you?"

"Mom was concerned about that as well."

"I can imagine." He fell silent for a minute.

"And speaking about your mother, she's the reason I was coming to see you."

"Oh?"

"She's told you she's moving in with me. How do you feel about that?"

Zanna knew with any other person she'd probably hedge her answer or come up with some platitude about the situation. But not with Henry Jenkins. He spoke straight from the heart and the head, too, and deserved the same kind of reply.

"I was surprised, of course, and a bit conflicted." She shifted her gaze away from his. "I worry about how you both will adapt to such a change, because you've been living as singles for so many years. Maybe one of you won't be able to adjust to such a lifestyle change. My other worry—and it doesn't reflect well on me I'm ashamed to say—is that I'm used to Mom being at a distance from me. Some of our ongoing issues have been mitigated by her living in another place."

He'd nodded thoughtfully through her entire admission and took his time responding. "I fell for Jane the first time I met her, at the engagement party for her and Fred. Of course, I kept that a secret for many years.

After their divorce, we reconnected, first by phone, then by email and text. It took Jane a long time to get used to the idea that she cared for me." His laugh echoed in the lobby. "We went from friends to…well…something better and more lasting. So, yes, we will have an adjustment period, but I know we'll get through it because we love each other. As to her living back in the Cove, near you. She told me you're having a baby—" he beamed and reached across the table to pat her hand "—which is something she and I are both incredibly happy for, and she's looking forward to being an active grandmother. I know she'll be a big help to you."

Zanna wiped her eyes with the back of her hand. "Thank you, Henry. And you know, Little Bean has grandmothers but needs a grandfather. Are you up to the task?"

It was his turn to tear up. "Next to finally being with Jane, this is the most wonderful gift I've had in my life."

Zanna's heart filled. At that moment, nothing could make her day happier. Except, she suddenly thought, to have Dominic walk through the hotel door and take her into his arms.

But it was Cora Stanfield with Mo who entered the hotel.

"Hello," Cora said, drawing near. "Mo and I have had a long walk and now I think we're due for a short nap before lunch."

Henry got to his feet. "Nice to see you again, Cora. And speaking of lunch, I have some grocery shopping to do." Turning to Zanna, he added, "Jane's coming back to town tomorrow and has promised to make me her famous eggplant parmigiana." He nodded at the two women. "Ladies," and headed for the door.

"He's such a lovely man," Cora murmured, watching him leave.

Zanna studied the older woman's wistful smile, and her mind jumped to the research Cora had obviously been doing on the town and the Winters family. Was there some other motive for her arrival in the Cove? It wouldn't hurt to get to know Cora Stanfield a bit better.

"After your rest, would you like to join me for lunch at Mabel's?" she impulsively asked.

"My goodness, I'd love to."

"Maybe you could bring Mo's crate down to the office? Rohan will be on duty, but perhaps Mo won't worry if someone he knows is around."

"That's a terrific idea!"

"Great. What's a good time for me to send Rohan up for the crate?"

"Maybe noon? Would that work for you, for lunch?"

"It's a deal." Zanna watched the small woman hurry toward the elevator. She liked Cora and hoped she was completely wrong in her assumption that she might be in town for something else besides sightseeing.

"THAT WAS DELICIOUS!" Cora set her spoon down next to the empty soup bowl. "And I'm sorry, but I couldn't possibly eat another bite of salad. Will they pack up the rest for me, do you think?"

"I'm sure they will." Zanna signaled their server. The lunch had been enjoyable, as she'd listened to Cora's stories of how she and her late husband, Maurice, met, along with tales of some of their overseas travel. But there'd been no hint of an explanation about visiting the Cove.

"I suppose Rohan might want some relief from Mo," Cora said once they'd left the diner.

"He'll be fine. Care to go for a short walk, before we head back?"

"Yes! I'm supposed to get as much exercise as I can handle."

"Can you handle the waterfront?"

"Definitely."

They headed down to Main Street and descended onto the boardwalk.

"It's a shame not to see the fishing boats come in anymore," Cora remarked. "I was here once, years and years ago, before I moved to Chicago."

Zanna was surprised. "Yes, there hasn't been any commercial fishing here for about fifteen years."

When Cora didn't add to her story, Zanna said, "Dominic's father was a lobsterman, as people called them. One of the last in the Cove, in fact."

"Are his parents still here?"

"His mother is but his father died when Dom was…" Zanna thought for a second, "about seventeen, I think. There was a freak storm out beyond the bay and his boat capsized. He and his one crew member were drowned."

Cora stopped. "How awful for him and his mother. How did he cope with such a loss at that age?"

"I don't really know to be honest. I was eighteen and excited about starting college, plus I scarcely knew him. He was in the grade below me."

They resumed walking but after a brief pause, Zanna said, "He's never really talked about it. I mean, to tell me how it was for him, as a seventeen-year-old."

"And is he an only child?"

"Yes."

"It must have been difficult for his mother when he left town for the navy."

They'd come to the end of the boardwalk and Zanna asked, "Want to go up to the beach?" At Cora's hesitation, she quickly added, "Not all the way to the lighthouse. There are benches."

"That's fine, dear. A bit of a rest will be good."

Once they were sitting on the nearest bench, Zanna asked, "Cora, you mentioned a moment ago that you're supposed to get mild exercise. Do you have a health issue?"

The other woman sighed. "Kind of. I have heart problems and I'm scheduled to have a valve replacement at the end of the summer."

That explained some things Zanna had noticed, like Cora's ashen face when Mo went missing and her occasional shortness of breath. "I'm sorry to hear that. If you ever need any help with anything, please feel free to call on us."

"You and Rohan have been wonderful, Zanna. Now, getting back to Dominic." She gave a sly smile. "I'm being nosy here, but I suspect you two are a couple. Am I right?"

Zanna felt herself blush, and not from the midday sun. Days ago, she'd have come up with a vague answer, but no need to now. "Kind of. We're going to have a child together. In late September." She grinned sheepishly but was taken aback at Cora's reaction. The older woman gasped and her palm flew to her chest.

Then she recovered, enthusing, "How absolutely wonderful! Congratulations!"

It was a nice change from Jane's worries after Zanna had told her, days ago. When

Cora began to pepper her with questions, she didn't mind at all. Until she asked the one question Zanna still had no answer for. "What are your plans? Will you and Dominic—"

"I don't know," Zanna interjected. "Things are a bit up in the air right now."

Something in her voice must have warned Cora off. "Oh. Well, I'm sure all will work out eventually. He clearly cares for you." After a short silence, she went on to say, "Shall we get back to the hotel? I'm sure Rohan will need rescuing by now."

Zanna thought Cora seemed a bit shaky and looped her arm through Cora's. They took the beach road to its junction at Main Street rather than the stairs down to the harbor. They were nearly at the hotel when Cora quietly said, "Maurice and I tried to have children, but unfortunately never were successful."

"You'd have made a great mother," Zanna said, touched by the woman's expression.

"Thank you, dear, I like to think that I would have." Another long pause and then, "Though I'll never really know."

Zanna squeezed her arm. "I trust my instincts about that. And there's the hotel just ahead."

As they went inside, Cora stopped to look up at Zanna, patting her arm affectionately. "This has been a very special day for me. Thank you again."

While Cora was being reunited with an overexcited Mo, Zanna thought back to her last words and felt a bit sad. What did it say about Cora's life, that a mere lunch could be so special?

THE CLASSROOM WAS almost full fifteen minutes before Dom's talk to the Cove's Eagle Scouts and he was nowhere to be seen. Zanna stood in the doorway, scanning the crowded room for an available seat. A caretaker had set up folding chairs behind the rows of desks and Zanna noted they were quickly being taken. She turned to the rear of the room and spotted a raised hand waving at her. Henry. He patted a vacant chair next to him and she rushed toward it.

"This is a nice surprise," he said as she plunked down on the metal seat. "Does Dominic know you're here?"

"No. It was a last-minute decision. And

where is he?" She straightened to look over the heads of people filling the room.

"He was in the hallway talking to a couple of the older Scouts when I arrived and so engaged in conversation, he didn't notice me." Henry peered around the room. "A good turnout for the Cove. Glen tells me there are more kids working for their Eagle Scout badges than ever. He credits it to the influx of people in the new part of town."

The low chatter in the room stopped suddenly as Dom, followed by Glen, entered. Zanna heard herself gasp and instantly covered her mouth in embarrassment. She scarcely listened to Glen's introduction and the light clapping, all her senses fixated on Dominic, in uniform.

Henry leaned over to whisper, "Striking, isn't he? I'm surprised and very pleased that he decided to wear his uniform. A super-motivator for those kids interested in the military."

The navy-blue suit, with gold-trimmed cuffs topped by a crisp white collar, transformed the Dominic she'd been spending time with into some kind of iconic poster for the navy. He was holding a white cap, decorated with more gold and the naval insignia.

"That's what's called a service dress blue," Henry added in a low voice. "Used for official functions that aren't as formal as those requiring dress whites."

Zanna was only half listening to his explanation, her attention on the man striding confidently to the front of the room. She'd never seen him in uniform, though she had a sudden memory of a framed photograph on the fireplace mantel at his mother's house. She'd intended to get a closer look at it when she was there for dinner but she'd left too abruptly.

Dom placed his cap on the teacher's desk and gazing out across the room, said, "Wow! I'm awed by this interest in Eagle Scouts and the ROTC program. I hope I can live up to your expectations." He smiled. "I started working on my Eagle Scout badges when I was fourteen…"

Zanna knew from the occasional bursts of laughter and the flurry of raised hands as he ended his talk that Dom's presentation had been a big success, but she'd spent much of the half hour thinking of all the other versions of Dominic Kennedy she'd come to know: the empathetic teenager comforting her at Brandon's funeral; the romantic man she'd reconnected with at New Year's and the more serious, committed father of her child. So many different images and now she could add this one—*the navy man*—to her collection. How many more sides of Dominic were there yet to be discovered? A shiver of anticipation coursed through her.

When he wrapped up his talk to a round of enthusiastic applause, Henry and Zanna wound their way around those heading for the front of the room where Dom stood chatting to a teenager. Henry motioned a goodbye and left. Zanna hesitated in the doorway, about to follow when Dom's voice stopped her.

"Hey, Zanna!" He said something to the youth next to him and rushed over. "This is a nice surprise. And I think I saw Henry, too?"

She nodded. "He just left. That was a great presentation, Dom, and I see you've got some eager kids waiting to ask questions."

He glanced quickly behind him. "Thanks for coming. Maybe we can get together sometime tomorrow?"

"Sure." She didn't move, wanting desperately to touch him, wrap her arms around this other Dominic and feel his warm embrace. Keeping her eyes on his, she quickly stroked the lapel of his suit jacket and murmured, "You look awesome."

His face reddened and he grabbed her hand before she could pull it away, giving it a quick squeeze. "Tomorrow then." He turned away and headed for the small group of people waiting at the front of the classroom.

The picture of Dominic in his dark navy-blue uniform stayed with her all the way back to the hotel and through the night.

CHAPTER SEVENTEEN

THE AROMA OF bacon frying got Dom out of bed. It didn't take much to revert to a teen when he was back home. Sleeping in was a rare occurrence for the adult Dom, but if anything could rouse him from bed, it was bacon. He had a quick shower and by the time he reached the kitchen, his mother was flipping the first of many pancakes.

"Late night?" She half turned and he saw the twinkle in her eye.

"Hope I didn't wake you."

"Not at all. I assume you and some friends went out after your talk."

"Yeah, to the Claw. Glen, the Scout leader, his brother Gary, and Ted Nakamura and Ben showed up. Plus, a couple of other guys from Ben's company—can't remember their names. They're newbies in town, didn't go to Portland High like the rest of us."

"Newbies?"

"You know, new to the Cove. They moved into the area about a year ago, when Ben hired them."

"Have fun?" She set two pancakes on a plate with four slices of bacon and brought it to Dom at the kitchen table.

"Not having any?" He asked as he poured syrup over the pancakes.

"I already had mine. But I'll have another cup of coffee with you." She brought two mugs over and sat opposite him. "So, was it fun?" she repeated.

"It was a good time," he answered through a mouthful of pancake.

"I'm glad you've reconnected with some of the old gang. I was just thinking that you've been more social this visit than other times when you've been on leave. You kind of stuck to home. Not that I minded," she gave a half laugh.

Dom held his fork midway to his mouth. "Hmm, I never really thought about that. I suppose I kind of lost touch with the old gang, so I never really tried to meet up with them when I've been home before." He continued eating.

"Or maybe it's because you've also been

out a lot with Zanna, and she's had a couple of years back home to…well…reintegrate, especially since last summer when all that hoopla about the lighthouse was happening."

Dom stopped chewing again. "Maybe that's it. Or maybe it's also because I'm a bit older now and being with friends is more important than—"

"Working all the time?" Marie teased.

Dom grinned. His mother had been nagging him for the past few years to get a social life. "I do have friends in Norfolk, and some of them even have children."

"That's good, because soon you'll have something else in common with them."

The image that rose in Dom's mind was daunting. He reached for his coffee and took a long swallow. "Guess so." He busied himself cutting and chewing bacon and pancake.

After a minute's silence, Marie said, "Tell me about your talk with the Scouts."

Dom was happy to redirect the conversation. "It was great! Lots of parents came along, too, with questions of their own. Of the four kids qualifying for Eagle Scouts, two were interested in the ROTC, and one especially, in the navy arm of the program. I really enjoyed talking to them. And guess who showed up? Henry and Zanna."

"Nice. Were you expecting them?"

"Not at all." Dom thought about how startled he'd been when he noticed them sitting at the back of the room. For a split second, he'd been speechless, mainly because of Zanna's presence. She'd given no hint about coming for the talk and he was both pleased with her interest and support and nervous about how she'd respond. But he'd quickly gotten into his topic as the enthusiasm of the teens caught his full attention. At least he'd managed to get her aside for a few seconds, though a big part of him wanted to leave with her.

"Dear? Was Henry an Eagle Scout?" His mother must have asked that question twice because she was frowning when he looked up.

"No, but over the years when he was the leader, he mentored a lot of kids who were working on their merit badges."

"Did you ever regret not completing yours? I mean, I think you had eighteen or nineteen of the twenty-one badges you needed."

"Just lost interest, I guess." Dom drank more coffee, avoiding Marie's eyes.

"Coincidentally, not long after your father died."

Dom waited a beat before saying, "Maybe." He finished the last of his bacon and looking up, met his mother's gaze.

"You've been avoiding talking about that day since it happened—nineteen years ago!"

He heaved a long audible sigh. "Talking doesn't change the facts, Mom. I should have been on the boat, with him. Instead, I was—I can't even remember! Doing something with friends? Nothing important!" He shook his head, thinking back to his seventeen-year-old self.

"I'm not judging the mindset of a teenager, Dominic. It was important to you at the time. Even if you had gone out with Jerry that day, the storm would still have come, the boat would still have capsized. It was old and needed spot welding. Remember? But your dad hadn't got around to it."

"I might have been able to save him."

His voice was so low she had to lean forward to hear. "No, that's not true. Even with life jackets and survival suits, neither of you would have been saved. It was a record storm!"

"Dad's crew member, Lenny, drowned, too. His family lost a son, a husband and a father."

"It was a tragedy for all of us, Dom."

"He wouldn't have been there if…"

She shook her head. "You don't know that. Lenny and your father always lobstered together and sometimes, you joined them. That's how it was." She reached across the table to clasp his hand. "If you'd gone, I'd have lost you, too. The story is as simple as that."

Few stories are as simple as they seem, he figured, but she'd been absolutely right about one thing—it did feel good to talk about it. He gently pressed her hand. "Thanks for this, Mom. I mean the talk—not only the breakfast. Maybe if I'd been able to open up back then, I wouldn't have been so much trouble afterward. The truancy, the arguments, the door-slamming and those long silences." He cast a sheepish grin at her. "How did you put up with me?"

"You were in pain, honey."

"So were you."

"But you were my son…my child. Parents don't let down their children." After a moment, she got up and began to clear dishes. "If you're seeing Zanna today, will you please return that baby book to her?" She turned around, smiling. "She may want to start reading."

"And maybe I should, too." He went over to the sink and wrapped his arms around his mother in a long hug. "You're the best."

She kissed him on the cheek before pulling away. "What're your plans today?"

"I'm going to spend the rest of the morning studying for my interview, then probably take Zanna's book to her."

"No pressure, but do you think you'll be home for dinner?"

Good question. He hadn't seen Zanna since Tuesday night at the Claw with Ben and Ella. Hotel and family obligations had been her excuse when he'd texted to see if she was free to meet up. He was hoping she'd receive good news about the hotel soon and they could start thinking—even planning—next steps around her move with him to Norfolk. Or wherever he was sent, if he got the promotion. "I'll let you know by this afternoon, okay?"

"That's fine. Now if you'll tidy up in here, I have an appointment at the beauty salon."

Using his father's habitual line, Dom said, "You're beautiful already!" and Marie blushed, as she always had. He loaded the dishes in the dishwasher and wiped down the counter and stovetop, as his mother had trained him many years before. *Funny how I never rebelled against this chore for Mom*, he thought. Even when he was at frequent loggerheads with his father, both on the boat and at home. He wondered what Little Bean would be like as a teenager, then realized how much that depended on the active role of both parents. *It was time to get Zanna on board moving with him.*

He poured himself the last cup of coffee and decided to drink it sitting on the front porch. It was a sunny day and warming up. On the way out, he spied the Friday issue of *The Beacon* on the small table in the entryway and took it with him.

The town's weekly paper had changed since Ella Jacobs took over as editor in January, including more community-based information and news along with local and some regional stories. Although it retained the tone of a small-town paper, its scope was broader and more sophisticated, Dom thought.

At the bottom of the second page, he was surprised to see a photo of himself standing in front of the Eagle Scouts at last night's meeting. He hadn't realized someone from the paper was in the room, unless a parent had written something and photographed him when the Scouts were taking selfies with him after he'd finished. It was a short write-up but nicely done. One comment from a Scout warmed him:

I had some doubts and questions about the ROTC navy but after listening to Lieutenant Kennedy talk about his work and his adventures, I'm feeling more confident about what I want to do.

Dom smiled. Despite his many experiences speaking to his crew, other officers and even superior officers, he'd never addressed teenagers. But he'd found their questions and comments both uninhibited and genuine. They didn't hold back, as adults might, and he'd liked that. Maybe when he and Zanna were finally settled as a family, he could invest some personal time engaging with other teens in a similar context. He turned the page and noticed the lead editorial with its headline, *The Cove Needs a Community Center*.

He was impressed that Ella had pulled together an editorial so quickly, using many of the points she and Zanna had discussed at dinner. Toward the end, one paragraph stood out:

The Brandon Winters Memorial Community Center Committee, chaired by Suzanna Winters, is seeking volunteers to work on this important project for Lighthouse Cove. Go to the attached link to take the survey or to volunteer.

Dom's head was buzzing. When did Zanna plan to tell him she was going to chair the committee, or had he been left out on purpose, in case he tried to dissuade her from the idea?

He had no answers, but he would get them.

ZANNA HADN'T BEEN prepared for the deluge of phone calls. Although the hotel copies of *The Beacon* had been delivered at the usual time and Rohan had placed them on the reception counter for guests, she hadn't read the article until after the first phone call, from Henry, who'd expressed his delight at the community center initiative—"Good for you for getting the ball rolling, Zanna."

Then her mother got on the phone. "The rest of the family ought to have been informed first, Zanna, rather than be caught by surprise from friends and neighbors wanting to know more about it."

"How is that a problem, Mom?"

"I've just been on the phone with Evelyn and she and Charles have been fielding calls all morning, people wanting to know where the center will be and if the company is going to build it and so on."

"That's silly. The information is on the website we set up. Why would Aunt Evelyn and Uncle Charles be expected to know all that?"

Her mother's sigh echoed along the line. "Because they're Winterses and Brandon was their nephew, and Charles—or I guess Ben, now—owns the only building company in the area." Another sigh. "And this is the Cove."

"I seriously don't think it's a big deal, Mom. Ella said she'd try to get the piece written for today's paper, but I wasn't sure she had. I haven't had a chance to see it myself yet."

"Are we still going ahead with the original concept for a memorial then, because I think Grace is due home tomorrow. How do you think she will feel about this change in direction?"

"We can go ahead with the plaque and maybe have a private ceremony just for the family. Didn't we discuss something like that, at our last meeting?" Zanna took a deep breath. She needed to calm down. "Why don't all of us meet up again this weekend and decide?"

"All right. I'll let Henry know and you can inform Dominic. Unless Grace will want to take over for him now"

Zanna ended the call. Clearly, she'd goofed by not informing her aunt and uncle ahead of time, but she felt that wasn't a serious oversight. Grace was another matter, because the lighthouse restoration and memorial plaque had been her idea. She'd forgotten her cousin was coming back from her honeymoon this weekend and decided to contact her to explain everything in person.

Right now, she needed to read the piece and wait for Dominic's inevitable phone call. She told Rohan she'd be in her office and began to skim through the editorial while taking more phone calls. Her mood lifted at these, because they came from friends and acquaintances expressing their pleasure along with offers to help out. Zanna hadn't seen the website yet, but one of her friends told her it had good information and she was then able to steer everyone else who phoned to the site. She was almost finished reading the editorial and high with excitement when Dom tapped at her open office door.

"Rohan told me to come on in," he said. "That okay?"

His subdued demeanor took her euphoria down a notch. "Sure." She folded the paper over and waited as he sat down, placing a bag that she immediately recognized, on the desktop. The baby book she must have forgotten at Dom's house. Her face heated up. What did that say about her potential mothering skills?

"Oh, thanks," she mumbled and before he could speak, blurted, "I'm sorry I didn't tell you about the community center plan, but things just happened very quickly and—"

"I knew about your community center idea, Zan, because I was with you when you and Ella were talking about it. The idea of naming it after Brandon is a nice one." He paused to rub his forehead as if he was trying to erase the deep frown on it. "I'm just wondering when you were going to tell me the part about you heading the committee. No, wait—" He held up a hand before she could interrupt. "Is your intention to continue with that job throughout the whole campaign—the fundraising and the construction—assuming it'll be approved?"

The fact that her mother had posed similar questions irked her. If she could own and manage a hotel with staff, why was it so incredible to think she could chair a committee?

"Dom, it's all up in the air. The center isn't even a 'thing' yet! I have a feeling you might be channeling me right now, getting ahead of yourself," she teased.

He gave a tight smile at that. "The point is, Zanna, that you can't be in two places at the same time. Are you and Bean going to be with me, wherever I end up, or are you going to be here in the Cove, helping to construct a community center?"

Zanna's mouth dried up. She hadn't actually considered that.

"I'm not pressing you for an answer this

minute," he went on, "but you know you'll
have to decide sooner or later. Maybe sooner,
once you hear back from that Gateway company."

His words washed over her, a tide of unhappy thoughts and confusion.

He waited a long moment and when she
failed to reply, he stood up. "I have to go.
I'm meeting up with Ben shortly." He started
to leave but paused in the doorway. "Zanna,
please don't see this as an ultimatum. You
have to decide for yourself what kind of future you want, for you and Little Bean. I
know I'll be part of it in some way, but I'm
hoping for a large part." Another pause. "And
I…I love you, Zanna. That's it. That's what I
wanted to say."

He was gone before she could say anything,
even if she'd been able to find the right response. Love hadn't been part of their vocab-
ulary up to now. They'd skirted around it the
past week, using less important synonyms
like *caring*. But *love*—that was a whole other
level, embracing different words like commitment, loyalty and honesty.

Zanna lay her head down on her arms,
folded on the desktop. If only she could nap

and wake up to all her problems solved, banished into the ether by some fairy godmother.

Minutes later her phone rang. *The real world was still there.* Her hello was groggy, heavy with fatigue, and there was a slight hesitation on the other end.

"Uh… Ms. Winters? It's Jeff Thomas from City Bank in Portland. I understand you need to set up an account for a fundraising campaign and I can fit you in about three this afternoon. Does that work for you?"

She cleared her throat. "Yes, perfect. Thank you, Jeff, and I'll see you then." After disconnecting, she sat for another ten minutes staring into space until Rohan rushed in to say Lisa had to leave early and it wasn't Cheryl's day to come in and could Zanna take her rooms because he had a noon dental appointment in Portland. Inhaling deeply, she said, "Right. I'm coming," and as soon as he left, she lay her head down again for one more second.

"Thanks again for seeing me on such short notice Jeff," Zanna said. "This was relatively easy."

"I recommend you find a joint holder for

the account and see a lawyer, too, about any legal conditions you might have to consider."

"I will." As she got up to leave, he quickly stopped her. "We also need to talk about the hotel's financials. Preferably right now."

She sat down and tried not to worry at the sober expression now replacing his smile.

CHAPTER EIGHTEEN

DOM CLOSED THE front door behind him and set off down the sidewalk for his morning run. He needed to clear his head, though he had a feeling it would take more than fresh air and exercise to erase the memory of yesterday's confrontation with Zanna. Now he worried he'd been too hard on her. Her claim that the community center idea had evolved quickly from the Tuesday night discussion at the Claw to the Friday editorial was reasonable. That wasn't the issue. She'd never once even *hinted* that she intended to head the planning committee herself! As he'd told her yesterday, she couldn't be in two places at the same time. She was either with him, away from the Cove, or here—without him.

He jogged across Town Square, which was fairly empty except for a few people with small children carrying plastic buckets and shovels, heading for the beach. One father waved and Dom saw it was Glen and waved back. He recalled what his mother had said about his reconnecting with old friends and knew she'd been right when she suggested Zanna had indirectly been responsible for that.

In spite of her many years away from the Cove, it seemed that Zanna had readjusted to small-town living. He figured her new sense of belonging in the Cove, along with her idea of a community center honoring Brandon, were compelling arguments for staying on, even if she sold the hotel. His stomach clenched again, and he stopped running, bending over to take deep breaths and ease the discomfort in his belly.

When he felt ready, he loped down a side street to Main where he decided to stay on the paved road rather than take the boardwalk below. Early Saturday morning traffic consisted mainly of dogwalkers and a few cars driving toward the highway and probably the big box stores in Portland. Passing the harbor, he noted a lineup for tickets at the Casco Bay cruise kiosk and thought of his mother's smiles the day they'd taken the cruise. He decided to spend as much time as possible with her before he left for his interview. Considering the scene with Zanna yesterday morning, that might be more time than he'd anticipated.

As if the unexpected complication with Zanna and the community center wasn't enough, his meeting with Ben late Friday afternoon had led to an unexpected offer, tossing another dilemma Dom's way. The reason for the invite to his office was apparent minutes after Dominic had his first sip of the coffee Ben had made.

"You have a degree in engineering, right?" When Dom had nodded, he asked, "What kind? Mechanical? Chemical or...?"

"Civil, but with a focus on mechanical and structural. Why?"

"I'm not sure how much you know about my company's business, but it's booming right now. We'll soon be finishing the green condo units on the other side of the highway, fronting the lighthouse peninsula, and six of the ten units have been sold. There's still room for development in the subdivision, now called Lighthouse View—" he grinned at the name "—and it seems from responses so far about the proposed community center that it could happen. In that case, Winters Building and Construction will likely be tendering a bid for the contract. Plus, we've got a new project in Portland, which I can't reveal yet.

"Frankly, all that's more than I can handle. Granted, I've got a solid team here and in Portland, and Glen is a great second-in-command. But his experience as a foreman connects more to the nuts and bolts of the business. I need an engineer with top-notch organizational skills and, most of all, the ability to lead. I've spent the last couple of weeks headhunting for such a person and haven't found anyone yet."

Dom's mind had been so fixed on the idea of the center actually happening, silently wondering if he should call Zanna that night, that he'd almost missed Ben's next words.

"Then you came to town," Ben had continued, "and it's taken me a few days, but I think you're exactly the person I'm looking for."

Dom had choked on his coffee.

Ben had held up a hand. "Let me finish. I know you have a career and the chance you might be interested in the job is remote. I'm simply putting the idea out there in case there's a possibility—as unlikely as it may seem right now—something might come up and you might change your mind about...you know...staying in the navy."

The meeting had ended soon after. The offer, though complimentary, was also completely unrealistic. Dom had no intention of giving up his navy career. But sometime in the middle of the night, he wished he wasn't quite so loyal.

When he reached the end of Main Street that connected to the beach road, he opted to continue on it, rather than run on the beach itself. Several yards along, he spotted Henry Jenkins strolling up from the beach. Dom slowed to a walk as Henry drew near.

Seconds after their greeting, Henry said, "Everything okay? You look a tad pale this morning."

"Rough night."

Henry's eyes twinkled. "Out with the lads?"

"Hah! I wish. No, just...thinking about some things."

"Let's have a sit over there." Henry pointed to an empty bench near the road. "I can use a few minutes after my morning walk."

Dom swiped his forearm across his sweaty forehead and followed Henry. He hid a small smile as the older man got to the point as soon as he sat down.

"Were you fretting about Zanna heading up this committee for the community center? Her mother and I were taken aback," he went on before Dom could respond, "but that's Zanna, you know. She gets an idea and runs with it, expecting others to follow along. Jane is concerned because this commitment is a big undertaking and Zanna's pregnant." He shifted his gaze, but not before Dom caught his sidelong glance.

After what seemed hours, he asked, "Had she spoken to you about her intentions? Jane isn't always privy to her plans, because Zanna also likes to keep things kinda private until she herself knows what she's going to do."

Dom could only shake his head.

Henry sighed. "Yes, that's Zanna. Correct me if I'm wrong, but I'm guessing you two haven't quite settled on a plan for when the baby comes, and you'll be leaving the Cove soon and it's likely now that Zanna will be staying."

"I've asked her to come with me, wherever I end up," Dom blurted. "I thought she was considering it, but now…"

"Uh-huh." Henry stared thoughtfully across the bay. "I'm not sure what kind of persuasion she'd need to change her mind, once she's decided on something. Compromise can be a good thing, but it's darn harder to achieve than people think." He paused for a long moment. "Don't know if you've ever heard my story, but I fell in love years ago. She married a friend so that was that. I never once let on how I felt, and I never felt that kind of love again for any other woman. Though there were one or two along the way."

Dom thought the man's light chuckle sounded more sad than humorous.

"The thing is," Henry went on, "even after she was free, I said nothing for years. See," he faced Dom, his eyes damp with emotion, "I'd given up. I made assumptions that she didn't feel the same, that our lives had followed different paths and later, that we were both too old and settled in our ways."

By now Dom had guessed the mystery woman was Jane.

"My point is—*finally*—" Henry's chuckle was more genuine now "—that we shouldn't make decisions based on assumptions. Talking has to happen. I know you're dedicated to your career, and Zanna's bent on this community center. Seems like there's no possibility of compromise. But I assure you, Dominic, that it's there. You just have to figure it out." When they parted, Henry clasped Dom in a quick hug and said, "I have complete faith in your ability to problem-solve."

Dom pondered the old man's words all the way home and as he got himself cleaned up. He decided to call the one person who might understand his dilemma—Uncle George. Minutes after the warm greetings and brief catch-up about Marie, Dom told the whole story to his uncle, starting from the search-and-rescue operation just prior to his leave, his return home only to learn about his imminent fatherhood and ending with the fact that he'd fallen in love with the mother of his child.

His uncle was silent for a long moment. "First of all, congratulations on being a father! Marie must be thrilled to bits."

"She is." Dom was about to say more when George added, "As far as the training exercise that seems to be bothering you, it sounds like your CO left the decision to cancel up to you. If he didn't initially agree with you at least he later confirmed that you'd been right. So I wouldn't spend any more time fretting about the incident."

Dom let out a long breath of relief.

"Now," his uncle said, "tell me more about what the promotion would mean to you."

"It's everything I've worked toward the past couple of years."

"And would you be willing to defer it, if you could?"

Dominic paused. "Defer it?"

"You've forgotten about a wonderful opportunity the navy offers." The answer came to Dom a second before his uncle said, "The Career Intermission Program, where you can shift from active duty to reserve for three years."

Dom was speechless. He ought to have thought about the program that he, as a lieutenant, had occasionally recommended to crew. "Obviously my mind has been on many things lately, Uncle George. From working on the material for my big interview to making plans for my new personal situation, I didn't think of the CIP."

"Well, there's an application process and I've no idea how long that takes. I think you can defer a promotion, but you'd have to confirm that. If you need a character reference, I'm sure your CO will happily do that."

Dom's energy level was starting to pick up. "This is great, Uncle George. It's an idea worth pursuing, for sure."

"Better than tackling a life-changing decision in a matter of weeks. And by the way, how're you feeling about fatherhood?"

"Now that I'm used to the idea, I'm both excited and awed."

"I've often thought how much more fulfilling my life would have been if I'd had someone to share it with. And I'm not talking about golf partners," he ended with a light laugh.

It was the closest his uncle had ever come to reflect on his bachelorhood. Dom promised to keep George informed and as he was about to say goodbye, heard his uncle say, "Whatever you decide, don't turn your back on love, Dominic."

ZANNA PICKED UP her phone for the umpteenth time Saturday morning to call Dom. Partway through the long night she'd realized that the entire time he'd been in her office yesterday, wanting an explanation for her decision to chair the committee, she'd focused on her own reasons and excuses. She hadn't considered how he might be feeling, especially after he'd talked so enthusiastically about having her and Little Bean follow him to Norfolk and beyond. She ought to have told him her intentions about the community center before her meeting with Ella. He'd told her he loved her, and she'd let him leave without calling him back to tell him that she loved him, too. At some point in the lonely hours of early morning, she'd asked herself, *What kind of person have I become, that I find saying those three small words so difficult?*

A cheery voice roused her from those dark thoughts. "Good morning, Zanna!" Cora and Mo were heading her way from the elevator. "Oh, have I caught you at a bad time, dear?" she asked as she drew closer. "You look as though you had a restless night."

"I'm fine, thanks, Cora. How are you doing? You seem energetic this morning."

"I am, indeed. I spent the night making some decisions and planning for my future." Her bubble of laughter bounced around the empty lobby. "And I must add that I read the editorial about the community center in honor of your brother. And you're running the committee! That's wonderful."

"Thanks, Cora, but obviously I won't be doing all that single-handedly."

"Of course not. Soon you'll have another very special project of your own—and, uh, Dominic's, too, I imagine."

Zanna merely smiled. As much as she liked Cora Stanfield, she wasn't about to spill her heart to her.

"I'd like to make a donation whenever you start fundraising. Meanwhile, would you be free sometime this afternoon? Maybe for tea, either in my room or at Mabel's?"

"I'll have to let you know when Rohan comes in later this morning."

"That's fine. I'm thinking of heading back home, maybe tomorrow or Monday, so I thought it would be nice to have a last visit with you."

Zanna was startled by an unexpected pang of disappointment. "Oh? I...I'm sorry to see you leave, Cora. I've gotten so used to you and Mo—you both have become such a big part of the hotel."

"Like a fixture?"

"In the best possible way," Zanna said.

They smiled at one another for a long moment until Mo started yipping and pulling on his leash. "Well, then, I'm off. I hope to catch up with you later." Cora let Mo pull her toward the hotel door and gave a hasty wave as she exited.

When Rohan arrived an hour later, Zanna was finishing dry mopping the lobby floor. "Uh-oh," he said, "are we shorthanded again today?"

"Lisa's coming in but she's going to be late. I thought I might as well do the floor. Except for Cora's room, there aren't any others that need cleaning."

"No reservations for today?"

Zanna shook her head. "And Cora may be leaving tomorrow or Monday."

Rohan's face fell. "Ah, too bad. I'm going to miss her—even Mo!"

They both laughed. "Okay," Zanna said, "let's get busy."

AN HOUR LATER Ella phoned to say that Grace had returned from her honeymoon and could Zanna meet them at Mabel's. Lisa had come in to work so Zanna arranged to take a break.

Both Grace and Ella were already drinking coffee by the time she arrived at the diner.

"You're positively glowing!" Zanna exclaimed, hugging her cousin. "Great honeymoon?"

"My enthusiasm for lighthouses did wane a bit," Grace confessed, laughing.

They chatted while the server brought Zanna's herbal tea and a plate of pastries. Then Zanna decided to get right to the point. "Speaking of lighthouses," she began. From the expression on Grace's face, she guessed her cousin had been filled in on some of the happenings in the Cove during the past two weeks. When she also revealed her plans for the community center, Grace's eyes lit up.

"That's such a wonderful idea, Zan! And the revised lighthouse ceremony is perfect.

"I'll ask Drew to make sure the lighthouse is all ready," Grace promised.

Walking back to the hotel, Zanna thought about Dom. He hadn't called, which worried her, but she knew once they were together, and she told him how she felt—*those three words*—they could surely work out some kind of compromise for their future with Beanie.

Turning onto Main, she glanced toward the harbor, where the sight of a small white furball got her attention. Then she noticed two figures on a bench near the Casco Bay cruise kiosk. She stopped walking, squinting against the reflection of the water to zoom in on the people. Cora and Jane, deep in conversation. Something important, Zanna guessed, from the hand gestures, Jane's patting Cora's shoulder and then an unexpected hug. Zanna hurried on to the hotel, giving them their privacy.

Since her meeting with the bank manager, she now had far more pressing issues to deal with than puzzling about her mother and Cora Stanfield—like finding enough money to pay next month's bills and wages.

CHAPTER NINETEEN

"I WANT TO tell you a story," Cora announced once Zanna, juggling a mug of tea, pulled the desk chair close to where Cora was perched on her suite's small sofa. Mo was napping contentedly on the bed.

Despite the random thoughts running through Zanna's head, such as the list of chores she ought to be doing that very moment, she was grateful for the excuse to sit for a few minutes. She hoped that she wouldn't doze off like Mo or lose track of whatever story Cora was about to relate, should her mind drift elsewhere. She sipped her tea, thinking what a good idea she'd had to provide electric kettles and hospitality baskets that included tea bags for guests.

"I've told you I grew up in a small town outside Bangor, and by the time I was seventeen, I was ready to leave for good. I planned to go to university but around Thanksgiving of my senior year, I went to a party where I met someone and...well...fell in love. He was the cousin of an acquaintance, from the West Coast, traveling around the States before being deployed to Iraq."

Her eyes shining, she added, "A marine, devastatingly handsome in his uniform. Once we met, things moved very quickly as they often do in young romance. He stayed in the area a couple more weeks before returning to his base and eventually, Iraq." Cora's paused. "I'm sorry to say that part of my story has a sad ending. I learned through friends of friends that shortly after his arrival, he and his unit were attacked. He didn't survive. Not long after, I found out that I was pregnant. That was thirty-seven years ago."

Zanna set her tea mug down, wondering why she was telling her this sad story when Cora looked meaningfully at Zanna. "I'm sure my wonderful parents hoped for a grandchild someday, but they also knew their seventeen-year-old only child had a big future ahead of her. So, the three of us went to a private adoption agency in Bangor and—"

"No!" Zanna cried out. Her heart was drumming against her rib cage, her head throbbing with random words and phrases that were impossible to gather into a single coherent question. When her breathing slowed, she asked, "I...I don't understand. Why are you telling me this *now*?"

"After Maurice died, I got the diagnosis about my heart condition, and I was not in a good way. I bought Mo and for a while my days were full of puppy love." She glanced at Mo, snoring softly on the bed, and smiled. "Then a dear friend suggested I make a bucket list of things I wanted or needed to do. It started as a therapeutic exercise, but soon I wanted to make it real. There were places to see and old friends to seek out, yet none appealed as strongly as finding my birth daughter. I'd kept track of you at the beginning. When the adoption agency told me they'd found a lovely home in a small coastal town near Portland, I began researching the area, even before you were born. Then during my last appointment at the agency to sign the rest of the paperwork, I overheard the secretary mentioning the surname of the couple—*Winters*—and the rest was relatively easy." Cora reached for a file folder on the table next to the sofa and handed it to Zanna.

She recognized it as the folder Dominic had picked up off the floor, the day of Mo's great escape. He'd mentioned newspaper cuttings and here they were, a sheaf of them dating over a period of years, the most recent ones from *The Beacon* but some, to do with Winters Building and Construction, from the *Portland Press Herald.* After Zanna shuffled through them, she raised her head.

"This is a lot to take in, isn't it?"

The softness in Cora's voice almost brought Zanna to tears. "It is."

"You must have questions."

Zanna reached for a tissue from the box next to Cora. "A lot, but right now they're a mishmash of thoughts and feelings."

"Take your time."

Zanna couldn't stop staring at the petite woman sitting so calmly opposite her. This was a different Cora from the cheerful woman devoted to her pet whom she'd gotten to know over the past two weeks. She'd assumed that person was the entire Cora Stanfield and she'd been wrong. "You don't look like me," she blurted.

"No, but *you* resemble your father. He was tall, ginger-haired, with the most wondrous smile. It was a fluke really, that Jane also had the same coloring." Cora reached over to pat Zanna's hand. "I know this will take time, and I'm leaving you my contact details for when those questions start coming fast and furious."

Zanna tried to focus on what she wanted to know right then. "What was his name? My father?"

"James McLeod. His family originated from Scotland and settled in Washington state. He, too, was an only child, but he may have relatives there."

"Did you ever try to contact them, after?"

Cora shook her head. "I considered it, but to be honest, I was only beginning to know him when he left. I'm not sure if we'd have gotten together if he'd come back from Iraq. But I remember him as a kind, warm man with a great sense of humor. Whereas I was his opposite, with a more cautious, organized approach to life." She smiled. "Maybe a bit like you?"

Some memories from the past few days were rising up now. "You mentioned the other day that you'd been in the Cove when the lobster boats were still in operation."

"When I graduated from university, I decided to satisfy my ongoing curiosity about you. I'd been visiting my parents and was about to move to Chicago for my first big job. I came here on an impulse. I never told my parents because I think they'd have worried. After you were born—and I had my time alone with you—they stressed the importance of getting on with my life." Cora's sigh echoed in the quiet, prompting Mo to raise his head briefly and look over at her before settling down again.

"Anyway, I came for the day, walked around, noticed that the Winterses owned the hotel as well as a big construction company. I knew you were a Winters but wasn't sure how you were connected. My visit told me a couple of things, though."

"Like what?"

"That this town looked like a good place to raise a child and that the Winters family was important and influential here. I felt like I could stop worrying about you. That you were in good hands."

"When did you start collecting those?" Zanna pointed to the folder on the sofa next to Cora.

"When I accepted the fact that Maurice and I were not going to have any children, I consoled myself with positive thoughts about you and your family. But I couldn't get you off my mind, and several years ago, after conferring with Maurice, I decided to reach out to you. I wrote you a letter with my contact information and asked the agency to forward it." Cora glanced across at Mo, awake now and sitting up, wagging his tail.

"And?" Zanna waited, every nerve in her body dead still.

"I never heard back from you or the agency, so I just let the idea go—until a few months ago when I revisited my bucket list. I'm sorry I didn't come out with all this right away, but I wasn't sure how I'd be received. I only knew a bit of your story before I came, but I needed to know you'd welcome this…this very unexpected news. When you told me you were pregnant, I decided you might like to know something about your heritage—well, mine, anyway."

"My mother—"

"Jane knows. I met with her this morning and told her."

The scene Zanna had witnessed was making sense now. "How did she take it?"

"She was emotional, of course, but happy for me. She was a bit concerned about your reaction." Cora frowned. "You look confused, dear, or maybe unhappy. What are you feeling right now?"

A good question, Zanna was thinking. *What am I feeling?* She rubbed her temples, easing the pressure of a beginning headache. "Overwhelmed," she whispered. There was one more detail she had to know. "When exactly did you write this letter?"

"You would have been about nineteen."

The dark time of the holiday weekend and Brandon's passing. Had her mother received it and never given it to her?

Mo's sudden yipping got Cora off the sofa, lifting the dog into her arms. The piercing barks also brought Zanna's mind back to the present. "I should go, Cora. There's a lot I have to do today." She stood on wobbly legs.

"Of course, my dear. Take your time digesting all of this." Cradling Mo, she walked Zanna to the door.

Zanna impulsively bent to wrap her arms around Cora and Mo. "Thanks, Cora, and…

we'll talk some more, okay?" It wasn't much of a goodbye, she realized, but the only one her dazed senses could manage.

Cora closed the door behind her and Zanna headed for the stairs. Her slow descent to the lobby felt like a trek along a fogbound and rocky path, unfamiliar and treacherous. All these years Jane might have known about the letter and yet had never uttered a word.

Rohan must have suspected something was up as he stared wide-eyed at Zanna when she brushed past him into her apartment, slamming the door behind her. She fumbled for her phone in the pocket of her slacks, and keyed in her mother's number with trembling fingers. A tiny voice of common sense warned her to wait, but she ignored it. Too many feelings had been tamped down and left unspoken throughout her life. She needed to deal with this now.

Jane's shaky first words told Zanna her mother knew why she was calling. "You've spoken to Cora."

"Why, Mom? Did you think I couldn't handle finding out back then? That I didn't deserve to know? Were you *ever* going to tell me?"

"Oh, Zanna, I'm ashamed to say it was all

about me. I got the letter just days after Bran died and you remember how chaotic and painful that time was. I just couldn't deal with it. I hid it away for a while and then later, when you were going back to college, I'd planned to give it to you. But…but by then I knew Fred and I were splitting up. I know I wasn't a very good mother back then. You needed comforting, too, but I was wrapped up in my own grief."

Zanna closed her eyes, picturing those cold, lonely days. She heard her mother blow her nose and waited.

"The thing is," Jane went on, "I was afraid of losing you. First Bran, then your father. That if you found your mother, you'd really like her."

And she did like Cora, was Zanna's immediate thought. But like wasn't love. She loved Jane, her mother. Why couldn't Jane have trusted her to know the difference, even at nineteen?

"Can we meet later, honey? And finish this talk in person?"

The taut coil of Zanna's anger was already loosening, giving way to exhaustion. The energy whipped up by Cora's revelation was fading and Zanna wanted only to lie on her bed and go to sleep.

"Yes. I'll call you later, Mom. I need to rest and…and think." She disconnected and tossed her phone onto the sofa. But on the way to her bedroom, she thought of the one person in the whole of the Cove who would understand her state of mind. The one who'd comforted her at Brandon's funeral. The one who proclaimed his love for her, despite her unyielding self. *Dominic*.

DOM HAD EMAILED his CO right after talking to his uncle. He figured he'd give him a heads-up about the plan percolating in his mind. The more he thought about the option, the more he knew this was the compromise that could work for him and Zanna. He could postpone his promotion and have three extra years to make a career-changing decision. Everything now hinged on two conditions—getting his application approved and getting Zanna on board.

He was so excited by this new development that he told his mother right after he'd sent the email. "I've just been talking to Uncle

George," he began. She listened while he summarized the possible option.

"Is this something you'd be happy to consider at this stage in your career? Without regrets?"

"Honestly, Mom, I don't know. But I do know if I can't work out a compromise, if I don't find a way to spend the rest of my life with Zanna and Beanie…that…*that* will be my lifelong regret." He choked on the last word.

"Then you'd best follow through, Dominic Kennedy—with your heart," his mother quietly advised.

He was almost out the door when he got the phone call from Zanna. Her voice was so thin and shaky that he could barely hear what she was saying. But her last few words rang like a warning bell.

"Can you come? Right now? I have to talk to you." She hung up before he could answer.

After a quick shout out to his mother that he was taking her car, he was on his way to the hotel. He had no idea what was happening or why, only that Zanna needed him.

As Dom marched across the lobby, Rohan looked up from the computer. He seemed about to speak but Dom kept striding on into Zanna's apartment.

She was pacing the small sitting area and when he walked in, stopped to stare at him.

He took in her flushed face and the dark circles beneath her eyes. "Are you all right?"

"I need to tell you what's happened, but I don't really know where to start."

"Here, come sit down." He clasped her by the elbow and steered her to the sofa. "Start anywhere, Zanna. I'll fill in the gaps."

"I owe so much money, Dom. I don't even know if I can make next month's payments. And what if Gateway decides not to buy? And Cora is my mother. My biological mother, I mean. My mother knew! And my savings are almost gone, how can I keep this place afloat?" She gave a light snort, in disbelief.

She was speaking rapidly, and her breathing was escalating, rather than slowing down. A fragment of memory flashed in Dom's head—the panic in his ensign's face as the inflatable boat for the training exercise was being lowered down to the turbulent sea. "Where's your phone?" He repeated the question at her blank expression and snatched it up when she pointed to the kitchenette counter. "Here, get your doctor or midwife's number. I'll talk."

"I'm okay. I just need to rest," she muttered, but she did as he instructed, handing him the phone when it rang.

DOMINIC KEPT UP a patter of talk on the drive to Portland, telling her about the complimentary messages after his Eagle Scout presentation on Thursday night. Zanna stared out the window through most of it, silent now. He'd managed to make some sense of her earlier story about Cora and Jane, although he was still having trouble with the Cora part. Why had she spent so long in the Cove before revealing her identity? He lost track of most of it, especially when Zanna complained how her mother had known something for years without telling her.

The sun was in its descent to the west when he pulled into the parking lot of the medical clinic where Zanna's midwife, Andrea, had arranged to meet them. Dom introduced himself and opted to wait outside the examining room, thinking Zanna might not want him with her. But minutes later Andrea opened the door.

"Suzanna wants you with her when I do the ultrasound." Then in a lower voice, she added, "Her blood pressure is a bit high, but I'll take it again before you leave."

"Everything's okay," Zanna said, sighting his anxious face when he followed Andrea into the room. He stood beside her where she lay on the examining table and took her hand. When the ultrasound image appeared, he heard himself gasp and both Zanna and Andrea smiled. He couldn't take his eyes off the pulsing image. Little Bean. His baby. *Their* baby.

"First time?" Andrea asked as she moved the machine's wand across Zanna's abdomen. "Everything looks good," she announced, finishing the exam. "I'll print out this picture for you two." As she left the room, she said, "Suzanna, get some rest and let this man of yours look after you."

Dom's gaze locked onto Zanna's. "Will you let me?" he asked when the door closed.

"Today, tomorrow and the day after, if you want the job," she ended, teasing.

"I do." He wrapped his arms around her and held her close for a long moment. "Let's go home."

CHAPTER TWENTY

ZANNA HANDED DOM a pillow and the duvet off her bed. "Are you sure? I'll be fine on my own and that sofa isn't long enough."

"I'm staying. And Rohan said there's nothing to report and he'll lock up at the usual time," Dom said. "Andrea said you needed hydrating, so I'll make some herbal tea. I'll bring it in when you're settled." He pointed meaningfully toward the bedroom.

Zanna didn't protest, happy to have someone else take charge. She was in pyjamas and propped against pillows when he brought her tea and cookies, which he placed on the bedside table.

"All I could find," he said, "but I'm happy to run out for something more substantial, if you want."

"No, don't leave."

He leaned over to brush a strand of hair aside and kiss her forehead. "Don't worry. I'm not going anywhere. First things first," he said, perching on the edge of her bed. "Tell me again about Cora and your mother?"

Zanna knew she hadn't been making much sense before. She started at the beginning, from her sighting of Jane and Cora at the harbor, and he didn't ask a single question as every emotion weighing her down over the past few days tumbled out.

"How do you feel now?" he asked when she stopped.

"About Cora?"

"About all of it. Especially the letter your mother disposed of."

"Confused and a bit sad that Mom didn't trust me enough to deal with the letter. I get her reasoning, but I wish she'd had faith in me."

"Maybe it's the other way around," he finally said. "Maybe she didn't have faith in herself, as a mother, to take that risk."

Zanna thought about his insight. She was only beginning to understand the complexities of motherhood. Perhaps it was time to give Jane some understanding. "You could be right. I know I have to set things right between us. I've carried this… I'm not sure what to call it…resentment maybe…too long."

"Sounds like it's all tied up with what happened that summer, with Brandon."

"Perhaps. I remember how awful I felt back then. That I hadn't been a good sister. That I'd let him down."

"You didn't let him down, Zan. What happened that night was the tragic result of a chain of events beyond your control and Grace and Ella's, too. Even mine." His voice drifted off.

She reached out to clasp his hand. "Thank you for today. For coming right away, no questions asked. I still don't know what happened and why I was suddenly feeling like I was swimming against a riptide." She waited for another surge of emotion to ease, then said, "I have a solution for the problem about the lighthouse ceremony, but need to pass it by Grace and Mom, first." She gave a sheepish smile, realizing that mere days ago, she'd have run with the idea on her own before consulting others.

He ruffled her hair, as if reading her mind. "Good, but we can talk about that later. Andrea said to rest and try not to worry about things you can't change. And I second that advice."

"She also told me I probably wasn't having a real panic attack, just what she called a stress attack."

"I think we were both having that."

She saw his face cloud at some memory. "What is it?"

"A few weeks ago, I had a similar experience. We were in the Mediterranean and I was conducting our last search-and-rescue training exercise. One of my men—a guy who'd been having serious family problems, I learned later—had a real panic attack."

Zanna listened while Dom recounted the whole story, imagining how he must have felt and at the same time, understanding the weight of responsibility on his shoulders.

"The thing is," he went on, "now I realize why I had such a visceral reaction to the fear in the man's eyes. I had a flashback to my father, fighting for his life in that storm, and even Brandon, struggling in the tide. I hadn't been there to help either of them, but that day in the Mediterranean, I could help someone. My CO accepted my decision, though he pointed out that the weather cleared in the end and the exercise could have still happened. But even now, my gut tells me I made the right decision to cancel."

"You're a good man, Dominic," she murmured. "But don't feel you have to take on so much. Especially for me. I don't actually need saving most of the time. When I'm not having a stress attack, I'm a very tough woman." She waited a beat. "But I do need loving."

"That I can promise." He leaned over and kissed her cheek. "By the way, I sneaked a peek at those two pages on your desk—your 'To Do' list. You know you can talk to me about anything, even your financial troubles."

"I thought I should be able to handle personal things myself."

"But sharing problems is what couples should do."

"*Are* we a couple?"

"When we saw Little Bean today, didn't you feel like a couple?"

Zanna's eyes prickled with tears. "I did, but I'm not sure how long that feeling will last. When you leave—"

"I may not be leaving. There's a possibility of a third option for us, Zan. A program I'd forgotten about until I spoke to my uncle today."

She leaned against the pillows, listening to his idea. When he finished, she asked, "Would you be willing to put your career on hold for three years?"

"Yes, if it means being with you and Beanie. It gives us time to work something out, but right now, it's the perfect compromise." His face shone with expectation.

She thought suddenly how lucky she was, that they'd both decided to go to that New Year's Eve party months ago and had met again, after so many years. All the worries of the past two weeks were beginning to take second place to a new emotion—one she hadn't felt in a long time. *Hope*.

"I love you, Dominic," she said and reached up to bring his face and mouth down to hers.

ZANNA HAD A DEEP, untroubled sleep. Like a newborn, she reflected as she showered. *Or maybe not*. She'd have to consult the book she'd purchased, still in its plastic bag on her coffee table—whenever she found the time. Right now, all she really wanted to do was to lounge around her apartment and think about the events of the last twenty-four hours that had changed her life. *Okay*, she amended, my *outlook* on life. She had Dominic Kennedy to thank for that. He'd told her he wasn't going to give up on her days ago, and he'd lived up to that promise.

Drying off from her shower, she scanned the note again that she'd found on awakening an hour ago. *I have some arrangements to make for this week but will be bringing coffee and treats midmorning. I love you.* Treats would be nice, she thought, toweling her hair, but seeing him walk through the door, his big, warm smile lighting up her heart, was more than she'd ever want. Along with Beanie, of course.

Rohan was already at the reception counter when she emerged from her apartment. He seemed to do a double take when he saw her. "You look…different."

If this was a scene in a Hollywood musical, Zanna figured at this point she'd be twirling around and breaking into song. Instead, she flashed the happiest smile she'd been able to manage in weeks. *Months or even years.* She could barely remember the last time she'd been this elated, without worries about how long the feeling would last. Of course, there were hurdles ahead, but Dominic would be there to help her.

"A good night's sleep." She tried not to smile at Rohan's skeptical expression. He was about to say something when the sound of the elevator opening distracted both of them. Cora was heading their way.

Zanna hadn't seen her since their talk yesterday afternoon. So much had happened since that stunning revelation that she hadn't been able to fully process it yet.

"I've decided to check out this morning," Cora announced as she drew near.

Her furtive glance at Rohan suggested she might want to speak to Zanna in private. "Well, that's a shame, Cora, but I'm sure we will see more of you. Why don't you and I have a goodbye chat while Rohan checks you out?" She gestured to chairs on the far side of the lobby.

When they were seated, Cora said, "You seem more relaxed today, Zanna. Happy."

"I am. It's a bit of a long story and perhaps I can tell you all about it later, by email?"

"I'd like that very much. I was hoping we might be able to stay in touch." Cora's eyes welled up.

"We will, definitely!" Zanna patted Cora's hand. "And will you let me know about your surgery? I'll be waiting to hear how you are, afterward. And if you need anyone to come and hold your hand, or help out…"

Cora brushed a tear off her cheek. "Thank you, dear. Fortunately, I have good friends in Chicago but would love to have a visit from you—and your baby—someday."

"Absolutely." Now Zanna's eyes were damp. "And before you go, I want to tell you that Dominic and I are making plans to be together. As a couple."

"Oh, my goodness! That is the best news I could want before leaving."

Zanna noticed Rohan signaling and miming holding a phone. "Oops, looks like I'm needed." When they were both standing, she leaned over and kissed Cora on the cheek. Walking arm in arm with her to the counter, she saw Rohan's puzzled frown.

She left Cora to pay her bill and, picking up her cell phone from the counter, went into the office. The voice message she played wasn't from Dominic, but from Alex Corelli. She took a calming breath before calling him back.

"We're ready to move forward, Zanna. I'm

emailing you the formal offer. We'll need to hear back from you within the week."

"I'll look for it," Zanna said, trembling.

"One thing you'll note, we'd like a later closing date. End of December, because our architect team is tied up with another project. I hope that works for you. If you have any questions after you've gone through the offer, please try to get back to me as soon as possible. We're very excited about a location in Lighthouse Cove."

Zanna was giddy with relief when the call ended. She was tempted to read the offer email right away but knew she ought to wait until she and Dom could go through it together. *That's another change right there*, she thought. Choosing *not* to handle a big decision on her own. She marveled again at how her whole life had shifted direction in a mere three weeks or so. Of course, the changes would continue to roll in, but as long as she and Dom could handle them together, she'd be okay.

By the time she returned out front, Rohan was helping Cora with her luggage and Mo. Zanna rushed to give her another hug and Mo, a pat on the head. "Text or email me when you're safely back home," she said.

Cora beamed. "I think I'm going to like the demands of my new life. That's what this is, my dear. A new life for me. I will be in touch." She motioned to Rohan that she was ready to go.

Zanna watched as Rohan led them to the door, turning around once to flash a very perplexed frown. He was only one of many people in the Cove who would soon learn about all the big news in Zanna's life. When he returned minutes later, assuring her that Cora was safely on her way to Portland in her rental car, Zanna suggested they have a long talk later that day.

"Okay, and will you need me for the next hour or so? I have some banking to do."

"Go," she said. *Banking*. The news from Alex had suddenly altered her serious money problems. Last night she and Dom had decided to go over the hotel accounts together and work out a plan with a financial adviser. Everything depended on a sale and now, that was going to happen. She could hardly wait to see his face when she told him the good news.

Lisa checked in for work right after Rohan

left and Zanna sent her to clean Cora's room. Every few minutes she looked at the hotel door, expecting to see Dom walk through. She considered texting him the good news about Gateway but wanted to share it with him in person. She also didn't want to distract him. She knew he was working on his application to the program he'd told her about.

Last night, he'd cautioned her that until he knew for sure about an approval—or not—they ought to keep the plan a secret. She'd teasingly scoffed at that, reminding him that some things had changed about her over the past several days, but she was essentially the same person—the Zanna who liked to keep her thoughts, plans and dreams close.

"Uh-huh," he'd murmured, embracing her. "I'm okay with living with that Zanna, so long as the new one—this one right here in my arms—shows up now and again."

He knew her so well, she thought.

Now for the final task of the day: making peace with her mother. When she and Dominic had returned to the hotel last night, she'd played the voice messages from Jane, sent while they'd been at the clinic. She'd texted that she'd be in touch the next day.

Zanna sighed. She hoped this new version of herself could handle what could be another emotional exchange and was about to call to arrange a meeting when she eyed Henry and Jane entering the hotel. They were both smiling as they came her way, which eased Zanna's nervousness.

"We've brought something to show you and…um…hope you'll approve," her mother began as soon as they reached the counter.

It was only then that Zanna noticed the box Henry was carrying. "Can we sit over there?" she asked, pointing to where she and Cora had sat minutes ago. "Rohan is taking a break."

When they were seated, it was Henry who took the lead, loudly clearing his throat and glancing quickly at Jane before saying, "Your mother and I want to show you the plaque for Brandon."

Zanna frowned. "The plaque? I saw it weeks ago when it arrived."

"True, but you haven't seen it since it's been engraved."

She looked from Henry to her mother, who seemed nervous.

"Jane and I noticed that you've had a lot on

your plate these past few days. This committee business has been going round and round without any progress. So Jane and I decided to go ahead and get the plaque engraved. We took it to Portland t'other day and were lucky to get a rush job. Would you like to see it?"

"Yes, please."

Henry removed the box lid and the tissue paper covering the plaque. Zanna read the inscription, unable to speak for minutes after.

Brandon Winters.

A Son and Brother.

"I like it," she finally said, hearing Jane's expelled breath at the same time.

"I wanted to keep it simple," Jane put in. "Without dates or a message. I wanted to sum up what Brandon was for us—my son and your brother. But if you think we should add something more, we can always take it back."

"No, Mom. This is perfect. Thank you both for taking care of it, because if we still want to go ahead with the ceremony on the holiday weekend, we only have a week left."

"That's wonderful, Zanna. Let us know what else you'd like us to do for you in the next few days," Henry said.

"I will as soon as I've figured out my own

plans." At their puzzled faces, she explained, "Dom and I...we're working out something that I can't actually go into just yet but what I can say is that we're going to be together. As a real couple. For good."

They were still hugging and kissing when Dom arrived, carrying a tray of take-out coffee and a paper bag. Zanna showed him the plaque.

"I like it," he said, echoing her own reaction. "I gather you two have heard some of our news? That Zan and I are reorganizing our future?" He grinned when Henry and Jane laughed, then went on to say, "I've been talking to Ben and Grace today and they're keen to go ahead with next weekend's plans. I'm also to pass on an invitation to lunch at Evelyn and Charles's place for the day of the ceremony."

"Sounds good," Henry said. "Now I think Jane and I will leave you two to continue on with those mystery plans of yours."

Zanna was about to fill Dom in on the conversation he'd missed but when she saw her mother about to leave, impulsively she rushed to her side. "Mom," she began, lowering her voice, "I want to apologize for my behavior yesterday, on the phone. I wasn't nice and I'm sorry."

"Darling, these few weeks have been overwhelming for both of us, especially for you, because you've held so much inside. Thank you for the apology, but I also want to say that mothers forgive their children. That's an unwritten code of motherhood. And by the way, I've spoken to your uncle and Charles is okay with your selling the hotel. So don't worry about his response when you make your decision." She reached up to hug Zanna and give her a quick kiss before joining Henry, waiting a few feet away.

"Have you had a busy morning?" Dom asked, watching them leave.

"Very, and there's a lot to tell you."

"Coffee and pastries then?" He motioned to the table.

Zanna took a long sip of her coffee before she spoke. "I don't know where to start, there's so much to say."

He leaned over the table to take her hand. "I know *how* to start. I love you, Zanna Winters, and I'm so happy that we're going to spend the rest of our lives together."

She bit her lip to stem the tears that threatened. "And I love you, Dominic Kennedy." She focused on his warm, dark eyes a full minute before adding, "Meanwhile, let me tell you about my morning."

He laughed and bit into his pastry.

CHAPTER TWENTY-ONE

DOMINIC HAD BEEN in Norfolk for a week, finalizing the arrangements for the special leave that would allow them to stay in the Cove. When he'd phoned yesterday after his promotion interview, his pride at how well he'd handled himself had briefly worried Zanna. Was he going to change his mind about his leave request? Or regret deferring the promotion, if the leave was approved?

She stopped herself from such futile speculation. Whatever happened, she and Dominic would figure things out when he returned to the Cove later that day. Details for the gathering at the lighthouse had been worked out, thanks to Henry, Grace and Jane, who'd rallied together. Zanna was apprehensive about the ceremony, fearing all the emotions of the past year would resurface. She'd envisioned it as a time to think and talk about her brother, rather than a sad reflection on how he'd died.

All of her family—Dom and Henry, too—had grieved his loss. Now Brandon deserved their happy memories. That was her goal for the weekend's gathering.

Shortly before she needed to drive to Portland to pick up Dom at the airport, Zanna got the phone call she was anticipating from Ella Jacobs.

"I managed to get the community center on the agenda for the next town council meeting," she announced. "The number of volunteers is awesome. It's amazing, Zanna, and so heartwarming! I don't think there's a person in town who isn't on board with this idea."

Relief swept through Zanna. How would she feel if Dom reorganized his career in order to help her with a project that wasn't going to happen? "That's fabulous, Ella. Thanks for getting the ball rolling. I guess we'll see you at Aunt Ev's luncheon tomorrow, before the ceremony?"

"For sure, and Grace asked me to tell you that the lighthouse beacon is ready for its revival tomorrow night."

Everything was coming together beautifully. She was especially pleased about the community center. Ben and Dom had drawn up preliminary plans, featuring a gym, meeting rooms for community groups, a preschool and daycare center as well as a large multipurpose room that could serve as a bingo hall for seniors or a dance floor for teens. Zanna thought she'd relocate the disco ball from the hotel ballroom to that new space. Dom told Zanna they were leaving extra acreage at the site, which was adjacent to the new subdivision at the highway. There would be space for a future swimming pool and other extensions that might arise.

As for the upcoming presentation, Zanna knew the support of the community to date was impressive and should garner more votes from councillors. She'd personally set aside a significant amount for the campaign, thanks to the large down payment she'd received from Gateway Living—with enough left over to pay her bills.

By the time Zanna pulled up outside the Arrivals area of Portland Jetport, her mind was buzzing with all the looming tasks on her current "To Do" list. But the instant she spotted Dom coming her way, a happy smile on his face, her worries vanished. She got out of her car, ignoring the impatient honking behind her, and flew into his arms.

DOM STUDIED THE hushed group clustered near the lighthouse, waiting for Grace to unveil the plaque mounted beside the lighthouse door. She'd asked Zanna if she wanted to do that, but Zanna had declined, saying that this particular memorial had been Grace's idea, and she had thanked Grace again for everything. Dom could tell from Grace's damp eyes that she'd been touched by the gesture.

Earlier, the family had congregated for lunch, hosted by Evelyn and Charles Winters at their home on a high hill above the beach and the harbor. When Dom was a boy, kids had called the place a castle, because of its turrets. It had always manifested an aura of magic and mystery for him, until he was a young adult and knew that houses were simply buildings. The families within them were what made them special.

At one point in the luncheon, he'd sat back in his chair, gazing around the room and the lively, chattering Winters clan, so different from his own small but close-knit family. He wondered briefly what his new family would look like. Larger for sure, more complicated probably—like the group around him at lunch. But loyal and loving, that he knew for sure.

Despite the general hubbub, a decision was finally reached that when they were at the lighthouse, each person should recount a happy memory of Brandon, because the day was meant to be a celebration of his life.

When Grace whisked off the silk scarf covering the plaque, there was a collective sigh, followed at once by smiles. Mixed feelings still, Dom thought, and that was okay. *That was life*.

He was surprised when Zanna stepped forward to lay the rose she was holding onto the concrete pad surrounding the tower. "I'll go first." She scanned the small family gathering, focusing on Dom, as she began. "My brother was a total nerd…"

Everyone laughed, and Dom blinked back tears.

Much later, after everyone had dispersed to reflect on the day privately, Dom and Zanna walked across the dune ridge to the highway, where they surveyed the nearly completed construction of the "green" condominium units. Dom told her more about the job he was going to start in Ben's company once his navy leave officially began.

"I have to report to base next week until mid-July, but after that I can take my accrued leave until September. I plan to earn plenty of frequent flyer points when I come back every weekend." He wrapped an arm around her and drew her in for a long kiss. She held onto him, so close he thought he felt the hammering of her heart against his. Eventually, they moved apart, grinning at one another.

"I'll never get tired of kissing you!"

"Not even when Little Bean is demanding your attention in the middle of the night?"

"A peck on the cheek will be enough to keep me going."

"That's a deal."

They continued walking along the highway, pausing across from the subdivision where Dom pointed out the proposed location for the community center. "We want it to be on the outskirts, so it won't have an impact on the residential area and will allow for expansion."

Zanna stared at the site for a long moment.

"I hope it *will* need room to expand. I really want this center to be a success, Dom."

"It will be." He hugged her. "Okay, let's keep going."

At the set of new traffic lights where the exit to the Cove branched off the highway, they turned down the slope of Main Street to the boardwalk where they stopped long enough to order take-out fish and chips from The Daily Catch. It was almost dusk by the time they reached what had become their favorite bench on the beach and dug into their food.

"Drew said the lighthouse beacon is automated to turn on at the same time from spring to fall and then an hour earlier in the winter," Zanna unexpectedly remarked.

Dom swallowed his mouthful of fish. "I like Drew. He's what's called a 'stand-up guy.'"

"He is—and he's the best thing that ever happened to Grace."

Dom set his Styrofoam container down and put his arm around Zanna. "And what about you, Suzanna Winters? What's the best thing that's happened in your life?"

"That's the corniest come-on I've ever heard," she grinned. Placing her container on the bench, too, she leaned into him, resting her cheek on his chest. "And you know the answer."

"I want to hear it," he teased.

"You are!" she laughed, tapping him playfully. Pulling away from him, she looked deep into his eyes. "I love you, Dominic Kennedy."

Dom lowered his mouth to hers and kissed her. "I love you, Zanna Winters."

The sudden shaft of light caught them unaware, though they'd come to the beach to wait for it. He drew Zanna closer, and they sat in the comfort of silence, watching the lighthouse's strong, fixed beacon of hope illuminate the night sky.

EPILOGUE

"If I'd known people were going to send flowers, I wouldn't have bought all these poinsettias," Zanna grumbled to her mother, as she held one of the plants and surveyed the small cluster of tables, each with a newly fashioned floral arrangement, in the ballroom.

"The good thing is the poinsettias will last and you can distribute them around the lobby tomorrow."

"True, though the hotel will only be open until the first of January."

Jane waved a dismissive hand. "That's still ten days away. Another option would be to send everyone home with a plant."

Zanna laughed and gave her a quick hug. "That's what I like about you, Mom. You always have a quick comeback."

The sound of footsteps got their attention and they both beamed as Dominic headed their way, Little Bean snuggled against his chest in the carrier strapped around him. A light dusting of snow covered his jacket and the toque he was wearing. When he yanked the hat off, a shower of wet snow flew into the air over them. Zanna and Jane covered their mouths, stifling giggles as Dom raised a warning index finger to his lips. "Shhh."

Zanna gently pushed back the edge of their daughter's woolen hat and marveled at her exquisite perfection for the umpteenth time since her birth almost three months ago. "It's about time," she whispered. "Do you think you can get her safely in her crib, without waking her?"

"I'll do my best," he whispered back, crossing his fingers. "Are you two almost finished in here?"

Zanna looked at Jane, then nodded. "I think so. The food is being delivered at five and Lisa and Cheryl are coming early to organize that. Oh, and Rohan offered to do the honors at the bar."

Dom flashed a thumbs-up and quietly headed for the door.

"I can't get enough of that precious girl," Jane said.

"Same here. Funny thing, I'd been a bit worried about what I'd find to do after the closing date for the hotel." She laughed. "Little did I know."

"Yes, a new mother's realization. Time either flies or crawls, depending on the kind of day you're having. Well, my dear, I need to go upstairs to unpack. That was a wonderful idea of yours, to make up rooms for all of us here in the hotel."

"I thought it would be kind of a goodbye to the place, from family and friends."

"Like a last hurrah," Jane said. "And thank you most of all for the wonderful namesake." She kissed Zanna's cheek.

They walked together out of the ballroom and Jane took the elevator to the room she and Henry were sharing while Zanna tiptoed into her apartment. Dom was tidying up lunch dishes and gestured that the baby was asleep. For convenience and less disruption of Little Bean's routine, they'd set up a makeshift nursery in her apartment bedroom for the night's celebration. The high school student that Zanna had hired during the summer as a room attendant was coming to babysit for the latter part of the evening, though Zanna suspected she and Dom would be sneaking away from the party to get to bed earlier than their guests. Right now, they had some time to make final preparations until everyone arrived.

Zanna plopped onto the sofa and smiled when Dom brought her a cup of tea. "I feel like I need some alone time with you," she said. "Well, with you and Beanie."

"Your mother and Henry have offered us a night off whenever we want," he reminded her.

"Hmm. Maybe soon, but not yet."

"That's what I told them." He sat beside her with his own mug of tea. "Let's have a quick catch-up right now. I've hired the cleaning company to go into the house tomorrow ahead of the movers the day after. Mom said she'd love to have Beanie while we supervise the move."

"Perfect." Zanna leaned against the back of the sofa and sighed. "I love it when you take charge," she teased. And she did. Taking care of baby, whom they still called Little Bean, was the only full-time job she wanted—for now. "We're so lucky Ben and Ella were willing to rent us their house. I don't think I could bear living in a hotel suite much longer."

"They're excited to move into Ben's new condo unit. I happened to bump into Drew on my walk and he told me he and Grace are taking over the big house."

"Seriously? Wow! Drew must be thrilled about that. What about Aunt Ev and Uncle Charles?"

Dom frowned. "Not so sure. Apparently, they don't want to move into the new condos. I think the plan is for them to stay on a bit longer, with Grace and Drew. Maybe this place will be an option for them eventually."

"Anything new about the community center?" she suddenly asked.

"On target," Dom replied. "I've handed over most of the work now to Glen because Ben needs me to oversee a project in Portland." He paused a beat. "It'll mean a little commute I'm afraid. That okay?"

"I think Beanie and I can manage until we see your lovely face at the end of the day," she teased.

"Has the family decided anything yet about Christmas?"

She pursed her lips. "No plans have been made yet for Christmas, but I think after tonight, plenty soon will be. And by family, I assume you mean the other Winterses, the ones famous for organizing?"

He laughed. "Are you implying that definition doesn't apply to you, too, because—"

"I'm technically not a Winters," she interjected.

"Hah! In all but birth."

"Speaking of which, Cora and her friend arrived while you were picking up your uncle from the airport this morning."

"All the out-of-towners are accounted for then?"

"Yes, unless you've invited some of your Navy friends."

He shook his head. "I decided I'd rather get together with them another time. Today is for family."

"And close friends."

"Who are like family."

"Are you excited about tonight?" He stroked her cheek.

"A bit but I'm feeling more—" she thought for a second "—deliciously happy and content. Is that good enough for you?"

"Whatever you're feeling works for me, my beautiful woman."

Zanna snuggled against him. "Funnily enough, I never used to like surprises."

"Yet you continue to surprise me," he whispered, pulling her even closer.

ZANNA GRIPPED DOM'S hand after placing Little Bean, in a pale green dress that offset her wispy ginger-colored hair, into the welcoming arms of Grandpa Henry. He strolled to the center of the U-shaped cluster of tables and, when everyone's attention was focused on him and the baby, said, "It's my privilege today to officially introduce all of you to little Alexandra Jane Marie Kennedy."

He waited for the light applause from everyone to die down. "Of course, most of you have met her already, but Zanna and Dominic wanted this occasion to be her formal welcome to the family. Wee Lexi, as they plan to call her—*if they ever decide to stop using Beanie*—" he joked, pausing again for the chuckles to subside "—is named for her three grandmothers—Jane, Marie and Cora, whose second name is Alexandra. Believe me, Lexi has outstanding role models to guide her along." A ripple of clapping echoed in the ballroom. "Her godparents, Ella and Ben, have signed up for lots of babysitting I hear."

Zanna laughed with the group, catching Ella's eye and winking. Then she nodded at Henry. He cleared his throat loud enough to elicit a tiny wail from Lexi and when the room quieted, announced, "Now I'm turning this part of tonight's celebration over to my notary public friend Leonard, whom some of you know from the Historical Society, for a surprise event."

Henry carried Lexi with him to the table where her grandmothers and their guests were sitting. Zanna and Dom, still holding hands, took his place and waited while Leonard worked his way around the tables. A buzz of conversation filled the room and Zanna saw the puzzled expressions of all the people she loved and cared for.

There was her mother Jane, who stood with her through the best and worst of days; Cora and the friend who'd urged her to compile the bucket list that brought her to Zanna; Marie, the best mother-in-law a person could want, with her brother, George; and finally, Henry, who'd been the acme of all father substitutes—for her and Dom. Finally, there was the rest of the extended Winters family: Grace, proudly flaunting her new baby bump, and proud father-to-be Drew; Ben and his wife, Ella, devoted godparents; and last, Uncle Charles, their resilient patriarch with his wife, Aunt Evelyn.

Friends were there, too. Ted Nakamura showed up with Julie Porter, Grace's friend.

Sam Hargrave, owner of Mabel's Diner, and his longtime partner, Dan. The Kowalski brothers with their wives. And Zanna's stalwart employees—Rohan and his girlfriend; Lisa and Cheryl with their partners.

Leonard stood in the center of the U and waited for the chatter to fade. "I am here tonight," he announced, "to marry Suzanna Winters and Dominic Kennedy."

Zanna scarcely heard Leonard's next words over the gasps and cheers that followed because she was gazing so intently into Dom's eyes. Then he winked, tightening his grip on her hand when she missed her cue. An image of the younger Dominic at Brandon's funeral flashed in Zanna's memory—the teenager who'd understood even then what she was suffering and had taken her into his arms for a brief moment she never forgot. Now she looked into the bright eyes of the man he'd become—a father, partner and lover. The man who'd never given up on her.

"Yes!" Her voice bounced across the now quiet room as she answered the repeated question. "I do. Oh yes, I do."

* * * * *

THE 2022 ROMANCE CHRISTMAS COLLECTION

In this loveliest of seasons may you find many reasons for happiness, magic and love, and what better way to fill your heart with the magic of Christmas than with an unforgettable romance from our specially curated holiday collection.

#455 HOME WITH THE RODEO DAD

The Cowgirls of Larkspur Valley • by Jeannie Watt

Former rodeo rider Troy Mackay has given up risk-taking and wants to settle down with his baby. He only teams up with local farmer Kat Farley out of necessity—but now he's ready to take the greatest risk of all.

#456 HER VALENTINE COWBOY

Truly Texas • by Kit Hawthorne

With her horse-boarding business barely staying afloat, Susana Vrba offers newcomer Roque Fidalgo a deal—twenty hours of work a week *and* she'll even board his horse for free. But falling for the cowboy was never part of that deal!

#457 A MERRY LITTLE CHRISTMAS

Return to Christmas Island • by Amie Denman

When Hadley Pierce tells her good friend Mike Martin that she's pregnant—and he's the father—Mike can't propose quickly enough. But Hadley won't accept *any* proposal that isn't based on true love...no matter how much she wants to!

#458 A FAMILY FOR THE RANCHER

A Ranch to Call Home • by M. K. Stelmack

Mateo Pavlic intends to buy back his family's ranch land from onetime friend and neighbor Haley Jansson. But the cowboy hurt her once before. How can Haley trust him now with her land, her newborn son...and her heart?

HWCNM1222